Dedication

Always have faith, hope and love! Soul mates exist and
yours is waiting for you somewhere!

Prologue

1990

I'm sitting in class wondering what the hell made me take Economics. Working hard isn't really something that I do at school. I spend too much time planning what I'm going to do in my next break or organising what's happening after school and who I'm going to be walking home with! So my mind regularly drifts and I have a tendency to stare out of the window a lot of the time just daydreaming.

Today things are no different except that when I'm lost in thought and looking out of the window I see HIM! I have to emphasise the word because he makes me lose my breath.

Oh my god! He is gorgeous! All I can hear is my heart beating, fast. I slowly pull my eyes away from him and look back in the classroom, looking around to see if anyone else has seen him. Thankfully, everyone is listening to Mr. Marsden drone on about economies of scale. I turn back to look out of the window just in case I imagined him. No, he's still there and I watch him walk past the window very slowly.

Suddenly he stops and looks into the classroom. He

catches my eye and he smiles at me. He continues to look directly at me. I can't tear my eyes away from him. I'm transfixed. I have never seen a guy look so good, so intense. I feel my breath catch; he has literally taken my breath away.

He nods his head at me and winks. Wow! I now know what they mean when they talk about having butterflies in your stomach. I have never experienced anything like it. I am holding my breath until he turns around and walks ever so slowly away. I let my breath out and at the same time I'm wondering who he is? I wonder why I haven't seen him before at school? I know that I need to know who he is, I can't wait to get out of this class and speak to the one guy who will know who he is – Jezza.

Jezza has been a really good friend to Bonnie and me, are best friend for the last six years. He is the captain of the school football team and he knows all the guys in the school.

Luckily for me the class is just finishing and Mr. Marsden is handing out the homework sheet for us to do tonight! My mind is on other things – I need to find out who 'HE' is and to be honest that is far more important than finding out how many boxes of cornflakes to order in a corner shop using the supply and demand model.

When the bell goes, I walk out of the classroom and straight into Bonnie. We are like chalk and cheese; she is an "goth" girl who wears doc martins and dresses in black and I like designer clothes and bright colours. However, we always have loads of fun when we're together and I can talk to her about anything.

"So, did you have a good French lesson? Economics was so boring I spent most of the class looking out the window."

"Oui it was c'est magnifique," she says laughing. She knows how much I hate French - I just don't get it! I dropped it as a subject as soon as I could.

"Where are we going to have lunch today? Canteen or outside?" I ask, enjoying the feeling of the sun beating down on me.

"I think we should eat outside today and watch the guys playing football," she says smiling at me. She knows my favourite pastime is watching the guys doing anything.

We sit down and start eating lunch when I see 'HIM' staring at me. I hold my breath, blush and turn around to face Bonnie.

"Erm … do you know who that guy is? The one over there staring?" I ask Bonnie, blushing and trying not to look in his direction.

She turns to look at him, he doesn't notice because he is still staring at me. "No," she says. "I don't know who he is, but I know that he is in the year below us! Why is he staring at you like that? Do you want me to say something to him?" She goes to stand up, I reach across and pull her back down to the grass to join me.

"No, no, don't say anything? I'm just curious that's all," I answer getting all embarrassed.

"The last thing you need right now is someone looking at you like that. Doesn't he know it's rude to stare!" She almost spits the words out. "You've been through enough this last year and you need to stay away from guys."

"Yeah I know but ..."

STOP!!

I just realised you don't know who I am or what I've been through.

Let's rewind to last summer!

"If I could Turn Back Time"

1989

It's summertime and the weather is amazing as usual! During the summer months we spend all day on the beach and most nights down the amusement arcades playing on the slot machines! I live in Newquay on the Cornwall coast and it's beautiful. I don't ever want to live anywhere else!

My name is Cassie and I'm sixteen, well nearly seventeen. I enjoy hanging out on the beach and relaxing with my friends. I'm an only child; some say I'm pretty with my platinum hair falling down to the middle of my back. I don't see it myself ! I do, however, get called the "Ice Queen" because I don't really let the guys into my world so they think I'm frigid. At least it keeps them out of my way, they just say it's not worth trying. This means that I'm actually good friends with a lot of the guys and hang out with them with no awkwardness.

Tonight we're going to a beach party and I'm so excited because there will be a big gang of my friends there. It's nearly time to go back to school and this will be our last one. Some of my friends are going to college this year so I won't get to see them as often, but I'm off to sixth form to continue with my A'levels, but I will be joining them in two years when I go to University.

We have made arrangements to meet at seven thirty this evening on the recreation ground, where the fair is – it comes to town every August and it is a great place to meet. We can all go to the beach together and we all like to bring something along with us like food, BBQ, drink etc. I'm taking my boom box with me so that we can have some tunes blaring to get the party in full swing - everyone expects me to be there with my cheesy music.

Tonight I'm going with my friend Danni., We've been friends with for the last five years at school. We enjoy hanging out together after school as we have our own set of friends in school. I know she'd look out for me if I needed her. Bonnie isn't going as she has to go and visit her grandma in Torquay. Danni is excited about tonight as Tony is going to be there and she has a big crush on him. He doesn't go to our school, but he has played football with Jezza and some of the other guys at school.

The night my life changed!

Danni and I are first to arrive at the fair and we wait for everyone else to get here. I love the sound and feel of the fair. It's loud, colourful and the air is always thick with the smell of candy floss and burgers.

When everyone has arrived we all walk to the beach together except for a couple of guys who have their driving licence and have borrowed a car. They drive and leave their cars on the road at the entrance to the park which leads to the beach. When we arrive there are already a few people here and they have started setting up the party. I notice there are some new faces who don't go to our school. We always love meeting new people and letting them join us at whatever we do, the more the merrier that's my motto!

Once the BBQ is set up, I organise the music and we get all the drinks together. Now, I should just say that none of us drink a lot, but we do like to have fun! Danni sees Tony and starts blushing when he walks towards her, obviously intent on talking to her. She has avoided him for the summer since she realised she liked him as more than a friend.

Us girls are a bit strange like that, we might be able to talk to a guy all the time but the minute we decide we fancy him – we just can't talk to him anymore. We get embarrassed, tongue tied and blush all the time.

"Hey Danni, how's things?" he says staring at her.

"Good Tony. What have you been up to lately? We haven't seen you around much over the summer," Danni says.

"I've been working in a hotel in Bristol for my Uncle. I'm back now though. I'm really glad I came tonight," he says winking at her.

Danni doesn't know where to look but she pulls herself together and smiles a really big smile at him. Then she looks at me with a look that says "do you mind if I go talk to him?"

I smile and look back at her saying "go for it." It's amazing how we can read a look, a nod or a smile and know what it means.

They wander off together and I move to the middle of the group that has now multiplied since I last looked over. I chat to everyone. I'm one of those people who gets on with everyone, a social butterfly and I have a really good night. There is a lot of dancing, drinking and laughing, it has been a great night and I can't wait to go back to school to spend time with my friends again.

Now, we have an unwritten rule between us girls - you always leave with the same person you came with. Never let someone find their way home alone. Newquay is quite safe but in the summer there are a lot of strangers around. So when everyone is getting ready to leave I go off to look for Danni to make sure we can share the same taxi home. She is with Tony, of course, and they seem to be getting on really well, kissing and hugging.

"Hey Danni are you ready to go? We need to get out of here and we'll have to walk quite a way to get a cab home," I shout as I'm walking up to the two of them.

"Yeah Cassie I'm ready to go, just give me one minute to say goodbye properly," she laughs.

I start walking back to the group, which has now thinned out. Danni shouts behind me that she is ready to go!

"I'll give you a lift home," Tony says when they've caught up with me. "I have to drop David home anyway."

"Who's David?" Me and Danni say at the same time.

"He's my cousin who I have been working with in Bristol. He's only here until Sunday, he was enjoying the party too. Let's go find him." Tony says looking around for David.

Everyone who is still at the party is ready to leave, so we gather up all of our stuff. I collect my boom box and tidy the rubbish up. Tony comes over to me and Danni and introduces us to his cousin, David. I hadn't really noticed him at the party, but he is quite good looking and I'd say he's hooked up with one of the girls because he has lipstick on his cheek and he certainly looks like he has enjoyed the party.

"Hi David, I'm Cassie" I say putting my hand out for him to shake.

"Hi" he says taking my hand and shaking it firmly. He holds it for a long time and just stares at me, it makes me a little uncomfortable so I pull it back off him quickly. He grins at me.

"I'm going to give the girls a lift home if that's ok with you David?" Tony says putting his arm around Danni.

David takes his time looking me up and down, it's like he can see under my clothes. "Yeah that's fine by me," he says. He then reaches over and takes my boom box and offers to carry it. What a gentleman, none of the other guys would have done that! Maybe I was too quick to judge him.

We are the last ones to leave the beach and all the streetlights are off so it is pretty dark. When we walk back to the road to get to the car, we have to go through the kiddies playground. Tony and David start running towards the slides and swings shouting "come on girls this will be fun". Danni looks at me, I nod and then we both run towards them, laughing as we go.

It's fun climbing on the fort and sliding down the slide, although it's a bit uncomfortable in my shorts and I can feel that I am getting burns on my legs. Danni and Tony have disappeared so I walk over to David, who is sitting on the swings, and I sit myself down next to him on the spare swing. I might as well get to know him a little bit better, because we are probably going to be here for a while.

"So do you live in Bristol?" I ask him.

"Yeah I live in Whitchurch Park" he says smiling at me. "I love it down here though. Everyone's so friendly, especially the girls." He looks at me with a hungry look in his eyes and wipes his mouth. He continues to stare at me for about five minutes and to be honest he is making me feel really really uncomfortable.

Before I can do or say anything he's pulled me off the swing and pushed me to the floor, face up. "I know you want me," he whispers into my ear. "I felt you watching me all night, admit it, you want me."

By this time I'm scared; I wasn't watching him at all and only just met him half an hour ago! What is he talking about?

"No, no I wasn't watching you. Get off me," I growl at him trying to push him off me. He is a lot stronger than me and it doesn't take me long to realise that he is serious and really thinks that I want him.

"Oh, I see you like it a bit rough do you? That's OK because I like it when a girl struggles." He's now pinning me down on the ground with all his weight. He leans down so that he is closer to my face. He takes my head in his two hands and holds it tight so I can't move. Then he looks me in the eye and kisses me, but it's not a nice kiss. I am trying to keep my mouth closed because I don't want his tongue to get inside, but somehow he forces it inside. I can hear him moaning, he's enjoying it! I can't believe he thinks I am enjoying this.

I struggle underneath him. I try to fight back but he's too strong for me. I try to bite his tongue when it's in my mouth, but he takes that as encouragement and I hear him groan again. I'm scared and I don't know how to get out of this. I think that maybe if I relax and don't fight him then he won't hurt me. It might be just the challenge he's after. As I stop fighting back he starts to relax, I can feel him move slightly upwards and then he pulls back so that he's looking at me.

I take this opportunity to look around me to see if I can see Danni but I can't. I can't even hear her. I'm really starting to panic. "GET. OFF. ME" I shout at him, spitting in his face. "If you don't I'm going to start screaming so loud that Tony will come running."

All of a sudden he puts his hand over my mouth and says "just you try it babe! I'll kill you before he gets here."

I'm really scared and I don't know what to do. Lots of things are running through my mind. I know he isn't really going to kill me because he's here with Tony, but I don't want to chance it. However, I am worried about what he is going to do to me next. He slowly takes his hand away from my mouth "don't you dare scream, I trust you not to make a scene. You know what I will do if you do."

He takes his belt off and grabs my arms and ties the belt around them. He then reaches above my head and fastens the belt around the pole of the swings, where only minutes ago I sat innocently swinging.

My heart is racing so fast that I'm amazed he can't hear it and it feels like it is going to explode inside me. His hands start rubbing down my body, he is making my skin crawl as his hands touch my boobs on their way down. With each stroke of his finger it feels like he is unleashing thousands of ants onto my body, it's like everywhere he touches has become dirty. I try not to show any emotion. I'm sure it will only encourage him more.

His hands move even further down my body and then they stop at my shorts. I start struggling again, trying to stop him from undoing them, but whatever I try to do he is ready for me. He has his knees on my legs pinning them down and he's trying to undo his own shorts as well.

Now I am really frightened! The only reason he would want to undo both of our shorts is if he is going to force himself on me.

I can't let that happen!

I'm sweating and try to think of something I can do to get him off me. Like now!

When he has my shorts undone he puts his hand inside them. I feel sick. I think I want to vomit. No one has ever touched me down there. I have kissed guys but never taken it any further. It's such a horrible feeling, I try to move my legs so that they are clamped shut, but his knees pin me down harder every time I try to move.

I struggle against the restraint, my wrists are killing me but I don't care, I pull on them as hard as I can. Nothing happens. Now his hand is trying to get inside my knickers and I can feel the tears starting to overflow from my eyes. I can't let him do this to me! I can't let him force me to do something that I don't want to do.

He takes his hand out of my shorts and then he has to move his legs to start taking his shorts down. I can see him moving his hand to his shorts and it's like everything moves in slow motion.

His hand moves into his shorts. I can feel him touching himself. Then he loosens his legs off mine so that he can take them down just far enough to …

I don't wait to find out what he is going to do. As soon as he has lifted his body weight off my legs I take the opportunity to knee him in the balls. I don't give him a chance to do anything else to me, I kneed him with all the force I have inside me. I know that this is my one and only chance to get away.

He screams. I start screaming. I have already loosened the belt around my wrists from all the tugging and pulling I had done. I turn over and am able to open the belt with my teeth. As soon as I am free I jump up and start running away. He recovers quicker than I hoped and runs after me. When he catches up with me he grabs hold of me roughly and shouts in my ear "What are you screaming for? You know you want me, I can see it in your eyes." He grabs my chin and makes me face him and then he says "no one is going to believe you with the way you dress, you little slut." I keep hitting him with my balled fists all the time he is talking. I start crying; he has made me feel so dirty, made me feel like it was all my fault and that I have led him on.

I know in my own mind that I didn't, but he makes me think that I had led him to do this and that I should just accept what he is about to do to me. I can feel the fight leaving me and I am finally ready to accept whatever fate has in store for me.

David keeps telling me that I deserve it. That I am a bitch for kicking him in the balls – who is he kidding? He deserved it. Yet the more he tells me it's my fault, the more I believe him and the more he makes me think that I'm a slut who is just asking for it, the more I believe him.

I am still crying when Danni and Tony come running over.

"Cassie are you ok, I heard screaming?" Danni says hugging me.

Before I have a chance to say anything David says "yeah we're fine, Cassie was screaming because I was pushing her high on the swing that's all, isn't it Cassie." I look at him, he still has his hand on my arm and he squeezes it tight. How can he lie so easily like that? I go to open my mouth to say something but David just glares at me challenging me to say something. He tightens his grip around my arm and I know that I will have some serious bruises tomorrow.

"Ok, let's go then," says Tony. I am very happy to hear those few words. Of course my happiness isn't going to last long, David still has hold of my arm and is steering me towards the car. When we get to Tony's car Danni says she is going to sit in the front and that I have to sit in the back with David. I don't want to sit next to him, I don't want to be anywhere near him.

"Ah no Danni sit with me, please!" I whine.

"Come on Cassie, I want to sit with Tony. I might not see him for a while," Danni moaned as she looks across the car to Tony.

I get into the car first and David follows behind me, not missing an opportunity to touch my arse.

"GET. OFF. ME" I growl high enough for David to hear me but not loud enough for Danni or Tony to hear.

David just chuckles behind me. I sit as far away from him as I can in the cramped car. I can't wait for this journey to be over, I want to get home, have a shower, go to bed and end this night.

On the journey home, David keeps rubbing my leg like he owns me or something. He keeps squeezing it really hard. I keep moving his hand off my leg and that makes him push harder to touch me. He puts his hand on my leg and starts to move it very slowly up towards the top of my shorts. I keep moving it away but he keeps pressing his nails harder into my skin. Marking me! He eventually gets his fingers underneath the leg of my shorts and starts to rub them on my knickers. I can feel the tears as I try to curl up into a ball in the back of the car. I am so scared, but I also know that I am safe in this car. David won't do anything too bad with Tony and Danni there with us.

I look over at him and see him sneering at me while he takes his fingers up to his nose and sniffs them. I groan again and turn to face away from him. I can feel the bile starting to come up into my mouth. I am going to be sick if this car doesn't stop soon.

When we get closer to my house, I ask Tony to stop the car because I don't want David to know where I live. Even though I know he doesn't live in the same town - I don't want him to know anything about me!

When Tony pulls over I can see Danni looking at me strangely because she knows we aren't anywhere near my house and she says "are you ok? What's going on?"

I look at her and just simply say "I feel sick I need to get out of the car. The fresh air will do me good." I can't look her in the eye. "I'll ring you tomorrow," I say, hoping that she believes me.

She looks at me and I can see her studying my face, she finally gets out of the car and pulls her seat forward to allow us to get out too.

"Thanks for the lift Tony, I really appreciate it" I say as I wait for David to get out of the car first. Once I am out of the car I try to walk past him as quick as I can.

As I do he pulls me closer to him, puts his hand around the back of my neck under my hair and brings me close so that he can whisper in my ear. "Babe, I'm going to finish what I started tonight. You won't know when, but you WILL see me again. I'm looking forward to sampling everything you have. Keep an eye out for me!" He leans towards me and kisses me on the lips, roughly. I squirm and try to pull away, but he keeps me kissing me. He eventually pulls away and just grins at me, before he gets back in the car. I know Danni saw him kiss me, she wouldn't believe me if I told her what he did.

I am petrified, but I just want this night to be over and I want to forget everything about David and his threats to me. I watch them drive away and it isn't until I can see the tail lights disappear that I actually move from the spot where I am standing, rigid and scared. I turn to lean on the wall and then I vomit everywhere. I just can't stop being sick. It's like my body wants to reject everything that had to do with David. After about five minutes of being sick there is nothing else to come up. I close my eyes and lean against the wall. I stay there in the peace and quiet for ten minutes before I feel that I can move.

I don't care that it's pitch black out, I walk slowly home thinking and replaying everything that happened. I try to think whether I had in any way encouraged him, but I know I didn't because I hadn't noticed him at the party.

When I get home I jump in the shower and stay in there until all the tears that are flowing from my eyes have dried up. I step out and I can see the bruises appearing at the top of my legs and on my arms where he was digging his fingers into my skin. My wrists have bruises around them from the belt and my waist from where he was trying to undo my shorts and on my legs I have huge dark purple bruises where he was resting his knees, using all his body weight to keep me pinned to the floor. They don't hurt because just thinking about what he did and what he could have done hurts an awful lot more. After drying myself off I put my dressing gown on and go to bed.

I stay awake for hours just so that I don't have to close my eyes. Whenever I do it is like a movie playing behind my eyelids, reliving every single microsecond of what happened in that playground.

Eventually my eyes start to close by themselves and the last thought that I have before I fall asleep is that I wonder whether I was to blame somehow? I think about David and how he threatened me and how he nearly took what I treasure the most – my innocence.

When I wake up I have a smile on my face, the party was great fun last night. I think about my friends and how we danced and laughed so much. Then my memories change and it all comes crashing down around me and I remember everything in great detail. What am I going to do? I cry some more and lay here thinking and rethinking everything! I don't get out of bed for hours, I just can't face the day. Maybe if I stay in bed all day then I won't have to face what actually happened.

"Are you ok Cassie?" Mum says when she comes into the room for the fourth time this morning.

"Yeah I'm just tired – it was a late night you know," I say, trying to be cheery like I usually am after one of our beach parties.

"Hmm … ok, well your Dad and I are going out so I guess we'll see you later," she says turning around and heading out the door.

At least I don't have to get out of bed yet, I can lay here and just try to forget what happened.

I spend the day ignoring the incessant ringing of the house phone, which rings on and off all day. It has to be Danni wanting to get the gossip on David, or Bonnie ringing to see how last night went. I really don't want to speak to either of them today! I eventually get out of bed around four o'clock just before Mum and Dad come home. We have dinner together, but I don't eat very much. I have lost my appetite. Halfway through dinner I have to run to the toilet to throw up the little food that I ate. I guess thinking about what could have happened and the food on top of that was just too much for me.

Mum and Dad are worried, but I just tell them that maybe one of the burgers wasn't cooked enough or something. Thankfully, they believe me, although I think Mum isn't totally convinced that there's nothing wrong with me.

Sunday is much the same, I only get out of bed when Mum makes me. "Cassie I'm really worried about you," she says at dinner time. "the burger is taking too long to get out of your system, are you sure it's nothing else?"

I can't look her in the eye because I don't like lying to her. Mum and I have a really close relationship. I can talk to her about everything and we have a lot of fun together. I'm not sure how she would take knowing what happened on Friday night, she might blame me for wearing those shorts. I sigh. "I'll be fine Mum honest, I just need some more sleep." I can feel myself withdrawing more and more into myself and I really don't know how I am going to cope at school tomorrow.

"The Confession!"

Bonnie's POV

I didn't go to the beach party this weekend so I can't wait to hear all about it from Cassie and the others. I tried to ring Cassie on Saturday and Sunday but there was no one home. It was a bit strange because we usually spend the weekends together either shopping or at the beach. I'm guessing she must have been busy with her Mum and Dad and getting ready for going back to school.

I don't see her walking into school this morning, which is also a bit strange, we usually meet at the bottom of the school drive and walk in together. Especially on the first day back at school. I hope I have a class with her later this morning then I can see her and ask all about the party.

I walk into our new classroom and she isn't there either. We have registration and we are given our new timetables and I head off to French class and see Danni on my way. I walk with her for a bit and ask her how the party was and she blushes and says, "it was a great night. I got together with Tony and he gave us a lift home with David," she's blushing.

"Who's David?" I ask her.

"Oh he's Tony's cousin, he seemed alright. Cassie will tell you about him, she spent quite a while talking to him" she says, smiling.

"Yeah I'm sure she'll give me all the information when she gets here. She's never normally late." I keep looking around trying to find her in the busy corridor. "It's so strange! Did you see her over the weekend other than at the party? I haven't been able to get in touch with her."

"No, I spent Saturday and Sunday with Tony before he had to go back to Bristol with his cousin. David was asking if I had spoken to Cassie though, I think he liked her" she smiles.

"I'm surprised she didn't mention him," I say to her. I'm sure she would have rung me if she had met a guy, we always tell each other everything. "Anyway, I have to go to French. Tell her I'll talk to her later if she turns up in your class," I say heading off to class.

"Yeah, see you later" Danni says heading off in the other direction towards her Economics class that she has with Cassie.

My day is like any other Monday except Cassie doesn't turn up. I don't like it because the teachers are asking me where she is, so her mum obviously hadn't rung in and said she was sick. I can't wait to get home and ring her to see if she's not well. Something just doesn't feel right, she is never distant, I hope everything is ok.

Just as I'm walking out of school to go home Jezza

catches up with me. He is one of our group of friends and he is so good looking. He makes me blush just looking at him. We have all been friends for a couple of years, but it is only in the last six months that I have looked at him and felt differently about him. "Hey Bonnie, slow down I'll walk home with you." He's a bit out of breath, he must have been far behind me and ran to catch up with me. I slow down and let him catch his breath.

"Hey Jezza how're you? Did you go to the beach party on Friday night?" He nods his head. "Did you have fun?" I ask him, not really wanting to know whether he hooked up with someone.

"Yeah it was a good party, but it would have been better if you were there" he says looking at me and smiling.

Wait! Did he really just say that? I shake my head because I'm sure I misheard him. I just ignore what he said and ask "Did you see Cassie there?"

He smiles and nods his head. "Yeah she was there. Why?"

"Did she seem alright to you? I couldn't get hold of her over the weekend and it's unlike her to miss the first day of school. I'm going to ring her when I get home, but just thought I'd ask." I know I'm waffling at this stage but I'm seriously getting worried.

"She was great, she brought her boom box with her and played her cheesy music. She was dancing around, laughing and joking and talking to everyone who was there. She looked like she had a great night" he says smiling at me.

"That sounds like Cassie alright" I say laughing. "Did you see this David guy? I heard Cassie was talking to him while she was waiting for Danni."

"Was that his name? He must have been the new guy that was hanging around. He seemed to be drinking quite a lot and having fun. I never saw him with Cassie though. He looked ok," Jezza says.

"Listen I have to get going, I'll talk to you tomorrow Jezza" I say wanting to get home to ring Cassie.

"Talk to you tomorrow Bonnie" he says smiling at me and I watch him walk in the opposite direction. He waves when he is about to walk up to his house. I wave back and can feel myself blushing even though he is so far away. I have it really bad I chuckle to myself.

I'm walking home and all of a sudden I decide that I want to go and see if Cassie is alright, rather than just ringing her. I just have a strange feeling in my stomach. I suppose that's what happens when you've been best friends for years. You know each other inside and out, I just wish I had been at that party. I can feel that something bad happened because Cassie would never ignore me, so the only alternative is that something is wrong.

I walk up to Cassie's door, knock and wait for someone to answer. Mrs. Thomas comes to the door a little bit surprised to see me. "Hey Bonnie how are you?

How was your first day at school?"

"I'm good Mrs. Thomas I just wanted to see Cassie. I need to ask her about some German homework." I don't know why, but I get the impression Mrs. Thomas didn't know Cassie hadn't been at school today and I didn't want to get her into trouble.

"Didn't you just leave each other?" she asks curiously. "She's gone for a walk on the beach to clear her head. She said she didn't have any homework" she's looking at me strangely. Crap, I don't want to get her in any trouble.

"I know. It was about something we did in class that I didn't understand. I'll go find her at the beach. We didn't get chance to talk much today." I say as I turn around to walk away.

"Can you tell her not to be too late home please?" Mrs. Thomas says.

"I'll tell her. See you Mrs. Thomas." I start walking away towards the beach. Something just doesn't feel right and the closer I get to finding Cassie, the more I start to worry!

I can see her sitting on the wall looking out at the sea. She looks like a mermaid sitting there dangling her legs over the wall, with her platinum hair tumbling over her shoulders. I stand there for a couple of minutes just watching her, she looks lost and I know instinctively that I was right to trust my feelings. There's definitely something wrong. She looks so sad and Cassie is usually a very happy, smiley person.

"Hey Cassie," I shout so she can hear me.

She turns to look at me, surprised I've found her. She looks like she's been crying. I hope she's ok! "Hey Bonnie what are you doing here?" She looks confused.

"I was worried about you, Cassie," I say pulling her in for a hug. "You didn't ring me after the party. It's just not like you. You always ring me if I don't go to a party and tell me all the gossip. Then when I rang your house you were never there to take my call. What's going on?" I ask gently because I can feel her sobbing quietly into my shoulder. "Come on we talk about everything."

"Oh Bonnie I'm sorry I just feel so … so ... I don't know how I feel," she says still nuzzled into my shoulder.

"Ok" I say. "Tell me about the party. Did something happen? Did someone say something to you?" I'm asking questions to try and draw it out of her. "Who's arse do I need to kick?"

"I don't know where to start really. You have to promise not to tell anyone. Please? I don't want anyone to know," she is pleading with me now and I am definitely getting worried.

"Of course I won't say anything. You know that we're best friends. I'll do anything I can to help you. I hate seeing you so upset like this. Come on Cassie, what is it?" I'm getting frustrated because I just want to know what has got Cassie in this state.

"You know I went to the beach party with Danni. Well I had a great time. It was so much fun. I was there with my music dancing along to Love Shack by the B52's and The Only Way is Up by Yazz and before I knew it it was time to go. I went to find Danni because she had disappeared earlier with Tony." She stops talking and looks up at me. "They got together that night you know. When I found her she said that Tony was going to give us a lift home with David, his cousin. I remember seeing a new guy at the beach party but I hadn't taken too much notice of him. You know what I'm like Bonnie when I start dancing." She is sobbing again.

"Yeah I know what you're like Cassie. You like to have fun. So, what happened then? It sounds like a normal beach party" I say, coaxing her to keep going.

"Well Tony introduced us to David who offered to carry my boom box for me, which I thought was very nice of him. Then after a few minutes him and Tony started running to get to the kiddie playground and they were laughing and joking. Danni and I ran after them and we all messed around on the climbing frames and slides. Danni and Tony sneaked off for some kissing and cuddling and left me and David sitting on the swings." She stops and starts sobbing, much harder this time. I wait for her to stop sobbing before speaking.

"Ok" I say, not really sure where this is going.

"I was asking David where he was from and all of a sudden he pulled me off the swing and dragged me to the floor." I don't think I've heard her right but the tears are flowing down her face. I draw her closer to me and rub her head.

31

"He pinned me down with his knees, kissed me by forcing his tongue into my mouth. Then he put his hand over my mouth and started to undo my shorts and his trousers. I was so scared Bonnie. I didn't know what to do and then when he was distracted with his buttons on his jeans I kicked him in the balls and started running."

"Oh my god Cassie, you poor thing" I say cradling her in my arms. "You must have been so scared. He's a bastard for doing that. Did you tell Tony? What did he do about it?" I ask because I know what I want to do to him.

"I didn't tell anyone." Wait, did I hear her right, she didn't tell anyone? I can see she wants to tell me more so I stay quiet. "He told me that I was a slut and that I had been looking at him all night – which I didn't Bonnie. I swear! Then he said that I deserved it. I started to believe him and was quiet on the way home. I asked Tony to stop down the road from my house, as I didn't want David to know where I lived. When I got out of the car, David had to get out of the car first. He whispered in my ear that I wasn't to tell anyone and that he would be back to claim what he considered was his."

She is full on sobbing right now. She can't breathe so I have to try and calm her down and I encourage her to take deep breaths.

"Come on Cassie, breathe in and slowly let it out. Breathe in and slowly let it out." She does and I can eventually hear her breathing getting back to normal with the odd sob in between.

She takes a deep breath and then continues. "So

after he said that he got back in the car. I said goodbye to Danni and then I walked home sobbing really hard. I got into the house, went for a shower and I just sank to the floor in the shower and cried. I was so scared. I got into bed and eventually went to sleep."

"When I woke up on Saturday I just remember thinking what a great party it had been and I started smiling. Then I remembered David and everything came crashing down. I didn't get out of bed till the afternoon, then I was sick and went back to bed. Mum and Dad went out on Sunday and left me in bed all day."

"I couldn't go to school today Bonnie, what if everyone knew about it? What if he told them I let him do those things to me? Oh my god!" She sobs a little.

"I just started walking to school this morning and ended up down here by beach, I've spent the day walking on the beach." She's trying not to cry anymore and she pulls away from me.

"What did I do to deserve that Bonnie? I've never been a slut. I've never put myself out there for guys at all. I'm the bloody Ice Queen for god's sake!" She's getting angry now and is shouting at me.

"You are so not a slut. You should have said something to Tony, he would have dealt with David. Did you tell your Mum? Did you say anything to Danni? She never said anything today."

Cassie doesn't answer any of my questions, she just looks down at the ground. This is going to be harder than I thought, I need her to open up to me and she needs to tell someone else.

"Come on let's go to the cafe and get a milkshake and we can talk properly." I link her arm, almost dragging her to the beach cafe 'Pebbles'. Mr. Stanley, who runs Pebbles, asks us what we want. After we order we go and sit down.

"I have to ask this question Cassie. I'm really sorry, but did he … did he rape you?" I can barely say the word, but I need to know. "Did he manage to get inside you?" I can't look her in the eye. What if he did? Oh my god I hope he didn't. I can't imagine how she would cope or how to even begin to process that information.

"No … no." She's almost shouting at me. "No, I got away before he managed it" she says looking in my eyes, tears running down her pretty face.

"Ok that's a start. So, how come Danni and Tony didn't hear you if you were screaming?" I need to keep asking questions to drag the answers out of her.

"They had gone round onto the green and were too engrossed in each other to hear me. They said they thought we were laughing and messing around. That wasn't the case. I didn't say anything to Danni because I didn't want to ruin her night. She was so happy getting together with Tony."

She's smiling now as she thinks of her friend. Cassie is just a selfless person, she would do anything to make her friends happy, but she has taken that too far this time.

"Cassie, did you think of telling your Mum? David

needs to be reported to the police". I say quietly.

Mr. Stanley comes over and puts our milkshakes in front of us. "Hi girls. How was school today?" He always makes time to talk to us and he never makes us leave when we have finished our drinks.

"It was ok, boring as usual. The first day is always about settling in the new classes," I say smiling at him.

He looks at Cassie and then at me "I'll leave you two to your milkshakes." He walks away to serve some more customers who have just walked in.

Her head lifts up quickly and she looks me right in the eye and says "I don't want anyone to know Bonnie, they'd all think I encouraged him and I know I didn't. I just want to forget it. Please." She is pleading with me and has reached across to grab my hand with hers. "Please Bonnie!"

As hard as it is to not tell anyone I can't see Cassie like this, but I understand where she is coming from. I don't think I'd want anyone to know either. I just worry how it's going to affect her by not being able to talk about it. "If it's what you want then I won't tell anyone. I think you should tell your Mum though."

"No," she shouts. "Especially not my Mum. Please Bonnie!" She's crying again. "I don't want my Mum to be disappointed in me Bonnie."

"She would never be disappointed in anything you do Cassie, but if it's what you want then I won't tell anyone. "Now drink up your milkshake and let's talk about something else. Jezza walked me most of the way home today" I say smiling.

She looks at me and smiles. "Wow that is fantastic Bonnie, I like Jezza, he has always been kind to us. I'm so happy for you."

"Me too Cassie," I say laughing. And then we are back to normal Cassie and Bonnie conversations but I can't shake this feeling that something bad will come out of this.

We finish our milkshakes, link arms and walk towards Cassie's house. I say goodbye when we get there and she hugs me and says "Bonnie you are the bestest friend in the world I don't know what I would do without you." She hugs me before she goes into the house.

I walk towards my house and all the time I'm thinking about how brave Cassie is and how could something like this happen to someone as nice and loved as her?

When I'm home I go to my room to finish my homework and try not to think about this David person and what he did to Cassie. I know this could have all been so much worse.

It's at this moment that I decide that I will protect Cassie and keep her away from guys. She doesn't need them in her life right now.

"First Day (back) at School"

Cassie

So, having decided to go to back to school to complete sixth year instead of college, I'm heading back into my old school. Except it doesn't feel like my old school. There is a separate wing for the sixth year students so it feels like everything is new, but some of my old friends are there which makes it even better. There are a few new kids but other than that it's just like last year.

I see Danni and I do my best to avoid her. Thank god we're not in many of the same classes and we usually don't spend time together at school. I don't know what to say to her and it's best if I don't say anything at all.

At break time everyone is talking about the beach party and what fun they had, it seems to have been the best party of the summer! I decide to join in and tell everyone what a great evening I had and how much fun it was. All I want to do is to be sick, go back to bed and not talk to anyone. I had to run to the toilet to vomit about three times already today.

I manage to get through my first day back by just keeping my head down and not really engaging with people. My friends think I am still sick after being off school yesterday. I let them think that, it makes things easier for me.

Danni sees me when I am on my way home and shouts "hey Cassie, wait up. I want to talk to you."

I wait for her to catch up with me. My hands are getting sweaty and my heart is racing.

"What's going on? How come you're avoiding me?"

"I'm not avoiding you Danni I'm just rushing around today. I wasn't in yesterday so I am trying to catch up," I say not catching her eye. "Honestly I'm fine – I had a great time the other night."

"Yeah looks like David was really into you. What happened with him? Why did you give him the wrong number?"

I stopped breathing for a minute, I don't know what to say, "umm what?" I spluttered. "What makes you think I gave him my number?"

"Well he said you gave him your number and when he tried to ring you on Saturday, it didn't ring so he asked Tony to get the right number for him. He thinks he wrote it down wrong." Something isn't right here. I don't like the way she is looking down to the ground and just kicking the stones. It's like she's nervous.

"Umm I kind of gave Tony your number to give to him. I thought you had already given it to him so I didn't think it was a problem. I'm sorry Cassie."

"Nothing happened between us." I can feel myself sweating and I still can't look Danni in the eye!

So, that was who was ringing me all day Saturday. "I didn't want him to have my number. I didn't like him like that Danni!" I'm getting angry and I know I shouldn't take it out on her, but god what was she doing? There is an unwritten code, where you don't give out someone's number until you've asked them if it's ok.

"Don't worry, he's gone back to Bristol so I'm sure he won't be bothering you, long distance relationships never seem to work out anyway" she says clearly annoyed with me.

"I hope you're right Danni, I really do. I'm going home I'll see you tomorrow."

So, this is how I spend the rest of the week, avoiding Danni and ignoring the phone when I'm on my own. When Mum and Dad answer the phone the other person hangs up without saying anything. The calls soon stop and I start to relax around my friends, life seems to be getting back to normal.

Or as normal as my life can be now!

My gang of friends and I, both guys and girls, hang around down at the beach at the weekends. Danni seems to always be with Tony but thankfully David is never with him anymore. We drink a little, well I drink a lot, more than I ever have before. I just want to forget what happened, never to have to think about it again.

Unfortunately, I can't forget. When I'm on my own it's all I think about. I know I was lucky and that I managed to fight him off in time, but what if I hadn't? What if he had forced his way in? I can't stop thinking about it and I just want to cry all the time. I don't, I just put on a fake smile and laugh and joke with my friends. No one is going to know what happened. I drink more and more each week in a bid to forget all about David and that awful night. Then out of the blue it all comes to a head!

The beginning of the end!

One weekend in November, we decide to have a beach party. I know it's a bit late in the year for a beach party, but we wrap up warm and light a fire - it's just what we do!

So we're having this beach party and I'm drinking heavily. Danni and I are talking again, I didn't stay mad at her for a long time because we have always been good friends and she didn't realise what David had done to me. It wasn't her fault. She is always telling me to slow down on the drinking, but I don't listen. I'm having fun tonight, over the last couple of months I hadn't let myself have fun! I hadn't let go of my emotions and just enjoyed myself.

Half way through the night I feel someone come up behind me and I hear something that I'll never forget, "Cassie, babe, I missed you." I jump a little and scream when he puts his hands on my shoulders.

No way was David here pretending that we're a couple and that I wanted him or something. No way was I letting that happen in front of my friends.

"What did you call me? I'm not your babe. Did you not get the message the last time?" I growl at him. People are starting to look my way, I don't want to draw attention to myself but I'm not going to be a pushover either! I finally decided that enough is enough. I am not going to be a victim any longer.

David grabs me roughly by the elbow and pulls me away from the others. "I think you're the one who didn't get the message the last time, Cassie. I will have you when I want to," he growls in my ear. "Whether you want me or not – you better get used to that idea."

I manage to pull myself away from him and run back to join the party. I sit myself down in the middle of them all and pretend to be having a good time. I pick up a bottle of vodka with the intention of getting drunk. I normally only drink beer but tonight I need to forget, tonight I need to take it one stage further.

Tony and David finally leave and I start to relax. Unfortunately, the vodka is having a bad effect on me and I start to feel sick. I walk down to the water and just breathe in the sea air. I can feel the tears falling down my face as I kick off my shoes and start walking into the sea with not a care in the world because tonight I'm going to forget.

Tonight I'm going to end it all and then I won't have to remember anymore because tonight I'm going to cease to exist!

I can hear shouting and my name drifting across the wind. One voice. Two voices and then more. I don't stop. Everything has become so clear now.

I know what I need to do to stop remembering.

The water is cold. As cold as ice. It's dark in the sea and the moon is beautiful shining in the dark sky. I walk closer to the moon, which is reflecting on the sea and inviting me to join it. It gets bigger and bigger the closer I get.

Then, all of a sudden the land shifts under me and I start to go under. It feels colder and colder the further I go under the water. My body is getting numb and all I can think about is that's it's all over and I don't have to think about it anymore! The world becomes so still and quiet then everything goes black.

This is it.

This is the end!

"A New Start!"

The sun must be rising in heaven because the light is so bright I can't focus.

"Cassie, baby girl wake up. Please wake up." Wow! That sounds just like my Mum. What is she doing here in heaven? I'm confused. I still can't open my eyes though.

"Cassie we love you, we can't lose you, you're too precious to us". Yeah that definitely sounds like Mum.

I try to open my eyes but they're so heavy and the sun is blinding me. "Did I make it? Is this heaven?" I croak, my throat is really sore and my voice sounds so rough! I thought everything was supposed to be beautiful in heaven – why do I feel so bad??

"Oh my god Cassie, can you hear me? Baby girl I love you, you're going to be ok. I'm here I'll help you, I'll take care of you." Yeah that's definitely Mum.

"Mum, where am I? What happened?" I say with tears running down my face! I've finally opened my eyes and I realise I'm in the hospital.

My Mum is crying; she never cries. "Baby girl you were at a beach party and you had too much to drink. Then Danni saw you walk down to the sea, you took off your shoes and then you ..." she's sobbing. " .... then you just walked into the sea. Danni shouted at you and then

44

Steve and Rob ran into the sea after you. They managed to get to you and drag you out. Jezza had to do CPR until the ambulance came. You stopped breathing Cassie. You stopped breathing." She can't say anymore because she is sobbing uncontrollably.

"Oh Mum, I'm sorry, I just wanted everything to be gone. I wanted the last few months to have not happened. I'm sorry I really am." I sob, I'm so sad that I didn't die because now I know that I will have to explain myself to everyone. They will all know what David did to me.

I sob because I love my Mum and I am glad that I am still here and I know she will help me to get through this.

Apparently I've been in the hospital for three days and Mum and Dad have been at my bedside the whole time. They are exhausted!

Once the doctor has checked me over, they send a psychiatrist in to see me to ask me about what I did and why I did it. I explain as much as I can without telling her anything, if that makes sense. I blame it on the drink and that I had felt depressed since my friends had moved on to college and I had gone back to school without them. They decide to put me on medication and I have to stay in hospital for another couple of days so they can keep an eye on me!

Mum told me that lots of my friends had been in checking on me and that they can't wait for me to go back to school. It made me happy that there are concerned about me, it means so much to me.

The doctors and nurses keep coming in and out doing my observations, then the psychiatrist comes in a couple of times explaining that it would be better for me to open up and tell them why I felt the way I did.

I am fed up of them all talking, prodding and checking everything and it is Friday by the time they let me go home. They have given me a prescription for some medication and told me to rest. I am so ready to go home, but also know that going home will make this all real and it will mean that I have to tell other people about David.

"You need to take it easy over the weekend, Cassie" Dad says.

"Before School on Monday we have a meeting with Mrs. Walker," Mum says.

I totally forgot about having to go back to school and seeing everyone and lots of people asking questions.

"Oh god Mum, I can't talk to her. She is going to ask lots of questions and make me relive everything." I hang my head in my hands and keep shaking it.

I close my eyes and say "everyone is going to be asking so many questions. I don't know if I can handle it."

"We are here for you," Dad says. "We have always been here for you." He stands up and pulls me into a hug. I get emotional because Dad never hugs me, so this makes it extra special.

Bonnie comes over and sits with me, we talk about

the party and David. "You know everyone has been so worried about you this week. I sat in the hospital all weekend, Mum and Dad tried to make me leave but I didn't want to. I needed to know you were ok. Your Dad rang the school to give me a message when you woke up. We all cried."

"I'm so sorry Bonnie. I didn't think about it – it just happened. I just wanted the hurt to stop. When I saw David at the party something inside me just flipped. I didn't want him to have control over me anymore."

"I know, but you know we're all here for you. You are so special to us all. You always were. You are the glue that holds our group together, we need you here."

We both cry for a long time then lay on my bed watching funny movies.

On Monday morning, Mum and I go to the school to meet Mrs. Walker.

"Cassie, we are so happy you are feeling better. We are here for you and if you feel under any pressure then you need to come and tell me, or any of your teachers, and we can deal with things there and then. Please don't let things build up again."

"I'm sorry Mrs. Walker. I didn't think about how this would affect anyone else. It was a spur of the moment thing, it wasn't planned. Honest!"

"I know Cassie, I had a deep conversation with Bonnie and Jezza to try and find out why you did what you did. Jezza doesn't know why and he was extremely upset. He saved your life you know."

I nod because Bonnie and my parents had told me the story of how Jezza had started CPR on me to try and bring me round while Steve ran to the nearest phone box to ring for an ambulance. I need to thank him when I see him; he saved me in more ways than one.

"I know he did and I will be forever grateful to him."

She smiles at me and after further discussion about how I am feeling she agrees that as long as I talk to my friends or to her if I get any overwhelming feelings, then she was happy for me to come back to school straight away.

I say goodbye to Mum and Bonnie is waiting for me outside Mrs. Walker's office. She hugs me and says "Come on everyone is waiting for you."

I feel nervous, but take her hand as we walk down the corridor to our tutorial class. When I open the door everyone starts clapping and I see they have some posters up on the walls to welcome me back into the class. I well up and the tears overflow, I didn't realise that this many people were my friends. The fact that they all participated in this makes me feel so happy.

"Thanks guys, this is a surprise. I'm sorry for what happened and Jezza, thank you so much for saving me." I walk over to him and he gives me a hug.

He squeezes me tight as he says "you mean a lot to us Cassie. The place wouldn't be the same without you to bring sunshine and happiness into it. Glad you are back." He kisses me on my cheek and pulls away. I see the glance he has for Bonnie and the smile that he gives her.

Everyone crowds around me until Mr. Smyth says "now give Cassie some space to breathe and let's finish tutorial, then you can all go to your classes. You can catch up with her later on." He smiles at me and I smile back to say thank you.

Jezza's POV

I am sitting around the fire at the beach party when someone says "Look, isn't that Cassie? What is she doing?" I look around to see her walking into the sea. I know she has been drinking a bit tonight and I have been watching her carefully. I stand up to go and talk to her to see if she is ok, when I see Rob and Steve running into the sea after her. She has walked really far out to sea and then she disappears very quickly.

The girls start screaming and the boys are shouting and all running to see if there is anything they can do. Steve dives under the water and we all hold our breath. He comes up for air and dives under again. Rob joins him and I start to run in after them. Steve comes back up and he has her, Rob joins him in pulling her up to the shore.

When they have laid her down, I start CPR on her. The two guys are bent over trying to catch their breath.

I push on her chest and then stop and breathe air into her mouth. "Come on Cassie, come on." I repeat my movements. I have tears running down my face, dropping onto hers. "Please Cassie, we all love you. Come on."

Someone must have rang for an ambulance because a few minutes later I feel someone touch my shoulder "come on move over, let us help her now. We can help her." I look up and see the ambulance man, I stop what I am doing and move back. We are still on the beach and I sit back and wrap my arms around my legs. Watching. Waiting.

It feels like forever before she starts spluttering and they roll her over so that she can throw up the water she swallowed. I can't stop crying.

"Cassie, oh my god. You're going to be ok, I promise you'll be ok. I'll always protect you – you don't need to feel like this. We need you, we all love you."

"Miss, miss, are you ok?" Cassie has been rolled back down, but she doesn't speak. Her eyes are closed and they try to wake her. They can't. They put her on the stretcher and carry her back to the ambulance. We all follow to make sure she is ok.

"Can someone ring her parents please? We need to get her to hospital fast – she isn't waking up, her body is in shock."

"I've already rung them," Danni says, crying.

"Good." The ambulance man turns to me "do you want to come with us?"

I nod my head and jump up into the back of the ambulance and just see everyone's worried faces when they close the back doors.

"Here" he says, handing me a blanket to wrap around me. I didn't feel cold, but now that the adrenaline is wearing off I am starting to shiver.

"Thank you. Is … is she going to be ok?" I am still

crying, the tears just won't stop flowing. She can't die.

"At the moment we just need to get her to the hospital and they will try and warm her up and see what they can give her to keep her stable."

Everything happens so quickly, the ambulance whizzes to the hospital with the lights and the sirens on. If I wasn't so scared I would be so excited because I have always wanted to work as a paramedic. When we get to the hospital I follow them in and it is only a few minutes later that Mr. and Mrs. Thomas arrive.

Mrs. Thomas hugs me and says "thank you for helping her and being with him. I would hate to think she was on her own in the back of the ambulance. I'll never be able to thank you enough Jezza. Thank you." They are both whisked off before I get chance to answer.

About ten minutes later my parents arrive at the A&E. "Oh my god Jezza are you ok? We got a call to come and get you from the hospital."

I run into her arms and sob. "Mum it was awful. I had to do something to help her, I couldn't let her die. Now it seems that she is going to die anyway."

Mum holds me and I hear Dad say "I'm going to go and see what I can find out Jezza, she will be ok."

Once we find out that she is holding her own in a coma, we say goodbye to Mr. and Mrs. Thomas and promise to come back the next day to see her.

I go back every day along with Bonnie and we sit and talk to Cassie, telling her how much we love her and want her to come back so that we can listen to her cheesy music one more time. I hold Bonnie while she sobs and we go down to Pebbles to have a hot chocolate and talk about Cassie.

I really like Bonnie but I don't want to lose her as a friend and we have become so close these last few days. She is such a lovely, genuine person and she loves Cassie so much. I know that I have to be here for her as much as she needs to be here for me.

When we find out that Cassie is awake and that she is going to be ok I am so excited I hug Bonnie and I kiss her. It is the most amazing feeling in the world, but then we both pull back. She looks at me, "I think we just got carried away there Jezza. Come on let's go and see Cassie."

"Yeah, it was just excitement." I wish I can tell her how I feel, but this is not the right time. We walk in silence into the room to see Cassie.

Cassie comes back to school a few days later and I am so excited to see her. We didn't get to spend any time alone with her at the hospital because her parents were always there. We have made some posters and put them up in the classroom to welcome her back.

When I see the door open and she walks in, I am speechless. She is so beautiful, so healthy and so alive that it makes me feel so protective over her. I love her and feel that I need to shelter her from any other pain and I vow that I will do that.

When she hugs me I say "you mean a lot to us

Cassie. The place wouldn't be the same without you to bring sunshine and happiness into it. Glad you are back." I kiss her on the cheek and then look over to Bonnie, she is looking at us with tears in her eyes. I smile at her and wink. She blushes, I love that I have that effect on her.

Back to Cassie

When we walk to our first lesson, Bonnie heads off to her French Class and I go to Business Studies. I sit at the back of the class and Jezza comes and sits next to me. "Can I sit with you?" he asks.

"Of course you can. You can give me the notes from last week so that I can catch up as well."

He smiles at me and hands me a folder with his photocopied notes. "Already ahead of you babe."

I laugh and it feels so good to laugh. I will tell him later how very grateful I am.

Business Studies is boring and I can feel myself drifting off, I think I miss most of the class because I am thinking about what happened and about how my class reacted to me coming back. I didn't really expect that kind of reaction and I smile. I really do have good friends.

As the weeks go on I notice that everyone is really protective of me, especially Jezza. We have formed a bond that I hope will last all through my life. I don't think I can ever imagine not being his friend; it would kill me.

STOP!

Now you know what happened and why Bonnie and Jezza are so protective of me! Now let me continue my original story.

"Learning to Live Again!"

1990, again!

I shake my head and it brings me back to sitting on the grass outside class, Bonnie is telling me that I don't need guys staring at me like HE is. "Seriously, Cassie I'm quite happy to go over and tell him to stop staring. I can even get Jezza to do it you know."

She turns to look at me and see's that I am blushing. I look at her and blush even more. "Cassie?"

"I'm sorry Bonnie, I don't want you to go over to him. I kind of like him staring at me."

She shakes her head. "If you're sure."

"I have never been so sure of anything in my life, Bonnie." I never once take my eyes off him. I just can't pull them away, it's like he is a magnet and I am being pulled to him.

He is so good looking. Breathtakingly good looking. He has dark hair, which is slightly longer on top and flops over his beautiful face. He is very tanned, like he has been on top of a surfboard all summer.

We sit in the grass enjoying the lovely weather and I can't help but watch him playing football with his friends. He is obviously in the year below me because I recognise some of them, but I can't believe I hadn't noticed him before. Then again, I was in an all girl's school until last year!

We have three schools on our campus; the girls school, the boys school and Sixth year – which is mixed. We were never able to mix with the guys, even though we were on the same campus, we were very well segregated.

Basically, we were fenced into our school and warned to stay away from the guys. It's no wonder some of my friends moved away to go to college instead.

I need to know who he is! I don't know why, but I just feel that I need to know.

"Hey, earth to Cassie, are you ok?" Bonnie says waving her hand in front of me trying to get my attention.

"Yeah sorry, I'm fine Bonnie, let's go to German class and ogle over the new teacher" I say laughing.

The German teacher, Mr Jones, is really old and ugly, so Bonnie knows I'm only joking. "Yeah come on," she says laughing back at me.

The German lesson seems to drag as Mr. Jones wants us all to talk German the whole way through each lesson. We're not used to speaking German for a whole hour and a half, so it's hard work. My brain is fried and all I can think about is Mr. Cutie. He is all I've been thinking about since I first saw him this morning. Was it only this morning? I'm not usually like this. I keep away from guys because they can hurt me and I don't need any more hurt in my life right now.

After German, I link arms with Bonnie and we start to head home when Jezza shouts over to us "wait up girls." He jogs over to us.

"You ok Jezza?" Bonnie asks him.

"Yeah I just want to invite you both to my house tomorrow night. I'm having a pool party and would really love you two to be there." He looks at Bonnie when he is saying it and I smile to myself. Then he turns to me and says "you can even choose some of the music, Cassie."

I laugh, because I do love my cheesy music and everyone groans when I put it on, but they all dance to it and have lots of fun too.

"Who's going to be there Jezza? Anyone we know?" Bonnie asks with a big smile. She's always fancied Jezza and can't keep the grin off her face.

"The whole gang and some new faces too," he says looking at me purposefully, what does that mean? "Don't worry Cassie we'll make sure you're ok!"

"What do you mean?" I ask aggressively. I feel like he's trying to tell me something. I know this is the first party I've been to since 'The Incident' but I hope he's not trying to tell me that David is going to be there. No one knows what happened except Bonnie and I know she won't say anything.

"We just want you to be at the party, Cassie. We missed you this summer and we like your company. It's not the same without you," he says smiling, trying not to laugh.

"Oh right, thanks Jezza. I appreciate it and yes we will both be going on Friday night. Thanks for asking us. You don't need to watch me all night though, I won't drink so don't worry," I say laughing.

He turns and walks the other way. We start walking home chatting about the party and what we are going to wear. "So," I say to her "are you going to wear something special for Jezza?" I waggle one of my eyebrows and she falls about laughing and then pushes me away.

"Ha ha very funny. Then again, I know he likes girls who wear belly tops so you never know" she says seriously.

We both look at each other and start giggling.

The next few days follow the same pattern:- going to lessons; sitting on the grass at lunchtime staring at Mr. Cutie and pretending not to; more lessons and then walking home.

Friday comes around very quickly because we are looking forward to the party. Everyone is talking about it, loads of our friends are going, so I know it will be good fun. If we don't hold beach parties then we have pool parties! I have just the new swimsuit to wear.

After school Bonnie comes over to my house as it's closer to Jezza's place. She is staying the night with me so that I won't be left on my own to find my way home. That is the only restriction Mum and Dad have put on me; that they know where I am, how I am getting home and that I have the money for a taxi should I need one. I don't argue with them because I know they only worry about me and I've caused them enough heartbreak!

"If I Could"

After we change into our swimsuits and put our little summery dresses over the top, we go out to talk to Mum and Dad.

"Hey Mrs. Thomas." Bonnies says smiling at my Mum. "I'll make sure to take care of Cassie and keep an eye on her," she says, as if I'm not even in the room. I know I should be annoyed, but I let her look after me because that's what Mum and Dad need.

"Thanks Bonnie, we know you will. Now both of you go off and enjoy the party, just make sure you come home together," Mum says looking at me and smiling, "there's no curfew tonight."

I go over and hug Mum and when I hug Dad he slips a fiver into my pocket. "That's for the taxi home," he says in my ear so that only I can hear him.

"Thanks Dad" I whisper back.

On our way to the party we meet Danni and Tony. I start to get sweaty and my heart starts to race when I see them. I always have this reaction when I see Danni, particularly when she is with Tony. I am constantly looking around to see if David is with them. When I see he isn't then I start to relax. I know Bonnie notices my behaviour because she takes my hand and squeezes it. They cross the road to join us and we walk the rest of the way to the party together.

When we get to Jezza's place, the party has already started. The music is blaring and there are loads of our friends in the pool already.

"Cassie! Bonnie! Come on, jump in its lovely and warm," says Steve. He was one of the guys who helped Jezza to pull me out of the sea. I smile at him; he is another good friend.

"Ok, give us chance to get changed," I say laughing. I feel so comfortable with these guys that all my worries slip away. Danni, Bonnie and I go upstairs and get changed. It's a good thing we put our swimming costumes on before we came, it saves a lot of time. I have my new swimsuit on; it's a little bit revealing as it has cut outs on the side and it is black and sparkly, but I love it!

"Wow, Cassie you look hot" says Steve when we get out to the pool.

I blush and jump straight in, splashing the others and laughing so much that I swallow lots of the water and I start gulping and choking, but all the time I am laughing. I'm not scared when I start choking because I know I am safe. I have been back to the beach and gone in for a swim; it took a few attempts before I got in but I was happy when I finally did. It means that tonight I can have fun and not think about that fateful night.

We are all splashing each other when I feel someone watching me. At first I think I'm going crazy. Then, when the feeling doesn't go away I start swimming round and round, looking around the side of the pool. I don't feel uncomfortable, but start wondering if it's David coming back for me. I get out quick, get a towel and cover myself up.

Bonnie and Danni get out quickly and run up to me. "Cassie what is it? You've gone as white as a sheet," Bonnie says looking around her.

"Danni, answer me one question and please don't ask why, but is David coming here tonight? I know you're seeing Tony, so you'll know whether he is coming or not." I put both my hands on her shoulders and start shaking her. "Tell me. Tell me!" I'm nearly shouting in her face.

She goes pale. "No Cassie he's not. Tony fell out with him the last time he was down. Tony won't tell me what it was about, but no he's not coming. Please calm down!" She's touching me now, trying to calm me down and I start to breathe again, deep breaths in and out.

"Are you going to tell me what that's all about?" Danni says staring at me and I can see the panic in her eyes. Shit! She's putting two and two together and coming up with the right answer. And to top it all off she's pissed with me because I didn't say anything to her.

"Danni, please don't get angry with me. I wanted to tell you but I didn't know where to start. Can we talk about this another day? I just want to enjoy myself tonight. I felt someone looking at me and I just panicked. I'm sorry!" I have tears in my eyes and she reaches out and gives me a big hug. Everything is going to be all right in the world again.

"I'm not angry" she says. "I'm just hurt you didn't say anything. I can't believe you went out with him and didn't tell me about it. We WILL talk another day, but tonight we are going to enjoy this party" she says hugging me. She obviously thinks we went out and it ended badly, well I'm not going to put her straight.

The three of us link arms and laughing we jump straight into the pool. Even though I am laughing, I know what I felt and I don't really understand it. It's unnerved me a little. We stay in the pool for about an hour when I decide that I want to get out, dry off and have a drink.

"Bonnie, I am going to get a drink, do you want anything?"

"No, I'm fine, I'll get one in a few minutes. Are you ok?"

"Yeah, I'm just thirsty and I'm starting to go wrinkly."

She laughs at me and I get out of the pool. When I do I feel it again. Someone is watching me, but this time I don't panic, because I know it's not David. I slowly turn around on the spot looking around me to see who is staring at me.

I turn and see HIM, I realise he is the one watching me. I don't know why I don't feel creeped out, but I don't. I put a towel around me and find myself walking towards him. I need to know who he is.

The closer I get to him the more of him I can see.
He is in his swim shorts and no top. His body is so
beautiful. All I can do is look into his eyes, they are the
most beautiful blue colour. They are turquoise and are
like pools that are drawing me in.

"Hi" I say, trying not to blush "I'm .. "

"Cassie" he says. "I know who you are, I was
hoping to bump into you tonight. I'm Jordan," he says
with the biggest and brightest grin I've ever seen.

"Hi Jordan. Why were you hoping to bump into
me?" I stupidly say to him. He's making me lose control
of myself. I feel really nervous and look down at the
floor.

"Erm I wanted to get to know you. I feel like I'm
drawn to you for some reason. I know that sounds
stupid, but everywhere I look I can only see you." He
puts his finger under my chin and makes me look into
his eyes. "Even when I have my eyes closed, all I can
see is you. Sorry if that sounds a bit stalkerish." He
laughs, but I can see that he's embarrassed about
showing me his feelings.

I laugh with him because I really don't know what
to say. I have to try and say something though because
he is looking at me with those mesmerising eyes. "Yeah
it does sound a bit stalkerish," I laugh. "But I'm flattered
and yes, I have seen you around at school and I did
wonder who you were too. So we are both a bit
stalkerish." We both start laughing.

"I'm going to go and dry off and get some more

clothes on. Then maybe we can grab a drink," I say really quickly so Jordan doesn't see I'm waffling on a bit. He is making me nervous but I don't want to stop talking to him. I turn and walk back into the house, towards the stairs to go upstairs to the bedroom to find my dress. I can feel him following me and I smile to myself. I am a little bit nervous though that I am in the house with him and my friends are outside, but he makes me feel safe.

"That's sounds great, although I don't mind if you don't put anymore clothes on" he says grinning at me. He is following closely behind me, I was right.

"No, seriously I would feel better if I had more clothes on." I laugh as I'm heading up the stairs.

Jordan's POV

I'm so glad I managed to talk Jezza into giving me an invite to his pool party. I arrive late on purpose. I want to people watch for a while. Well, really I want to watch one person in particular. Cassie! She is the one girl who has captivated me from the first time I saw her. I was walking past Mr Marsden's Economics class and I saw her looking out the window. I looked at her and felt that I couldn't move. I just had to keep looking into her eyes. She was beautiful and she had a huge smile that brightened up her face. I could also see a sadness in her eyes. I just felt that I wanted to make her happy and take away her sadness.

The problem is that she is a year above me at school and those girls don't normally talk to us. I'm not going to let that stop me making this girl happy though.

I smile and wink before walking away. I can feel her looking at me as I move away from the window and that makes me smile.

Over the next few days I see her watching me playing football, when she thinks I don't notice her there. I do though, because it's like my whole body is tuned into her frequency. I see her regularly talking to a guy named Jezza, so I try to talk to him to find out who she is.

"Hey. It's Jezza right?" I say walking up to him.

He looks me up and down and says "yeah, why?"

"I heard you captain the school football team and I was wondering if I might be able to get a trial" I say starting off with general conversation.

"Yeah I do. We've got trials on Thursday after school, you can come along then and we can see how good you are," he says.

"Cool I'll see you Thursday. Oh and I'm Jordan!" I'm so happy I got a trial for the football team and chance to find out more about Cassie.

On Thursday I go to the football field and try out for the school team, it goes well and Jezza tells me that I have a place on the team. I get in the team and I'm delighted.

After the trials when we're getting our stuff to go home some of the lads are talking about a party at Jezza's. This is an opportunity I can't resist so I chance my arm and ask him myself. "Hey Jezza, I heard you're having a party on Friday night and wondered if me and a couple of mates can come along aswell."

"Yeah Jordan that's fine, there will be a good gang of the football lads there so it's a good way to get to know your team mates," Jezza says.

I cross my fingers behind my back as I risk asking "so erm will there be many hot girls going?"

Jezza starts laughing, "Yeah of course. Have you seen the girls in this school? They're all freaking hot."

"Will erm … will Cassie be there?" I'm stuttering

and I can feel myself blushing, what the hell is wrong with me.

"She is a good friend of mine, so of course she will be there with Bonnie and Danni too. Don't get too close to Cassie though, she is very fragile. We all look out for her. There was some major shit that went down recently with her and we are all protective of her. You mess with Cassie - you mess with all of us."

I wonder what happened, maybe that is why she looks so sad all the time. "I hope you understand that and I hope you take note." Jezza says warning me off.

"Is she your girlfriend or something?" I ask, just to make sure I'm not stepping on anyone's toes.

"No she's not. She is a very good friend who has been through a lot and she needs a break. That's all."

"I don't intend to mess her about, I promise." I can't believe my luck, I am going to a party and Cassie will be there. I can't wait.

So, here I am waiting at the bottom of the stairs thinking back on how I got here. I'm really nervous, but I can feel that she wants to get to know me too. While she was upstairs I put my t-shirt back on and went into the kitchen to get a drink for both of us, I rushed back so that I didn't miss her.

I see her now at the top of the stairs and she just takes my breath away. I don't think she knows how beautiful she really is. I smile so wide and I'm rewarded with a big smile back. I take a deep breath and hold a drink up for her.

"Another Day in Paradise"

Cassie

When I get into Jezza's room, where I had left my clothes earlier, I close the door behind me and lean up against it. I take a few deep breaths in and out to try and calm my racing heart down. I can't believe the guy that I have been staring at all week is here at this party. More to the point he wants to get to know me better and have a drink.

I quickly dry myself off and put my little white sundress back on. I put my wedge sandals on, roughly towel dry my hair and try to make it look nice. I grab a bit of lip gloss and head back down the stairs. Jordan is waiting for me at the bottom of the stairs with a big grin on his face.

Jordan … I like the way his name sounds on my lips.

"Actually, I take back what I said earlier. I don't mind you putting more clothes on at all. You look gorgeous," he says as he watches me walk down the stairs. He has put pair of surfing shorts and a tight t-shirt

71

on. Mmm he looks good enough to eat.

"Thanks" I blush not knowing where to look.

"I got you a drink, but I wasn't sure what you wanted, is a beer ok?" he asks handing me the plastic cup.

"Erm … yeah that's fine. I don't really drink," I say.

"Sorry I didn't know, come on let's go in the kitchen and get you a coke or something." He smiles and reaches out and takes my hand to lead me to the kitchen. As soon as he touches me I feel a jolt of electricity shooting up my arm, he must feel it too because when it happens he turns to look at me. He smiles and grips my hand tighter. When we get in the kitchen he takes my beer off me and pours me a cup of coke.

"Let's go and sit outside by the pool," Jordan says as he guides me towards the back door, he puts his hand on the curve of my back. Well he's not quite touching it, but I can feel the warmth of his hand through my dress. I shiver a little at the thought of his hand touching my back. "Are you cold?" He says. "You're shivering, do you want my jumper to keep you warm?"

"No, I'm fine thanks. Honest" I say not able to look at him.

Just as we are heading into the kitchen towards the front door, Danni and Bonnie rush through the door and almost bang straight into us.

"Cassie, we were getting worried! I know you said

you were going for a drink but you were gone for ages." Bonnie looks at Jordan and then back at me. "Are you ok?"

"Yeah girls I'm fine. I just wanted to get dried off because I was getting cold in the pool. Sorry I didn't say anything to you guys." I look at them and then look towards Jordan. "This is Jordan. He just got me a drink and we were coming back out to the pool. Sorry girls." I say, embarrassed that the girls had been looking for me and I hadn't even realised.

They look at him and smile, Bonnie says "Hi".

Danni does the same.

"I know you worry about me and I should have told you where I was going. I'm sorry. Now turn around and get back outside so we can get this party started," I say ushering them to move outside.

"I'm going to go and choose some of my cheesy music to get everyone in the mood." I move out of their way and walk over to Jezza's stereo to see what CD's he has. I see he has Now That's What I Call Music 17, it has all the latest songs on it.

I find the number of the song I want to put on - Opposites Attract by Paula Abdul. Everyone starts groaning and I hear loads of people shout "Cassie, turn it off."

I start laughing "no way, you know I like this kind of music" and I start dancing around the edge of the pool singing away to myself with my eyes closed.

"I take two steps forward,

I take two steps back,

we come together as opposites attract"

I'm laughing and dancing when all of a sudden I crash straight into someone. I open my eyes still laughing and start apologising "Sorry, I didn't …."

"See me?" Jordan says laughing. "That would be hard when your eyes are closed. I was waiting for you over there and it didn't look like you were going to come back to me anytime soon, so I decided to come to you instead." He grins at me.

"Sorry, I get caught up in the music and just lose myself," I say blushing. "Come on, let's go sit over there," I say grabbing his hand. It feels comfortable to hold his hand and I'm not ready to let go. I like how my hand feels in his. I can see Bonnie looking at me with her eyebrows raised. I smile so that she knows it's OK. That I'm OK.

We move over to one of the sun loungers at the side of the pool. I can still hear the music, but it's not too loud so I'll still be able to hear Jordan. I put both legs up on the lounger and cross them and then sit down on them. My sundress rises up and shows more of my legs, but I don't care he saw me in my swim suit for god's sake. We sit there looking at each other

"So, I want to ask you something, but I don't want you to answer if you don't want to," he says, but he isn't able to look at me when he says it. I don't know what to expect but I'm not sure I like it.

"OK carry on," I say feeling a little bit apprehensive. Had he heard what I did that night on the beach? What did he think about it all? My heart is racing and I can feel my hands start to sweat.

"Your friends seem to be very protective of you. I always see them looking around when you are with them, like they are looking for something. Then when we were in the kitchen, they rushed through the door looking for you. They looked petrified. Why is that?" He says it all very quickly, like he wanted to get it over and done with.

How do I answer that question? I don't know him well enough to tell him my story and what happened to me. I just need to come up with something else to say, because I just know that I don't want to push him away or start lying to him. I take a deep breath.

"Girls stick together you know. We're all protective of each other. Something happened to me last year and it's made the girls over protective. I don't really want to talk about it, but let's just say that I'm very grateful for my friends."

I can feel that I'm on the verge of crying, so I take a couple of breaths to calm myself down. When I'm calm, I eventually look at Jordan. He is looking at me strangely and I can feel myself staring into his eyes, they really are beautiful.

"Your friends are very lucky to have a friend like

you too. I don't want to push you into telling me your story, but I hope that if you want to get to know me better, then one day, when the time is right, you might tell me about it," he's smiling at me. I don't know what to say, I just keep looking at him.

It's in this moment that I know he will be there for me and that I will let him in. Don't ask me how I know this, but I just do.

I smile back and whisper "I hope so too!" He takes my hand and just smiles at me. I can feel the heat and sensuality from just touching his hand. It feels like a defining moment in my life. Something that I will remember for the rest of my life.

Neither of us has anything else to say and we just sit there holding hands and watching everyone enjoying the party.

The music has slowed down and I can hear Jam Tronik with Another Day in Paradise. I can feel myself swaying slightly and singing along:-

Oh, think twice,

it's just another day for you and me in paradise Oh, think twice,

it's just another day for you. You and me in paradise

I feel like I'm in paradise right now. Jordan has moved behind me and he is pulling me back so that I am sitting between his legs and leaning up against him. I lean back into him and I inhale his scent. I can smell a bit of chlorine from the pool and something tropical. I love that smell already!

"We are in paradise Cassie! This is what I have wanted all week. To talk to you, feel you and just to be with you." He whispers into my ear, "I can't believe how lucky I am." I can feel his breath on my neck and feel my body shivering and goose bumps are forming on my arms and neck.

"You're cold again," he says rubbing my arms. "Let me get you my jumper," he starts to move off the lounger.

I put my hand on his thigh to keep him in place. "No, I'm not cold I was just enjoying what you were doing," I say not removing my hand.

What am I doing? How can I even think about touching a guy, when the last guy who touched me tried to do something really bad to me. I have to stop thinking about it. I can't blame Jordan for what David tried to do.

"Cassie, are you ok? I think I lost you there for a few minutes. You've just been staring ahead not listening to me and you're not relaxed anymore. Where were you?" Jordan asks.

He obviously sensed a change in me because he isn't touching me anymore. Did I move away from him? Did I say something to upset him? Why am I thinking about David when I'm here with Jordan?

"Erm … I'm fine. Honest. I was just lost in

thought. Can we move closer to the party? I feel like I need to dance and I could do with another drink." In just that one moment I shut Jordan out. I start to get up from the lounger and I can't look him in the eye.

"OK, if you're sure that's what you want to do. Let's go and party!" he says with a big smile. He gets up and grabs my hand and we walk over to the pool where the party is in full flow.

We dance and laugh for the next hour or so and then Bonnie comes over and says that it's time to go. I know she's right, but I don't want this night to be over. I don't want to have to leave Jordan. I feel like I can't breathe at the thought of leaving him, what is going on with me?

"I'll be five minutes Bonnie. Do you want to go and see if Danni is ready to go? Then the three of us can leave together." Bonnie walks off towards Danni, who is slow dancing with Tony.

I look up at Jordan and smile. "I have to go – thanks for a great night. I'm so glad you just had to talk to me."

He laughs. "I wish you weren't going, but I know you girls stick together." He smiles. "What are you doing tomorrow? Can I meet you? I'd really like to get to know you more." He's blushing now. God, can this guy get any more beautiful?

"I'm not doing much tomorrow" I reply, I look around for a piece of paper and a pen, I have one in my bag. "Here's my phone number, ring me tomorrow when you've had time to think about tonight and whether you still want to meet me. Sometimes things look different in the morning." I smile weakly, I don't want him to change his mind.

"Oh I already know I won't be changing my mind. So, I'll ring you at ten o'clock in the morning Cassie." He's moving closer to me as he's saying it. He puts his arms around me and draws me closer to his body. I can smell him and he smells just gorgeous, he leans down and kisses me on my forehead. His lips are boiling hot and feel like they have left an imprint on me. I moan a little because I am feeling all sorts of things that I don't understand.

"Until tomorrow Cassie. Sweet dreams and remember *"it's just another day for you, you and me in paradise!"* he sings in my ear.

I peel myself away and just look up at him with a large grin on my face; this guy has made me so happy by just being in his company for a couple of hours. I walk over to the two girls and link arms with both of them. I'm in the middle and I know that I'm smiling liking a lunatic. I look over to Jordan and he is still looking at me, his smile matches mine.

"Girls Just Wanna Have Fun!"

The three of us are singing and linking arms as we leave Jezza's house.

"So Bonnie, come on tell us, did anything happen with you and Jezza? We need to know," I say laughing and pulling Bonnie closer to me.

"Well …. We kind of talked and admitted that we fancied each other and then he kissed me." She just drops that one into the conversation and runs ahead and then turns to face us. She has the biggest smile on her face.

"WHAT!" we both say at the same time. "Come on you need to tell us more. You can't just leave it there" I say running towards Bonnie.

"Well, I'll tell if you promise to tell afterwards. I want to know all about Jordan," she says laughing at me and making kissy lips.

"Ha ha ok you go first," I say while we walk down the street to look for a taxi.

"Well" she says. "We were talking and dancing like we always do and then he put his arm around my shoulders and pulled me closer to him. I was so excited and nervous at the same time. Then he just whispered in my ear, "come on Bonnie you know you feel it too," then he leaned down and took my chin in his hand, tilted my head up so that he could look in my eyes and then he kissed me very gently and very slowly."

She's smiling and looking all dreamy, "so then we said that we would meet up tomorrow and just hang out." She has the biggest smile on her face. "Now it's your turn Cassie, come on I want to hear all about Jordan."

"OK, OK, OK" I say laughing at the two of them dancing around me.

"You know that Jordan is the guy I've been staring at in school and the one I've been day dreaming about. Right?" They both nod at me. "Well what I didn't know is that he has been watching me too. He'd heard about the party at Jezza's and he asked if he could go too. Jezza said he could and then he asked him if would I be there." The two girls start squealing and jumping up and down, clapping their hands.

I carry on, "Jezza told him that I'm a great girl but that I didn't need a guy in my life to mess me about. He's always so protective of me." I laugh thinking of Jezza acting like my dad.

Jordan told him that he wasn't going to mess me around and that he just wanted to meet me and talk to me. I can't believe he told me all of this, but he wanted me to know that he had asked Jezza about me, before I heard it from him."

The girls are looking at me like I've just told them something epic. "What?" I asked and the two of them start giggling.

"Oh my god, he sounds so dreamy," Danni says smiling at me.

"We didn't really talk much, we just listened to the music and danced a little. He didn't even kiss me." The girls are now standing with their mouths open in front of me. "Well, he did kiss me, but it was on my forehead! I was so frustrated," I say with disgust in my voice.

Bonnie starts laughing and then Danni joins her. "What?" I ask them getting annoyed with them.

"You were frustrated that he didn't kiss you. That is so funny! You never go near anyone or have been interested in anyone for so long and then you get frustrated because he doesn't kiss you," Danni says, hugging me and laughing in my ear.

Bonnie then joins in the hug and says to me, "so what now? Are you going to see him again?"

"Yes, I am. He is going to ring me in the morning and then we're going to make some plans. I'm nervous and excited all at once. What am I going to say to my Mum? She isn't going to like me going out with a guy, she will be worried about me." I say starting to come down off my cloud nine.

"Your Mum is going to be happy for you babe, she wants you to be happy. You have to understand that she will be worried that you'll get your heart broken and how you will deal with that. Just make sure you talk to

us and to your Mum if you feel you need to. OK?"
Bonnie says while hugging me tight.

We all know what she is talking about and it was
hard for her to say it, but I have been at my lowest and I
never want to go there again. Ever!

We hail a taxi and the three of us slip inside. We
are going to drop Danni home and then go back to mine.
We sit in the back of the taxi and sing along to "Just
Like Jesse James" by Cher, which is playing on the
radio. The taxi driver turns it up, but I think that is more
to cover our bad singing voices than because he was
enjoying it.

After dropping Danni off and arranging to meet up
on Sunday lunchtime, we arrive back at my house. We
pay the taxi driver and walk up to the house. When we
get in we go straight to my bedroom and get ready for
bed. I'm tired now, but I'm also so excited about
spending the day with Jordan. I wonder what we will do
or where we will go?

When we get into bed, I ask Bonnie "are you happy
you finally got a kiss off Jezza and was it everything you
wanted it to be?"

She rolls over onto her side facing me with her
hand holding her head up. "Cassie, it was the best kiss
ever! I've wanted him for so long and always pretended
that I just wanted to be friends, I never thought it would
happen. I just hope that he can live up to my
expectations."

I smile at her. "I'm sure he's wanted to be more

than friends for a long time too, but he didn't want to do anything about it because it might risk your friendship. I guess he decided he couldn't wait any longer." She smiles at me and I can see she is getting sleepy.

"Come on let's try and sleep, we've both had a good night and have a busy day tomorrow, we need our beauty sleep ha ha." I lean over and give her a hug and then roll on to my side facing away from her.

"Night Cassie" she says as she rolls to face away from me too.

I lie there for a long time thinking about Jordan and how I feel about letting a guy into my life after what David did to me. I'm not sure how I'll feel when Jordan goes to kiss me properly – I can still feel David's rough lips on mine and his tongue forcing its way into my mouth. I lay there and hope that what happened with David won't affect my feelings for Jordan.

I can feel a lone tear slowly making its way down my face. All I want to do it to go through one day without something triggering a memory and then I want to wake up one day and believe that it never happened.

I don't get much sleep, all I can see when I close my eyes are turquoise eyes and a beautiful smile. I am so excited that I will be seeing Jordan again tomorrow. I hope he rings me. I try really hard to sleep and eventually, with a smile on my face, I manage it.

"With Every Beat of My Heart"

When I wake up in the morning, Bonnie tells me that I was talking in my sleep. She's laughing when she tells me that I have been moaning and saying, "Jordan mmm".

"Ha ha very funny" I say back to her, laughing.

"Seriously you were. I had to throw a pillow at you to get you to shut up," Bonnie says laughing.

"That's why I woke up cuddling an extra pillow then ha ha." I pick the pillow up and throw it at Bonnie. "Come on let's get some breakfast," I say to shut her up.

When we are having have breakfast, Mum sits with us and we tell her all about how great the party was. Halfway through the conversation the house phone rings. I jump out of my chair and run to answer it. "Hello!" I'm panting, I'm so out of breath.

"Hi Cassie, did you sleep well?" I hear Jordan speaking from the other end of the phone. All I can think is 'yay he rang. He rang.'

"I did, eventually. I kept thinking about all the fun we had, did you?" I ask.

"I went to sleep thinking about you and I had the

best sleep in a long time." He is quiet for a minute to allow me to take in what he just said. "So, do you want to spend the day with me today?" He asks and I can hear the nervousness in his voice.

"Em let me think about that for a minute." I laugh. "Yes, yes I do."

"That's great," he says, and I am sure I can hear him smiling down the phone.

"What do you want to do?" I ask him, hesitantly.

"It's a surprise! I want to spoil you today and show you what I like about our town!" He says. "Can you be ready to meet me in an hour?"

"Yes I can, where will I meet you? Do I need to bring anything with me?" I can feel myself getting excited.

"Meet me at Hunter's in town at eleven o'clock. You know where that is don't you? You don't need to bring anything with you, just your beautiful smile. I'm hoping to see it all day long!" He says with lots of sincerity.

"Yeah I know Hunter's. Ok I'll try my best," I say laughing. "I'll see you in a bit."

"See you soon, Cassie," he says laughing when he hangs up.

I hug the phone to my chest and stand there smiling, it takes me ages to replace the handset onto the base. I take a deep breath. I have a huge grin on my face. I know that Bonnie and Mum were listening to every word I said and that I'll have to explain myself to Mum. I don't know how she's going to take it. She's been very protective of me since the beach party.

I turn around and see the two of them shuffling back to their seats. "I saw you, there's no need to hide," I say laughing and go back into the kitchen. They are both sitting down staring at me.

"Do either of you want a cup of coffee?" I say innocently, trying to draw out the inevitable.

They are both looking at me as if I am mad!

"Sit down Cassie and tell me about that party again, you seem to have missed out some things earlier," my Mum says laughing.

"Ok! Well we had a great time, everyone was there. The music was great, the pool was warm and we had lots of fun." I'm smiling at this point, I just can't hide it.

"And?" Mum asks.

"Well I met this guy, Jordan. He just rang and asked did I want to spend the day with him and I said yes, that's all!" I say all of this really quickly because I'm nervous she won't let me go.

"Mum he's really nice, he's thoughtful and I really like him," I say because she is staring at me.

Bonnie says "Mrs Thomas, he seems really nice, he's really good looking as well," she laughs. "I'm still going to ask around at school and see what people know about him. Jezza let him into the football team, so he's keeping an eye on him. Don't worry, I have Cassie's back," she's smiling at Mum because she knows she just said the right thing.

"Ok, that makes me feel a little better Bonnie, thanks" she says looking at me.

"Mum I really want to go and meet Jordan and see what today brings. It might not work out, but I want this chance. He's the first guy I've been interested in for a long time, you know that. Please can I go?" I'm pleading with her now.

"Of course you can go, I'm not going to stop you Cassie. I know you've had your fair share of problems to deal with, but you're nearly seventeen and you need to start living your life again! Go and enjoy yourself just be careful that's all," Mum says with tears welling in her eyes.

It's in that moment that I realise how tough it's been for her and Dad. I think about what they must have gone through this last year, watching me retreat into myself and shut myself off from my teenage years.

I move closer to her and give her a big hug as I say, "I love you Mum and I'm sorry." I have tears streaming down my face.

I look at Bonnie and she's crying too. I start laughing. "What are we all like? We look like we're going to a funeral instead of the two of us having hot dates today." I start laughing.

Bonnie laughs too and Mum says, "so Bonnie, you've a hot date too do you? Who's that with?"

Bonnie says, "it's with Jezza. I've liked him for a while and it seems he feels the same way too," she's blushing now.

Mum reaches over her and gives her a big hug too. "Now you both need to hurry up and get ready for these hot dates." We all fall about the place laughing.

Once we are dressed we walk into town together then go our separate ways, promising to ring each other tonight.

"Here and Now"

I'm nervous walking down to Hunter's to meet Jordan. I've not really been on a date before, not one that I was this excited about. I don't really know him and it will be the first time I've been in a stranger's company since David. I don't know how I feel about that. How am I going to react to Jordan if he tries to touch me?

I can see him leaning up against the wall waiting for me, he's looking around searching for me. He eventually looks in my direction and I'm rewarded with the biggest and most beautiful smile. It is a smile all the way from his heart. I can feel my heart speeding up as he walks towards me.

"Hey Cassie, I am so glad you agreed to meet me. I hope we can get to know each other better and I'm looking forward to seeing your beautiful smile all day." He's still smiling and I can see he has a dimple on his left cheek. I didn't notice that last night in the dark.

I feel like I've died and gone to heaven. I smile at him too and say "well it's working already." I can feel myself blushing. "So tell me where are we going and what are we doing?" I walk up to him and link his arm.

He looks at me and lifts my chin up a little and kisses me on the forehead. "Follow me, we're going to have fun today."

We have a lot of fun; he takes me bowling where I whoop his arse, but secretly I think he let me win! Then he takes me to the cliff overlooking Fistral Beach where he unpacks the rucksack he's been carrying all day. He wouldn't tell me what was in it, but now I can see for myself. There's a picnic blanket and a small picnic. I don't know what to say I'm stunned.

I watch him unpack everything and he looks at me smiling. "Are you going to stand there all afternoon or are you going to park your gorgeous arse down here next to mine?"

I smile and walk towards the rug and sit down. "Did you pack all of this yourself?".

"I'd love to say that I did, but I told my Mum that I had a date with a beautiful and special girl and asked her to make it up for me," he says, blushing a little bit.

"It looks amazing. Thank you and make sure you thank your Mum for me. I've had a great day so far," I say looking out at the sea. I decide I want to know more about him. "So, Jordan I don't know much about you. I know you're at my school and you're in lower sixth year, but that's about all," I say lying down to look at the clouds rolling by.

"Well, em … that's about the most of it really. I have a younger brother. I like football and I'm going to play for the school team." He's laid down as well, looking at the clouds. I get the impression there's more to Jordan than what he's telling me, but we all have our secrets and I'm happy to keep mine to myself for a bit longer and he's probably the same.

After we've eaten the picnic, we talk a bit more about school, we talk about what we want to do when we finish school and just about our friends. By the time we start to tidy everything up its four o'clock and I can't believe we have been here that long. "Wow Jordan it's four o'clock, the time just flew past," I say looking at him.

"Yeah it sure did," he says smiling at me as we fold up the blanket. I hope you enjoyed your day so far because it's not over yet," he says staring into my eyes. My heart is flipping and flopping all over the place as he reaches down and takes my hand. He brings it up to his lips and kisses it very gently. "Are you ready for some more fun?" he says with a big smile on his face. He keeps hold of my hand; it feels good, so I don't take it away.

"What else do you have planned, Jordan? This has been amazing already today" I say holding his hand a little tighter.

"Well the football lads have arranged a little bit of fun at the "old rec ground". I know Bonnie is going to be there with Jezza and I thought we might go and see them for a bit, that is if you don't mind being seen with me," he asks looking sheepish. Why would he think that I'd mind being seen with him?

"Why would I be embarrassed to be seen with you Jordan? You're gorgeous." I put my hand in front of my mouth. "Oh my god did I just say that aloud?" I can feel myself blushing, but I know the best thing is just to continue to talking. Hopefully he didn't notice. "If you're worried about the age difference then that doesn't bother me, age is only a number." I'm laughing because I'm embarrassed by what I had said.

"Yes, you did say that aloud and I'm flattered coming from such a hot girl," he smiles and rubs my hand with his thumb. "Yes, I didn't know if you were worried about the age difference. I'm not and I'm glad you're not either." He's looking at me intently and he leans over and kisses my cheek.

I make a small little moan, I hope he didn't hear me, oh my god I'm so embarrassed. What am I doing?

We walk over to the "old rec ground" and all the gang are there, including Danni and Tony. As usual, when I see Tony at the weekends, I always look around to see if David is there, I notice that he's not. I know I was holding my breath while I was looking around, but then I release it when I realise he's not there. I hope Jordan didn't notice anything.

We have a great time with our friends and then it's time for me to go home. I told Mum that I won't be too late, because I know she'll worry.

Jordan walks me to the door and introduces himself to my Mum, which is really funny. He is quite confident considering his age. We both agree that we have our own things to do on Sunday, so I tell him that I will see him at school on Monday.

As I watch him walk down my drive he turns and says, "See you Cassie, thanks for a great day. I'm glad you came out with me. See you Monday" and then he is gone.

Mum is watching me and I am expecting the third degree, but it doesn't come. All she says is "he's very nice Cassie, I can see he will treat you well," and she has a tear in her eye.

"I'll be your everything"

Life has never been so good. I hang out with my friends and Jordan as much as I can. I didn't see him on the Sunday after we had our first date, but he rang me on Sunday evening and we stayed on the phone for hours. I can feel myself falling for him more and more each time I talk to him or see him.

You know when life is going good; you just know that it will all come crashing down at any minute.

We have been seeing each other for about three weeks and we are at Pebbles Beach Café having a milkshake. This has become our favourite place to spend time. It's very welcoming and we just like to sit and chat for hours.

We are saying goodbye to Mr. Stanley when Jordan grabs my hand and pulls me outside. We're leaning up against the wall watching the sea, when Jordan says, "Cassie, I really like you and I really want to kiss you, but I don't want to push you."

I just look at him with tears in my eyes. I really want this with Jordan and I have to push any image of David, that I might have, to the back of my mind. "Jordan" I say leaning closer to him. I know he is waiting for me to tell him its ok, but I just take the lead by leaning in even further and taking his lips between mine.

Very softly I kiss him. I have my eyes open and I can see the surprise in his eyes, but it's only for a split second. Then he is taking my lips between his. I feel his tongue slowly forcing its way into my mouth. I have mixed emotions right now, because I'm really enjoying it, but it's bringing back memories that I have long since buried.

Jordan is a great kisser and I concentrate on his lips, my hands go up towards his neck and I pull him even closer to me and I moan into his mouth. He has one hand on my lower back and the other one wrapped in my hair pulling on it slightly. I hear him groan and then he stops kissing me but he doesn't pull away.

He rests his forehead against mine and whispers into my mouth "I've wanted to do that since the moment I first saw you in your Economics class. Do you know something Cassie? It was even better that I thought it would be. You are an amazing and beautiful person," he says pulling away slightly to look me in the eye. He has my head in between his hands so that we are looking directly at each other.

I can feel tears welling up in my eyes; because what he just said is so beautiful and I am overcome with emotion. I pull him closer to me and kiss him again, just so I don't have to say anything back to him.

We've been kissing for a while when we both pull back and start laughing.

We see a lot of each other over the next couple of weeks because we don't like being apart. My friends have accepted Jordan and he is now good friends with Jezza and Tony.

One night we are at a beach party having a dance, laughing and generally having fun when Tony turns up, Danni is sick and has to stay at home. He comes over to us and then says, "Oh Cassie, you remember David don't you?" Everything seems to happen in slow motion, he steps to one side and there is David, looking at me with the type of grin that will make you vomit.

"Hi Cassie, remember me? How've you been?" he says, he's a real slimeball. I can feel myself tensing all my muscles and I don't realise that I have dug my nails into Jordan's arm.

"I'm fine thank you David," I say through clenched teeth. By this time Bonnie has come over to see who it is that Tony has brought with him. She stops dead when she hears his name, then when he talks she comes over to me and holds my spare hand.

"Breathe Cassie, breathe in and out," she whispers in my ear then she steps back slightly so that I can turn to walk away. I just need to get away from him; just hearing his voice is bringing back all the memories. Memories that I have tried to suppress.

I turn to walk away from David when he puts his hand out to stop me. "I thought I might have heard from you after the last party." He has a disgusting smile on his face, well it's more like a sneer. "I tried to ring you but you were never there. I was very disappointed."

He looks angry, but I can only look at him with contempt on my face and anger in my eyes and say "you obviously didn't get the message then I see." I turn and run down the beach.

I don't turn around, I don't want to know what is happening behind me. I can hear shouting; Tony is one of them. "What the hell is going on David? What are you talking about?"

Bonnie is shouting too. "So, you're David! Well let me tell you something, you made a big mistake turning up here tonight."

Last of all, I hear Jordan, "Who are you? What did you do to make Cassie run away like that?" I don't hear his reply but I hear Jordan saying "I'm not finished with you, when I've calmed Cassie down you and me are going to have a chat."

Jezza is shouting at him too. "Yeah Jordan, I want to be part of that conversation. You go and check on Cassie and I'll make sure HE doesn't disappear."

I can't hear anything else except the blood pumping in my body and I can feel myself holding my breath. I know that my lovely quiet life is about to come crashing down and I don't know if I can handle it. I start sobbing and sit on one of the big rocks.

I can hear Jordan running up the beach to get to me as fast as he can and Bonnie is not far behind him.

Jordan reaches me first and pulls me up and just engulfs me in a big hug. I try to wriggle free at first until I can smell him and I know it is his arms around me. "Hey, I'm here for you. Just breathe slowly in and out nothing bad is going to happen to you, I promise" he says quietly into my ear.

I feel myself calming down. I don't know how he does it, but I always feel calmer when he is with me.

Bonnie has reached us at this stage and she starts rubbing my back. "Come on Cassie, it'll be ok. Please just calm down. He's not worth it."

She is getting a little bit hysterical now and I say "I'm ok Bonnie honestly, it's just a shock to see him again. I thought I'd never see him again." I'm nuzzling into Jordan, knowing that I'm delaying the inevitable but enjoying this moment of closeness.

"Ok look Cassie, you need to sit down here and take some deep breaths. We can talk when you're ready, only if you want to," Jordan says taking control of the situation.

I sit down and hold his hand and Bonnie's hand too. I think about what I can say. "I can't, I can't, I'm sorry." I stand up and just run and run and run as far as I can. I hope they don't follow me, but I suppose I know they will.

I can hear shouting back at the party and it's getting closer too. The next thing I know someone is pulling at me and trying to push me down on the sand. Why is David doing this to me again? I start fighting, kicking and punching at him. I fall to my knees. "Leave me alone David! Why are you doing this to me again, why? What did I ever do to you?" I'm full on sobbing now still kicking and punching with all my might.

"Cassie stop. It's me, Jordan, please stop. I'm here and I'm going to protect you. I promise I won't let anyone hurt you, come on please, it's me." He puts his arms around me now to try and stop me from kicking and punching him. "Please Cassie?" I can hear him sobbing as he tries to calm me down. I stop thrashing around and just lie face down in the sand crying. I can feel Jordan's heart thumping really quickly and then he lifts himself off me and pulls me onto his lap, kissing my forehead and rubbing the top of my head.

Bonnie is there too, trying to calm me down. I start to breathe normally and I know that once I look into Jordan's eyes I'm going to have to tell him what happened last year and I really don't want to. He likes me for the person I am now. How will he feel towards me when I tell him? I don't know what to do.

I look up at Bonnie first and she looks at me with eyes that tell me to tell him. She smiles to make sure I'm alright and then says "I'm going back to the group to make sure David is still there and to make sure he doesn't go anywhere. Everything is going to be fine Cassie, I promise." She starts walking over to the group and I can hear voices and then shouting.

Jordan is still rubbing my back and when I dare to look into his eyes all I see is his love for me. I open my mouth to start talking and Jordan shakes his head, lifts his finger and puts it to my lips. "Let me talk first Cassie, while you get your head sorted" he smiles and I nod.

"Cassie, when I met you I felt a pull towards you. I didn't understand it, but the more I've got to know you the more I feel it. I believe you're my soul mate and that we are meant to be together. I love you Cassie and I know it's not the right time to tell you this, but I do and I need you to know it." I can't stop looking at him. Did he really just say he loved me? I can feel a tear rolling down my face. Jordan uses his thumb to wipe it away.

"I'm not finished yet. I asked a lot of people about you before I got to meet you at Jezza's party. I wanted to know you and understand you. I heard rumours about a beach party, but they were only rumours and I knew you would tell me when the time was right. I think now is the right time. You need to stop carrying this burden by yourself, whatever it is. I'm here for you and nothing will change that. You're my soul mate, my other half. I love you Cassie."

What can I say to that? "Jordan I ... I ..I love you too and I'm sorry to burden you with my problems, and I know I have to open up and tell someone."

I take a deep breath and tell him what happened to me that night in the playground. I don't stop talking for fifteen minutes and I can see his eyes cloud over. "Jordan, I'm sorry, but there's more." I go on to tell him about the beach party in November last year when I tried to kill myself. I'm sobbing so hard that I can't see through my tears. What I can see though is that Jordan is getting angry and I put my arms around him because I don't want him to be angry with me.

"Jordan, I'm sorry. Please don't be angry with me, I don't want to lose you because you think I'm a liability," I say, because I'm so worried about the look in his eyes.

I see his eyes change; they become turquoise again. "Cassie, you're not going to lose me, I told you I would be here for you, whatever happens. I'm just so angry with that guy who's standing over there and I'm trying to control my anger. I feel like I want to kill him for what he did to you Cassie. I... Love... You," he says kissing me on my forehead between words. "It's my job to protect you and that's what I want to do. I haven't done a good job though I'm sorry," he says looking at the ground.

"Jordan, this happened before I met you, it's not your fault," I say not understanding what he's saying.

I hear Bonnie approaching us; she says that we need to ring the police and my Mum because we can't keep this to ourselves any longer. "Cassie I know you don't want to do this, but you need to confront him and you need to ring your Mum. She will come down here and she will make this all right! They are waiting for you to make your way over to the group and David is still there with Jezza and Tony. He won't hurt you Cassie, I promise," she says looking at me and I know she's right.

"I won't let David or anyone else hurt you, remember you're my soul mate," Jordan says and kisses me on the top of my head while pulling me in close. "No one!"

I know that I have to go over to them, I've put it off too long already. I take Jordan's hand and Bonnie links my spare arm and we walk back over to the party.

When we get there, I can see that Jordan is struggling between hurting David and protecting me. I stand in front of him and pull his arms around me like a comforting blanket. I can see that Jezza and David have been fighting and Tony now has hold of David so that he can't run off.

Tony is the first to say something. "Cassie, I'm so sorry. I didn't know anything happened that night. I thought you both liked each other and that you were laughing not screaming. I feel so guilty, I'm so sorry," he's crying now and I have to stay strong or I'll collapse on the ground. "I can't believe you tried to kill yourself because of my stupid cousin, I'll never forgive myself Cassie. We could have all lost you and you are the one who keeps our gang together. You mean so much to all of us."

"Tony, it's not your fault. You didn't do this to me. HE did," I spit towards David. "He ... He .." I need to try and compose myself. "He told me I was a slut and I that had wanted him all night, I hadn't even noticed him until you introduced us. Just ask Danni. He pounced on me and started ... he started to touch me and then undid my shorts and then when he was undoing his I kicked him in the balls and ran. That's when he grabbed me and told me I was a slut. Then he said he would come back for what was his. I was so petrified that he would come back and finish what he started that I couldn't live with it any longer."

I stop to control myself and feel Jordan pulling me even closer and he whispers in my ear. "Cassie, I'm so sorry. I love you." I can hear him crying. What have I dragged him into? A sorry messed up life that's what.

I don't know how long we stand here, I don't say a word to David and he never speaks to anyone, he just looks down at the sand. Everyone is looking at me and all the guys have tears in their eyes. I don't know what to say to them, they all love me and that makes me so happy.

I hear a noise behind us and when I turn I see my Mum approaching us. I fly into her arms, sobbing hysterically. Bonnie and Jordan come up to us and they tell her what happened that fateful night and everything that happened after. My Mum is sobbing now and she holds me even tighter. "Baby girl, why didn't you tell me? I would have helped you and we could have talked about this. Are you ok? Did he try anything tonight?"

"No, Mum he just showed up and was looking at me, I freaked and then when Jordan followed me down the beach I thought he was David and I started kicking and screaming. Mum what am I going to do?"

"Well I rang the police on the way over here and they're pulling up now, so we are going to walk over to talk to them. I see Tony has already taken David over to them."

My Mum is holding me up while I walk over to the police. How am I going to manage going through it all again? Will they even be able to arrest David? Yes he assaulted me, but he didn't rape me, even if that was his intention. It was so long ago, how can they believe me? I start sobbing harder and harder and I feel Jordan come up to my Mum and pry me off her.

"Cassie, come on breathe in and let it out, breathe in and let it out. Come on you know you can do it," he says and he sounds like a broken man.

I look up at him and smile to let him know that I appreciate him being there for me, he leans down and very gently touches his lips to mine. He pulls away and passes me back to my Mum. "I'm not going anywhere. I'll make sure I can be with you when they question you, ok?"

"Why?"

When we get over to the Police I can see David has been handcuffed and is being put into the back of one of the police cars. At least I don't have to stand there and look at him any longer. Mum has one hand and Jordan has the other.

A female police officer comes over to me. "Are you ok? It's Cassie isn't it?"

"Yes it is and yes I'm ok. I'm just a little shaken up that's all."

"We need to bring you down to the station to tell us what happened and then we can take this from there."

"Will … will he see me talking to you?"

"He won't. He knows we are taking you in though. Are you worried about something?"

"No. It's just he said that he would come back and finish what he started and I'm worried that this might make him worse. That's why I didn't do anything at the time. I don't want to make things worse." I start to sob and Mum pulls me into her. Jordan doesn't let go of my hand.

"It's ok Cassie, the police will look after you." Mum says.

"We will, so let's go to the station and we can

interview you there. Are you going to take her Mrs. Taylor?" the very kind officer asks Mum.

"Yes I will, I want to be with her when you interview her as well." She says.

"Me too," Jordan says so that everyone can hear him.

"And who are you, sir?" the officer asks.

"I'm her boyfriend and I promised her I wouldn't leave her while you are talking to her. I never break any promises to her. She doesn't need that on top of everything else that has been going on." Wow Jordan can be very authoritative.

The police officer looks at Jordan and says "OK we won't be in a formal setting anyway because Cassie hasn't done anything wrong. I don't want you getting upset and angry when she goes through all the details with us. Is that understood? If you do then I will have to ask you to leave," she looks at him with a furrowed brow.

He smiles, "that's fine, I promise I won't get angry. My priority is to protect and take care of Cassie and that's what I intend to do."

She smiles at him. "OK, see you down the station, my name is Officer Pettigrew, just ask for me at the desk and I will bring all three of you through to the interview room."

We nod and walk over to Mum's car. Jordan opens the front door for me to sit and then gets into the back.

As Mum drives over to the station it is very quiet in the car. No one really knows what to say.

Jordan almost whispers, "I'm sorry you had to go through that Cassie and now you have to go through it all again. I'm really sorry."

"Jordan, it's not your fault. It was before I even met you. David is a very unpleasant person and I'm glad that he is going to get what he deserves in the eyes of the law. I didn't do anything about it last year because I didn't think anyone would believe me. I should have known that Mum would have. I'm sorry Mum, I just thought that I had to deal with it all myself."

She moves her hand onto my lap and takes my hand in hers. "Cassie, I am your Mum and Mum's are supposed to protect their daughters. I let you down and you couldn't tell me about it, that's the hardest part for me to understand. We talk about everything. Why didn't you tell me?"

I sob a little. "He kept telling me I was a slut and I started to believe him and I didn't want you to think of me like that. I'm not a slut Mum, honest."

"I know that, I just wished you could have told me and we could have dealt with it when it happened. Maybe then you wouldn't have tried to leave us when you couldn't bear it any longer." She has tears running down her face, I don't know how she can see to drive.

Jordan reaches forward and rests his hands on my shoulders; I can feel the heat radiating from them, calming me down. "We will all protect you Cassie, until our dying breath. Remember that!"

Mum pulls up outside the police station and the three of us get out of the car and walk inside to the desk.

Officer Pettigrew collects us and takes us into a room where there are seats for us all, she offers us a drink and we all take one.

"So, Cassie most of this conversation will be between me and you. I will ask your Mum and boyfriend a couple of questions, but mostly I will be talking to you. Is that ok?"

"Yes that's fine." I mumble.

We spend the next forty-five minutes talking about the night at the playground and the ride home in the car. Then we talk about the night I tried to kill myself and eventually we talk about what happened tonight to bring everything to a head.

I am exhausted and just want to go home.

"OK I think I have everything down, I will type up my report and give it to the arresting officer and then it will be taken further."

"What … what do you think will happen to David?" I ask, stumbling over my words.

"These type of cases are very difficult because it happened over a year ago, but I think we have a strong enough case for some kind of a conviction. It won't surprise me though we get him for attempted rape and he will get a suspended sentence. This means that he will be charged but allowed to walk free. I know that isn't what you want to hear, but he will have a record against him and it is very hard to get anywhere in life with a sexual offence against you."

"I hadn't really thought about what would happen next. What happens if he comes to get me? What do I do then?"

"You will have a restraining order against him and if he breaks that then he could go to jail."

"OK, well that is something I suppose."

Mum stands and holds out her hand to Office Pettigrew. "Thank you for your help, I think Cassie needs to go home now."

The officer stands up and shakes Mum's hand, then she shows us out the door. When we get back into the car, we all sigh a big sigh of relief.

"Jordan, will I drop you home or do you want to stay at ours tonight? In the spare room of course?"

"I'd like to stay with you if that isn't a problem. I just need to ring my Mum when I get to your house. Is that ok?"

"That's fine. We can all talk a little while longer when we get home. It's going to be difficult to tell your Dad. He heard that I was needed at the beach and I rang him to say you were ok, but that we would be a while. He is waiting for us to get home."

"I forgot about Dad. Mum, he is going to be so angry. I hope I haven't let him down." I can feel myself getting a little bit panicky and upset.

Jordan squeezes one of my shoulders, "don't be stupid Cassie, your dad loves you and will protect you as much as he can."

"I know, I just hate the thought that I might have let him down."

"Cassie, your dad won't think that at all, if anything he will think that he let you down because you didn't go and talk to him about it."

We go quiet again as we pull into our driveway. Dad is waiting for us at the door and he hugs me tight when I get up to the door.

"Cassie, what is going on? I have been out of my mind with worry. Let's get you inside you must be freezing. Come on Jordan, come on in."

I step inside and I know that I have to talk about this all over again. Each time I tell the story, the burden eases and it becomes easier to talk about. It's like therapy I suppose.

"All I Wanna Do Is Make Love To You"

Life gets back to normal after that. Jordan and I are even stronger and we are madly in love. Our relationship is progressing well and I know it's time to take the relationship to the next level. I love Jordan and he loves me, so sex is the next step right? I know I want it so bad and I'm guessing he feels the same.

We are at yet another party, but this time it's in a friend's house and we have both arranged to stay out for the night, so I guess we are both ready. I know Jordan is worried that I'm going to panic but I think I'll be fine because I love him.

The party is good and there is lots of dancing and laughing and then we sneak off up to the spare room, where we are staying the night. As soon as we close the door we start kissing passionately. Jordan pins me against the door and I can feel how excited he is to be staying the night with me.

He takes my clothes off, it's like we are both in a rush, and so I start pulling at his. He stops kissing me and takes my chin in his hands, then he looks me in the eye and says "Cassie, we can stop if you want to! It will be hard, but if it's not what you want, then we can stop." I can see the desire in his eyes and I know that they are only reflecting what is in mine.

"Jordan, I really want this. I want you now, don't make me wait any longer. Take me to bed or lose me forever," I say winking at him. I love the film Top Gun and that is one of my favourite quotes from it.

He smiles and it reaches his eyes. "Get on the bed wench," he says laughing, pushing me towards the bed.

What happens over the next couple of hours is so beautiful that I find myself in tears. It was everything I wanted and more. Jordan makes sure everything is about me and he keeps reassuring me and making sure I don't freak out.

"Cassie, why are you crying? Did I hurt you? Do you regret it?" He looks sad at the thought.

"No Jordan, it was amazing. I think I love you more. I'm so happy, that's why I'm crying."

"I'm glad you're not hurt Cassie. Now we need to get some sleep. This is what I've been dreaming of, holding you close while you sleep," he says pulling my naked body into his. He fits exactly around me and hugs me tight.

"Night night and thank you" I say as I start drifting off!

"How Am I Supposed To Live Without You?"

Six months Later ...

I'm sitting in Pebbles with Bonnie and Danni trying to understand why life keeps putting obstacles in my way. Why can't life be simple? I have Jordan in my life and we love each other. David has been convicted of attempted rape, but he was set free with just a record against him. I have a restraining order against him so he can't come anywhere near me. So why now, when everything seems to be coming together perfectly does life through me a curveball?

"Come on Cassie, you know this is a great opportunity that is hard to turn down. Anyway, it's only for ten months. It's not forever." Danni is saying. "You know Jordan won't stop you going and if it was the other way round then you'd encourage him to go too."

I've been offered a ten-month placement in San Francisco working as an intern in a book publishing company. This is my dream job and the first step towards my lifelong dream of being an editor. The only fly in the ointment is that I don't want to leave Jordan and I can't ask him to give up school to come with me.

"I know girls, I really do. It just breaks my heart to have to be apart from him," I say with tears in my eyes. "I know I have to tell him tonight, before he finds out from someone else."

"Wish me luck" I say standing up and walking slowly out of Pebbles.

"I'll call you tomorrow," Bonnie says.

Danni says "yeah me too."

Jordan and I have been together for a year and today is our anniversary. As usual he has planned something special. I'm so lucky. He's so romantic and is always thinking of me and doing really nice things for me. This is going to be so hard. I don't want him to hate me.

I walk along the beach, thinking about how far I've come over the last two years and how my life has changed. I attribute a lot of that to Jordan. I smile and make my way home to get ready for him.

He collects me, looking gorgeous as usual, and he takes me for dinner in the fabulous Upper Deck Restaurant. The food is amazing as always.

We finish dessert, pay the bill and leave the restaurant holding hands. We walk down to the beach and lay down on the grass next to it, just holding hands and looking at the stars. Just like our first date!

"Cassie, I love you and you've made me so happy this last year. I know we've been through a lot, but I've loved having you next to me. I can't believe that I fell so hard and so fast for you. You mean the world to me, but I need to tell you something," Jordan says rolling onto his side to look at me. I roll towards him and he takes my hands in his. He kisses me on the forehead and I feel dread in my stomach.

"I need to talk to you too," I say looking into his eyes.

"Can I go first, please Cassie? And we won't discuss it until you've said your bit too. How's that for a deal?" He says with a small smile.

"Ok" I say softly.

"So you know how I play football for the school. Well I've been offered a scholarship to teach young kids how to play football." He holds up his hand before I can speak. "Wait, let me finish," he says. "It's in Toronto for six months and it starts in eight months' time. I want to go but I don't want to leave you. I don't know if I can do it, I wanted you to know though, so that we can discuss it together. Right, it's your turn now" he says rubbing my cheek so that I nuzzle into it. I have tears in my eyes because I can see what's going to play out here. Well here goes nothing.

"Jordan, I love you so much and you've helped me through a tough time in my life and for that I will be forever grateful. I truly believe you're my soul mate and that we are meant to be together." I smile kissing him very gently on the lips.

"I've been offered a ten month placement in San Francisco working for Plume who are a Penguin Group Company. I will be going in as an Intern in the Editorial Department. It's the job of my dreams, but I don't want to fulfill my dreams if I don't have you with me," I say with a tear dripping down my face.

"When does it start Cassie?" He has a tear in his eye too, I think he knows that our lives are changing right in front of our faces.

"Next month, they've brought the placement forward and want me to go as soon as possible, but I want to talk about us Jordan, I need to know where we stand. I love you and you're my soul mate and I can't really be without you." I'm whispering this last part because it is so hard to say.

"Cassie, we are soul mates and we will be together, I won't let distance stand in my way. I'll be in Canada and you'll be in San Francisco. That's closer than Newquay, babe. Our relationship is so strong we can do this." He's pleading with me with his eyes.

"I know Jordan, but I don't want you to go to Canada and keep thinking about me and worrying about what I am doing and how I would react to things that you are doing. You have to go and live your life and if we are true soul mates then our souls will find each other again." I'm crying now but I realise that I need to let him go and follow his dream. We are both ambitious and we need to do this to really find ourselves.

If it's meant to be, then it's meant to be. I'm a big believer in that.

We cry a lot, we hug and make love under the stars. We want to be together until the last minute. We love each other and know that we have to let each other go to do this or we might regret it and blame each other and I'd hate that. I love Jordan too much to hate him.

When he walks me home, we stop outside my house and he pulls me close. "I love you Cassie, I will always find you and look after you. It's only for a year and then we will be together again. We can keep talking all the time and write letters. It will be fine, it will work." I don't know if he is trying to convince me or himself.

I kiss him really passionately and then when I reach my front door I turn around and wave to him and watch him walking down the street. I walk to my bedroom and climb into bed without even getting undressed. I cry myself to sleep and know that yet again my life is about to change. I'm not sure I want to embrace it.

We see as much of each other as we can before it is time for me to leave. Jordan agreed to sign up for the scholarship for teaching football in Toronto, but I will be leaving first.

The day before I have to go to London to catch my flight, we go on one of our magical dates. We cry for most of the night and he gives me a gift of a necklace, which has the infinity symbol in cubic zirconium, it's beautiful. He places it on my neck and kisses it and continues upwards towards my earlobe. He whispers in my ear, "Cassie, wear this every day and when you think about me just touch it and I will be thinking of you. One day, I will buy you one made of real diamonds, you are my diamond."

He spins me round and kisses me passionately, neither of us wants to be the one to walk away. "Jordan, I'll think of you every day. We need to say goodbye and in a year's time we can try again."

"No, we can still be together even though we are miles apart, we can ring and talk to each other, we can write letters. Just think of all the letters you can keep and show our grandchildren. Please don't push me away Cassie, it will all work out. I know it will. I want it to."

"Jordan, it's not fair for you to wait for me, you should be enjoying your life in Toronto without thinking about me all the time. It will spoil your experience."

"No! Not having you in my life will ruin my experience. Cassie I need you, I love you."

"I love you too Jordan, but I know I have to let you go. As you said, if we are true soul mates then our souls will always find each other." I can't stop the uncontrollable sobbing which leaves my throat.

"Cassie, I will find you and I will be with you – together forever, that's us." We hold each other tight and then I have to walk away and go into the house, not knowing what my future holds.

San Francisco

Have you ever had to give away something that you really love? You know like an old doll or a memento? Well, that's what I had to do with Jordan. I had to give him away so that he can enjoy his dream of teaching football in Toronto.

I've been in San Francisco for four months and I love it. However, I'm so sad and home sick. I miss my Mum and Dad, Bonnie, Danni and even Jezza. But most of all, I miss Jordan. He's rung me loads of times but I try not to talk to him if I can help it. It makes us both so sad, but I know I have to push him away. It's the best thing for both of us. I need to concentrate on my job here, it's my dream job and I absolutely love it. It's hard work, but I know it's the right thing for me. Jordan needs to concentrate on his football, because he will be going to Toronto in two months and this is a once in a lifetime chance for him.

We will see each other when we are both back home, who knows what will happen then. When I talk to Bonnie or Danni I don't ask about Jordan, but they tell me anyway. He's missing me so much and he's hanging around with my friends so that he can hear what I'm up to. I know he doesn't hate me, he still loves me and I know he agrees with what I'm doing, but it does hurt. So much!!

Work is unbelievably amazing! I have always wanted to work in editing and I'm doing a lot of running round and skivvy work, but I don't care because I'm working in the perfect environment. I love reading, making sure that anything written is at its best and is an enjoyable experience for the reader. I feel that I have to give one hundred per cent to this because it will help me get my dream job when I get home in four months and counting. I gave up a lot for my dream job but it was the right thing to do, it hurts though. Every day I think of Jordan when I wake up, when I go to sleep and so many times during the day. My heart feels like it is breaking every day. I am wearing his necklace and instinctively I touch it when I think about him. It makes me smile and I vow never to take it off.

1992

Two months and counting ... I'm looking forward to going home, but I know that life won't be the same. I'm not the same. I just miss everyone so much. I still think a lot about Jordan, but it's getting easier because I'm so busy and think about nothing but work all the time. It was for the best!

Bonnie and Danni are coming out to see me when my placement is over and we are going to just relax for a week. I can't wait!

My boss, Claudia, has given me a really big project to do. I can't believe it; she's trusting me with this new author and has given me her account. I'm so excited I just want to cry. The first thing I do is ring my Mum, "oh my god Mum you are never going to guess what happened today," I'm shouting down the phone.

"What happened, baby?" she's laughing.

"They gave me my own account at work. I'm looking after Donna Tartt, Mum you know she's amazing." I'm laughing and crying at the same time.

"Oh Cassie that's amazing I'm so excited for you." I can tell she's really proud of me.

"I can't wait to come home Mum. I miss our hugs and chats," I say going quiet on the phone.

"Me too Cassie, me too, but I'm so proud of you and what you are achieving. It was definitely the right decision for you to make. I love you." She's crying now.

"I love you and Dad so much. Thank you for giving me this opportunity." I have to finish off the call because I feel so homesick. I go to bed crying my eyes out!

"If Wishes Came True"

This is my last week on my placement and Bonnie and Danni came out a week earlier than I expected. They've been sightseeing while I've been working.

I arranged to meet them in the local bar after work to let our hair down and have fun.

I usually finish work late, but Claudia knows it's my last week and my friends are here so she has let me go early these last couple of days. She rings me about four o'clock and I think she's going to let me leave extra early.

"Cassie, can you come into my office please?" she says down the phone and she sounds so serious that now I'm worried.

"Sure Claudia, I'll come over now." I get up from my desk, smooth my skirt down and walk slowly over to her office. My heart is beating really fast and I can feel my hands starting to get sweaty. I hate confrontation and I hope she isn't disappointed with something I've done. I've tried really hard to prove myself and show that I really wanted to get as much out of this internship as possible.

I stand outside her door and take a deep breath. "OK Cassie," I say to myself "you've done nothing wrong, just go in there and see what she wants."

I knock on the door and wait for her to tell me I can go in. I open the door and walk over to the desk and sit in the chair opposite Claudia. "Hey Cassie," she says. "I can't believe your placement is nearly over. You've done a fantastic job and we have been delighted to have you here with us."

"Thank you," I say looking at the floor. I was never good with praise. "I'm hoping that the unbelievable experience I've had here will help me get my dream job when I go back home." I say, hoping she will understand that I'm asking for a good reference.

"I'm sure it will. Have you any idea what your dream job is though Cassie? Do you know what you really want to do? Have you thought about the opportunities available to you when you get home?"

She looks at me and smiles. I don't think she is going to tell me off, she is smiling too much. I don't get chance to answer her questions as she continues.

"I want to discuss an opportunity with you! Donna Tartt has said that she was amazed with the work you've done for her and she wants you to be her personal editor. This is a phenomenal opportunity and one that is very rare, particularly at your age."

Is she still talking? I lost her somewhere at phenomenal.

"Oh my god are you serious? Wow! I don't know what to s.. s.. say." I'm stuttering now.

"I know, it's amazing and something I would have loved when I first started out. Hell, I'd have loved that at any age." She says smiling at me.

"Now obviously, if you take this opportunity it would mean staying in the States and not going home at the end of next week. I know you want to go home so badly." Crap I hadn't thought about that, now I just want to cry.

"Your friends are staying with you, so I'm giving you the rest of the week off to have some fun and think about this offer. This can be a turning point in your career if you decide to stay, so think long and hard about it. Talk to your parents and your friends and then we can meet up on Friday to discuss your decision. Whatever you decide to do, I will back you one hundred percent" She's smiling at me because she knows how amazing this is.

"Claudia, wow! Thanks." I'm gushing now. "I really can't believe it, what an amazing opportunity. Obviously, it's something I really need to think about, not the job – that is my dream, but my family and friends. Thank you so much Claudia." I get up and walk around her desk and give her a hug. I can see she is shocked but then she relaxes into it.

"Cassie you deserve it. You've worked so hard during your internship and this couldn't have happened to a nicer person. Now off you go and have some fun," she says pointing at the door.

I walk over to the door, but before I walk out of the room I put my hand on the door handle and turn around with the biggest smile on my face. "Claudia, thank you for believing in me," and then I walk out. I go back to my desk in a daze, collect my bag and walk out of the building. I head over to the bar and luckily Bonnie and Danni are there before me. They smile when they see me.

Danni says, "wow Cassie you're early, we were just going to grab a table and order a drink before dinner."

"Ok let's do that" I say with a huge smile on my face.

Bonnie looks at me and says "Cassie what's going on? You've got a huge smile on your face."

"Let's grab this table and I'll order the drinks." I see a waiter passing by us so I stop him. "Can we have three San Francisco cocktails please?" The two girls look at me. We usually only drink a couple of beers and never get drunk, especially when I have work the next day.

"Girls, I have something really important to tell you and I need you to help me make a decision. This is something life changing for me and I want your advice. I love you guys so much and I know you'll tell me what's best for me." They both look so confused.

"You know my placement is over at the end of this week and then we are going travelling for a week, well Claudia called me into her office today and has offered me a once in a lifetime job. To be sole editor for Donna Tartt." I stop talking and look at the two girls. They are staring at me with their mouths open. Bonnies starts clapping her hands really fast, she is so excited.

"It would mean staying here in the States; so it's a big decision and I need you both to help me make the right decision." I look up and they both have tears in their eyes, they look at each other smiling, then both stand and come round the table and hug me.

"You are amazing do you know that? You have come all the way over here, put your name out there in a really hard industry and now you've been offered a job of a lifetime. Oh my god Cassie I'm so proud of you," Danni says crying.

"Me too Cassie. I wouldn't have been able to do what you've done in a million years. You're so strong. I know in my heart that you've got to take this job and see where it takes you. I'll miss you so much, but look at the great holidays I can have." She pulls back so that she can see me, "Cassie, this is your rollercoaster ride babe, and it's not time for you to get off yet," Bonnie says and I'm sobbing.

Our cocktails arrive and we have a toast "To best friends," I say and we clink our glasses.

"To dream jobs," Danni says and we clink glasses again.

"To the right decisions," Bonnie says and we clink for the last time.

We look at each other and start laughing then down our cocktails in one.

As we order more San Francisco cocktails I think about what the girls have just said and it reminds me of the decisions I have already made. I start to feel sad and I look at the girls and say, "sometimes the right decisions are the hardest ones we have to make. I miss

Jordan you know, and now I won't be able to come home and accidentally bump into him. Not for a couple of years anyway. It hurts so much. I really want to have him close to me, holding me and telling me that I'm doing the right thing and that it's OK to pursue my dream without him here with me."

They both smile at me. "You know Cassie, the hardest thing you ever did was to walk away from Jordan. You didn't need to do that, he wants to be with you and he wants to move here to be closer to you when his scholarship ends." Bonnie takes a sip of her new cocktail, which the waiter has just put down on the table. "That can still happen you know."

"I know Bonnie, but I want him to enjoy every aspect of being in Canada. He's still young and needs to lead a normal, healthy life – full of girls, drink and parties. He doesn't need to be thinking of me all the time, he needs to go out and have lots of fun. I told him that if we were truly soul mates then our souls will always find each other."

"In my opinion, I think you are really silly to be thinking like that, he doesn't want to have fun, he just wants to be with you," Danni says.

"I know, but I don't want him to wait, I want him to enjoy his freedom." I can feel the tears starting to form in my eyes because letting Jordan go was the hardest thing I have ever done and thinking of him enjoying his freedom with someone else just kills me. I need to stop thinking of him because it just upsets me.

"Let's not worry about that tonight, I don't let

myself think about him very often because it hurts too much," I sigh. "Tonight I just want to get really drunk and celebrate my good news."

We clink glasses again, "to a good night!" We start laughing again and it sets the atmosphere for the rest of the night.

I have a funny feeling, I've had it a few times since I've been here but it's a lot stronger tonight. I look around me because the hairs on my neck are standing up.

"Are you ok Cassie?" I turn slowly and look at Bonnie. I look at her strangely, I heard her say my name but I don't know what she said.

"Sorry, did you say something?"

"Yeah I asked if you were ok. You looked a bit spooked."

"Sorry Bonnie, I'm fine. I just had a feeling someone was looking at us. I can't see anyone I know, so I guess I just need more drink."

She laughs and we throw our cocktails down and order more.

"Release Me"

We had a great night, lots of cocktails and dancing and I can definitely feel it in the morning as my head is really sore the next day. I'm not used to drinking and don't usually get hangovers. Thank god I don't have to work today.

We sleep in and over breakfast we decide to go sightseeing for the afternoon and we head down to the bay to get the ferry across to Alcatraz to see the amazing prison. It is a fantastic place and it feels really eerie, especially when you walk into a cell and they close the cell doors. You are trapped inside the small cell and it made me think of all the inmates who used to be inside and how they must have felt living inside these small rooms all day and night.

I feel all shivery and look out from between the bars. This is what it would have been like for David, if he had been sentenced. I shudder – I don't like to think about him but sometimes he just pops into my head and I get nervous thinking about his comment that he would find me and finish what he started.

Thankfully, the "warden" doesn't leave us inside for long and we all sigh with relief. I look around me because I have the feeling that I am being watched. Why does this keep happening to me? Maybe I was just kidding myself that I could move on without it affecting me.

"Are you ok Cassie?" Bonnie asks me.

"Sorry I was just a little spooked back there, the thoughts of people living in those cells just made me think of David. I'll be fine." I sigh.

"Come on let's explore the Island before we sail back." I say linking their arms and walking back outside the prison.

We walk around the Island but there isn't a great deal to see, so when the ferry comes back to drop more visitors off, we climb on board and enjoy the short ride back to the bay. It is a sunny day and we make the most of it by having lunch outside. I love being by the water, it remind me of home. I regularly come down to the bay and sit, drinking coffee thinking about Mum and Dad.

I can't fully relax though today, because I know I have to ring them and tell them about my amazing job offer and that I might be staying in the States. We have thrashed through every eventuality and I know that I just have to stay. This is something I have wanted for so long and it is being handed to me on a silver plate. I have to grasp it with both hands and see where it takes me. This is a one in a million opportunity and I don't want to regret not taking it. No regrets remember.

When I speak to Mum and Dad they agree that I have to take the offer. There are tears, but they are so proud of me and know that I need to do this. They tell me that they are going to come out to visit me at the end of the month so they can meet Claudia and see where

I'm living. I miss them so much.

We go out to a restaurant overlooking the Golden Gate Bridge, which is so beautiful and I realise how lucky I am to be given this opportunity. I also know how hard I'm going to have to work but I don't mind, this is what I want to do.

I go back to work on Friday and tell Claudia that I am taking the position and that I am delighted to be working with her for longer.

When I meet the girls after work I tell them that I still have the following week off work. So that means we are still going travelling, as planned. The only difference is that I am not going home with them. That will be a sad day when I have to say goodbye

We have a really good night but when we got back to my apartment I have a message on my answer phone. I press the play button without thinking about it.

I stop dead in my tracks.

"Cassie, I heard your great news. I wish I could be there to celebrate with you. I miss you so much and love you even more, but I know it was the right thing for both of us. I'm in Toronto and it looks like they're going to take me on here too." I smile and touch the answer phone as if by touching it I am touching him. My other hand reaches up to touch my infinity chain that Jordan gave me. It makes me feel closer to him.

He continues to talk. "Looks like we both landed our dream jobs. Thanks for pushing me into making the right decision."

I smile at the phone. "I hope I get to see you soon." He hangs up!

Wow Jordan rang me. How did he find out so quick?

I sink to the floor sobbing. I miss him so much and I was just starting to get through a day at a time without thinking about him. Hearing his voice and feeling the answer phone vibrating when he was talking made it feel like he was here in the room with me. I thought I was getting over him. How stupid of me to think like that, I'll never get over him. I know that now!

Bonnie and Danni hear me sobbing and sink to the floor with me. They both hug me and rub my back.

"Sorry Cassie, I told Jezza your news and he must have told Jordan. I didn't think he'd ring you. I'm sorry babe," Bonnie says through her own tears.

"I'm not mad Bonnie. It was hard leaving him, but we both needed to concentrate on our futures. It was the right thing to do, we have both been offered our dream jobs because we left Newquay. That means the world to me," I say meaning every word of it.

I go to bed that night thinking of Jordan. Who knows when I'll see him again - if I ever will! I am heartbroken because this is so final, the door was always left open to meet when we both go home and now I have closed that door on this chapter of my life.

I have a dream about my wedding; I'm standing on the cliffs in Newquay looking out to sea. I'm there on my own in my beautiful white wedding dress. I turn around slowly to see where everyone is, but no one is there. I turn back to look at the sea, it's quite rough. There's a storm approaching and soon enough I can feel the spray from the sea reaching up to the top of the cliff. I look down at my dress, I don't want it to get wet, this is an important day; this is the day I get to marry the man of my dreams.

I turn away from the sea and slowly walk back down the hill where I can see Jordan waiting for me at the bottom. He is reaching his hand up to me for me to take so that he can help me down. He is smiling at me and I smile back at him, I am so happy.

Every time I reach out to take his hand though he becomes more and more out of reach. I start to cry as I try to take his hand, I can feel the tears falling down my face. Everyone is stood behind Jordan and they are all reaching out for me, but they just seem to get further and further away as I walk closer to them. I can feel myself starting to panic, I become frantic running down the hill and yet they still get further and further out of my reach.

All of a sudden I stop running and when I turn around I am back at the top of the hill looking out at the raging sea once again. If I can't get to Jordan then what is the point of being on this planet? I turn once more and look at Jordan and my friends and family reaching out their hands to take mine, they are shouting at me but I can't hear what they are saying.

I say goodbye and then I jump into the raging sea, it is the only thing that calms me as I fall deeper and deeper into the depths of my own despair. I am thrown around the sea like a jumper in a washing machine, but still I keep falling. My dress flies up over my face as I take my last watery breath, and keep falling, spinning out of control.

I hear a scream and I wake realising it's me, but I can't breathe. I can't see. I start thrashing around in the bed screaming, it really feels like I am drowning.

All of a sudden I hear a thud as my door crashes open. "Cassie, what's wrong. Wake up Cassie." It's Bonnie and she is holding my hand. "I'm here."

I can feel myself calming down and then I can breathe again, and I can see. "What happened? Why was your nightdress over your head? Your face is wet. Cassie what did you dream about?"

I realise that my face is wet because I was crying in my sleep and when I jumped into the sea I must have moved around so much my nightdress flew up above my face, just like in my dream. My necklace, that Jordan gave me, got caught and was pulled really tight against my throat, which is why I thought I couldn't breathe.

"Bonnie, just hold me please." I wasn't ready to tell her about my dream; I know it will bring back unpleasant memories from the beach party when I walked into the sea ready to give up on everything. Thank god for my friends or I wouldn't be here in San Francisco, being offered the job of my dreams. I owe them so much.

She holds me for about twenty minutes before I feel I am ready to tell her what happened, then she pulls me close and cradles my head in her hand and holds it close to her head. "I know this is hard Cassie, all the old memories were brought up last night. Do you have these dreams often?"

"No I don't Bonnie, I promise. I haven't had a dream like that in a long time; you don't need to worry about me honestly. I'll be fine now I promise." All the time I am saying this I can feel my heart hardening, I need to get past this. I was the one who was insistent that we didn't have a long distance relationship. I need to move on and the thought of that just breaks my heart.

Bonnie climbs into bed with me and holds me tight and eventually I fall into a deep, dream free sleep.

"White Wedding"

2000

Today is the night before my wedding. I am unbelievably nervous and keep wondering whether I am doing the right thing?

I'm only twenty seven and I met Chad two years ago, I love him and I know that he will make me happy. So, why am I thinking about Jordan? I know everyone says you never forget your first love and I can honestly say that is true. He creeps into my thoughts when I least expect it and then I get sad. I don't regret anything about my life, I have an amazing time here in the States and it was the best thing I have ever done. However, it is also the worst thing I have ever done. Jordan is my one regret in life. I wonder how things would be if he were in my life. I know that he won't be there for me ever again as I am closing yet another door to prevent us being together, but I need to move on and it took me a while before I could do that. I met Chad and he is perfect for me, he is a wonderful man.

I need to keep my mind on him. We have a lot of fun together, we want to be together. I love him and I know he loves me. I know it sounds like I am trying to convince myself, but I'm not really.

We've talked about starting a family after we get married and I would love to have a couple of children. I can see myself surrounded by nappies, day trips, and babies and I know my parents would love grandchildren.

We are going to Australia for our honeymoon and I am so excited, it's a place I've always wanted to go. Danni lives there now with Tony and after the wedding we are flying home with them and we are staying with them in Perth after we have been to Sydney for a week. We have two months off work to enjoy and I know that I will enjoy the rest.

Work has been unbelievably hard, but I have risen in the ranks and have quite a few authors under my belt. I also do some freelance editing and particularly like working with Indie Authors. I'm not really fussy on the genre I work with because, as a reader, I like almost all genres.

I now work in New York, which is where I met Chad. Time flies when you live in New York, everything happens at a fast pace and I suppose that's why we're getting married after this short time together. It's the most natural thing to do.

I go to bed thinking about Jordan and how my life would have been so different, but I like my life now and tomorrow I'm getting married. Mum and Dad are here with me tonight and they love Chad, they can see how much I mean to him and how much he takes care of me and loves me. That's all Mum and Dad ever wanted was for someone to love me as much as they love each other. Isn't it?

MY ONE REGRET

"It's a Nice Day for a White Wedding!"

Today is my wedding day. It's beautiful outside and it's a perfect day to get married. However, I spent the night dreaming of my wedding but to a very different man. Jordan. I wake up crying and feel a loss like I've never experienced.

I am truly closing that chapter of my life.

This is a milestone for me.

Why does it feel like my heart is breaking all over again?

The wedding is amazing, Bonnie and Danni are bridesmaids and they look so beautiful. I am feeling really emotional today and keep crying, both for my loss of Jordan but also for Chad and how much of himself he has given to me. He loves me unconditionally; I love him back but never as much as I loved Jordan. It is enough though; enough to make him happy.

The party after the wedding is so much fun and I can't wait to spend the night alone with my husband, Chad.

Chad is gorgeous, he used to play American Football at college and he goes to the gym every morning before work. He has blonde hair, which he keeps tight to his head, he is naturally sallow skinned and he has blue eyes, everything I love in a guy. He is such a gentleman and knows how to treat a lady. I remember the first time I met him, I was speechless because he was so gorgeous and then for him to come and talk to me was just amazing.

We were at a work ball and he was there with his company. He came up to me and said, "please may I have the pleasure of this dance?"

I thought to myself, wow so old fashioned and romantic. So far removed from the men in my life since Jordan. My love life now fits into two categories. "Before Jordan" and "After Jordan". I am a different person "After Jordan", it was a major turning point in my life.

"Why of course," I said with a twinkle in my eye and a slight grin. He took my hand and led me into the middle of the dance floor.

"Hi," he said taking my hand and kissing my knuckles. "I'm Chad," he looked intently into my eyes.

"Hi," I blushed. "I'm Cassie and I'm really glad you pulled me away from those old cronies," I laughed.

We danced for a few songs and I couldn't help but notice that when he put his hand on my lower back I could feel an excitement building up inside me. I could feel myself blushing and I tried not to look at Chad.

After a few dances he said "Do you want to go and get a drink, I'd love to talk to you for a while longer. I don't feel like I'm ready to let you go back to your group yet." He was stroking my lower back as he spoke to me.

"Yeah that would be good, its getting warm in here anyway," I said looking directly into his eyes. What I could see in his eyes was desire and lust, I felt that my eyes mirrored his and couldn't wait to spend some time alone with him. He made me have feelings that I hadn't had for such a long time.

We had a few drinks and I didn't talk to anyone else at all that night, it was like the whole of the room just disappeared and it felt like we were on our own. When it was getting late, Claudia had come over to me and said goodnight with a twinkle in her eye. She whispered in my ear "go off and enjoy yourself Cassie, you work too hard. Tonight is your night to play hard!" She winked at me and walked away.

I knew she was right; I had a reputation for "all work and no play." That had been my defence mechanism for the previous eight years and I had not let anyone into my life in all that time because I hadn't wanted my heart broken a second time. It had hurt so much the first time; even though it was something we had both decided to do.

"Do you want to go and get some breakfast Cassie?" Chad said and I looked at him and then looked at my watch.

"Oh my goodness, we've been talking for the last four hours. Where did the time go?" I laughed, it was amazing to talk to someone who understood me and I had known when we went for breakfast that Chad would be someone important in my life.

I'm brought back to my wedding by the signal for the start of the speeches. The food is fantastic and everyone seems to be having a great time. Chad stands up to say the first few words, "Ladies and Gentleman, I think you would agree with me that my wife, Cassie, looks amazing." There are rounds of applause and wolf whistles when he calls me his wife and I gaze up at him with love in my eyes.

"Cassie" he says looking down at me. "I love you so much and would do anything for you. You have become my one, my only and my everything." I have tears in my eyes looking at him now and I can see he has some tears too. "I have bought you a wedding present with the help of your parents and Bonnie. I just hope you like it." He looks worried when he hands me an envelope.

I open it slowly, because I have no idea what is inside. When I open it there is a piece of paper with a picture on it and a key. I'm confused so I open the piece of paper and see a photo of a house in Newquay that I've always loved, it stands on a little island on the beach. It's beautiful and I've always fantasised about living there.

"What? …. Are we going there for our honeymoon? I thought we were going to Australia?" I'm really confused, but then the thought of going home to Newquay after all this time for a trip makes me start smiling. "Are we going to rent it after Australia, babe?" I ask and everyone is silent.

"Yes, Cassie we are. However, I've bought the

house for you. I was told that this is a house that you have always dreamt about and I wanted to give you an amazing wedding present as you have given me the best present a man could ever want. You walked down the aisle today and agreed to be mine," he has tears coming down his face at this stage and I know that I am sat with my mouth open just staring at him.

He leans over to kiss me and says, "say something babe, please. Do you like it?" I reach up, grab him and pull him close to me and then give him a really big passionate kiss and I can hear everyone wolf whistling in the background, but I don't care.

"I love it. I can't believe it. I love you so much Chad, thank you so much." I have tears streaming down my face and he wipes them with his thumb before he gently places a kiss on my lips.

The rest of the wedding is fantastic and everyone has a great time. I can't believe I have my own house in Newquay to stay whenever I get to go home and visit. My thoughts stray to Newquay and the fact that I didn't go home for about 6 years after moving to San Francisco and even then it was only for a short trip to see my parents, Bonnie and Danni before she moved to Australia. God, I miss them girls, but now that we have mobile phones and email it is so much easier to keep in touch.

It soon gets to the time that Chad and I have to leave the wedding party to go to our honeymoon suite as we have an early flight in the morning. We also both want some time on our own to reflect back on the day and of course to truly become man and wife in the biblical sort of way.

"My Heart Will Go On"

2005

Today is our fifth wedding anniversary and life has been amazing for us. We'd been trying to start a family for the first three years and enjoyed "trying" in every possible situation and position. Then after various tests we found out that Chad was unable to father any children. This hadn't bothered us that much as there were always other options, but we decided that we had so much fun together and wanted to live out our dreams. We made a decision the night that we were given the test results, that we would see as much of the world as we could. Obviously, we were both still working, so could only go to these places when we had holidays from work.

So far, we have been to all my favourite places in the world like Paris, Milan, Rome and of course Newquay. We only manage to get home once a year and usually it's for Christmas. Mum and Dad come over to us once a year too, so it doesn't seem too big a gap between seeing them. I miss them a lot, but they are so proud of me, and everything I have achieved.

Today we are going to the airport and we are heading off to Disney World. I have always wanted to go to there and we had been waiting to take our children, but seeing as we can't have any we are just going to go anyway. I am so excited. I'm like a child in a sweetshop and Chad is laughing at me about how giddy I am.

He hasn't been feeling well this last week and we talked about cancelling the trip. "You know it's not too late to cancel Chad. I know you aren't feeling the best. We have all the time in the world and can go anytime. You need to concentrate on getting better so we can plan where else in the World we are going to go."

He walks up behind me and wraps his arms around me. He rests his chin on my head, "no, we are going baby. I know how much you want to go to Disney. This is one of those things on your bucket list and me sharing it with you is on my bucket list too."

"Ah, thank you. I'm so excited and can't wait to meet Mickie, Minnie and the gang. I feel like I am about ten years old all over again."

He chuckles and pulls me tighter to him. "I love your enthusiasm for life, you really inspire me. When I met you I knew you were going to be someone special in my life, I just didn't realise how special. We are going to set Disney World on fire this week, see everything and go on every ride. I can't wait for the night time shows, they are supposed to be spectacular."

"I know, I can't wait either. You need to take it easy though, this bug is really wiping you out. You look so pale. Seriously Chad, are you sure you are well enough to go? I love you, but I want you to enjoy it too and we can always reschedule."

"I love you, Cassie. Do you know that? You are truly selfless and I couldn't have wished for someone better than you to share the rest of my life with."

He seems upset and I realise that this bug really has been kicking his arse.

We get the suitcases and take a cab to the airport. We have plenty of time before the flight and I leave Chad looking after my carry-on bag while I go and do a bit of shopping.

One of the things I love about America is Victoria Secret and I am so lucky there is one at the airport. I walk in and while I am looking around I spot the perfect outfit I need to buy. It is red with white spots just like Minnie Mouse and it is just the thing that will lift Chad's feelings when he sees me in it. I might even buy some "Minnie" ears to go with it. He will love it!

I smile to myself and put it into my bag. When I get back to Chad he is asleep, he seems to be doing a lot of that lately.

We get on the plane, first class of course, and Chad sleeps for the whole journey. Bless him he is going to need his energy for the remainder of the trip, because I am going to take him on every ride in the park. I smile thinking about the two of us on the rides behaving like children.

I'm browsing through the in-flight magazine when I come across an article about Rape and Sexual Abuse

Victims. My heart starts beating really quickly as this is a part of my life I have pushed to the back of my mind and forgotten about. Well, it's not fully forgotten but I try not to think about it anymore. I glance over at Chad to check he is still asleep because I don't want him to ask me any questions about the article that I want to read.

It is a really good article about a new charity, Pebbles that has been set up to help victims to move on with their life. Their motto is 'Pebbles – the Stepping Stones to healing.' They provide counselling, workshops, online forums and support groups to help victims to get their lives back on track. I wish I had had that kind of help when I was younger; maybe I wouldn't have tried to take my own life. I look over at Chad worried that he might be able to see my guilt at reading the article.

Reading it has made me think about David and how easy it would have been to just let him do what he wanted to. How many girls go through this and think that they deserved it? Maybe they were flirting, maybe they had given off the wrong signal, but it is still wrong. God, I wonder how my life would have turned out if he had raped me. I don't want to think about it, I usually do a good job of blanking it out, forgetting that it ever happened. I realise now that I was so lucky that he hadn't taken it all the way and raped me. I feel a lone tear over spilling from my eye and rolling down my cheek.

Thinking back to this part of my life, makes me

think of Jordan and I wonder what he is doing, how he is and did he ever find love again? He would have made a great Dad and I wonder whether he has any children. This makes me a little sad; bringing up lots of memories that I have tried so hard to bury in my life. I look across at Chad and it reminds me of what I have now and how lucky I am. My life is perfect!

I fall asleep for the rest of the journey and when we land I gently wake Chad and we disembark the plane. We hold hands as we make our way through the airport, collect our bags and go out to arrivals, where a limo is waiting for us. "Wow," I say. "I wasn't expecting this," I turn and look at Chad and kiss him.

"It's our anniversary baby, I can't have you getting into a cab on our anniversary," he says kissing me on the forehead. We get into the limo and settle back for the short ride to the hotel. Chad falls asleep in the limo, all he seems to do is sleep these days. This bug is really hard on him. I know he is conserving his energy for the rest of the trip, so that's fine, I am tired too. We pull up at the Polynesian Village Resort and go to check in. The Hotel is like being in the South Pacific and there are tropical palms, lush vegetation, koi ponds and white-sand beaches. I can just imagine moonlit walks along the torch-lit waterfront. When we get to the room, I ask "Chad babe, are you ok? You've not been yourself all day."

"Yeah I'm fine, I'm just really tired. Can we just go for dinner in the hotel? I've heard the restaurants are fantastic. Then after a good night's sleep we can head off to the park and start living out your childhood dreams," he says wrapping his arms around me and pulling me in for a chaste kiss on my cheek.

"MMM if you keep doing that I won't make dinner," I say wrapping my arms around his neck. "I'm actually hungry, we can finish this later," I pull away and turn to the door to make our way down to dinner.

The food really is fantastic and we sit by the window where we can look out and see the beautiful beach. However, Chad is very quiet, I just put that down to the tiring journey. I can't get enough food, it's so tasty and I'm starving. I even eat some of Chad's because he doesn't seem to be able to finish his dinner. "Mmm babe, this is amazing, are you sure you can't eat anymore?" I say looking at him and touching his cheek.

"No, I think I just need to get to bed, then I'll feel so much better tomorrow Cassie," he says yawning. We finish up and go back up to the room, normally on the first night on our trips we take our time making love and then fall asleep in each other's arms. When I go into the bathroom to get changed for bed I hear Chad getting into bed. I come out of the bathroom about ten minutes later and he is fast asleep on his side of the bed.

I climb in next to him and give him a kiss on the cheek. "I love you Chad, sleep tight." It takes me a while to fall asleep because my mind is working overtime. Why is Chad so tired? I will have to make sure he goes to a doctor when he gets home. Why didn't he make love to me? Why was I thinking about Jordan after all this time? I have loads of images of David in my mind after reading that article on the plane.

I finally fall asleep and have a mad dream about the night when it all happened. Although, in my dream, David manages to rape me and I didn't get away from him, but then Jordan came and rescued me. I was screaming at him to help me, save me and to get David off me, I was sobbing and screaming at the same time. The next thing I know someone is pinning me down to the bed and I start thrashing. "Cassie baby stop, stop, it's me Chad. What's the matter? What are you screaming for? Calm down," he sounds petrified.

I sit up and look around me and then grab hold of Chad and hug him like my life depends on it. "Sorry Chad, I was having a nightmare, I'm sorry if I woke you."

He holds me at arm's length and says "what the hell Cassie, that didn't sound like a nightmare."

"Sorry Chad, it was just a nightmare. I read an article on the plane about rape and sexual abuse victims and it must have struck a chord with me, that's all. Now come on let's go for breakfast, I'm starving and I want to get out to see Mickey and Minnie." I laugh.

Chad looks at me and then laughs with me. "Come on then princess, let's go meet Mickey and Minnie."

We go down to breakfast and I notice that Chad still looks tired and he isn't really saying much. The twinkle in his eye has disappeared. I'm worried about him now. "Did you not sleep well?" I ask him. "I didn't keep you awake all night did I?"

"No, you didn't, baby honest. I'm just tired, this bug has been at me for what feels like weeks and it's just wearing me out" he says. I can see he's not feeling the best today either.

"If you don't feel well, then you can stay here and hopefully you will feel better after a day's rest. I'd still like to go though if you don't mind, I've dreamt of this for years," I say feeling guilty for suggesting that I still want to go even though he wants to stay here.

"Cassie, I really don't want you to go on your own, but you might be right, a day's rest might be what I need. We can go to the show tonight and watch the firework display. I'm sure I'll be feeling better by then. Now you have to promise to send me a picture of you with Mickey and Minnie though, just so I can see that you're enjoying yourself," he says with a smile.

I leave the Hotel and get on the monorail which takes me straight into Disney World and I feel like I am a small child looking at all the shops, the rides, the cinemas everything. I stop at lunchtime and send a picture of me with Mickey Mouse to Chad.

"Me and Mickey. Are you jealous?"

"Looks like fun!"

"How are you feeling? Are you able to come and meet me?"

"I've been asleep since you left. I still feel tired though. Carry on without me and you can tell me all about it this evening over dinner."

I get worried. Something just isn't right here, but I have to admit that I get easily distracted by the Parade. Wow, if you've never seen this then you have to put it on your bucket list. It is amazing and I am so happy. I just wish I could share it with someone I love.

I think I must be really emotional after my nightmare because as I am stood in front of the Disney Castle I feel like someone is watching me. It's the same feeling I had a few years ago in Alcatraz, when Bonnie and Danni were visiting. I've had it a few times, but I just put it down to the fact that I was going over the whole David thing. I twirl around but don't see anyone I recognise so I take a photo of the castle and then walk off looking for Minnie Mouse.

I get my picture with Minnie and send it to Chad.

"Me and Minnie, I just love her dress. What do you think? Will it suit me?"

I'm thinking of my Victoria Secret dress that I am going to wear later for him.

I don't get a reply, so assume he is asleep. I decide to go back to the hotel at about six o'clock so that we can have dinner together. I am really giddy with excitement when I get out of the lift and walk over to our room. As soon as I open the door I can sense that something isn't right. I can't put my finger on it but I start having flutters in my stomach and my heart starts palpitating. I don't know what to expect as I walk into the bedroom. What I find will haunt me for the rest of my life.

I walk around the corner in the room and there in the middle of the bed is Chad. He is as white as a sheet and there is blood and vomit all over the bed. I'm shocked! I stop and stare for a few seconds and then run over to the bed. "Chad, Chad, wake up, what's going on?"

I can feel myself getting hysterical. I'm shaking Chad and he's not answering me, I start shaking him even more. "Chad, come on. Chad, wake up, let me help you. Please come on, wake up. I love you. Don't you dare leave me." I'm crying now.

I walk over to the telephone and ring down to reception. "Please can you call an ambulance, my husband isn't responding please help me, please!" I'm sobbing on the phone now.

It only takes about ten minutes for the ambulance to get to us, but it feels like an hour. By the time they arrive, Chad still hasn't woken up. "Chad, come on the ambulance is here and they are going to take you to the hospital. I'm coming with you and I am going to hold your hand all the way. I'm not going to leave you. Please Chad don't you leave me, please. I'm sorry I left you today, I should have been there to help you." I'm kissing him but the paramedics are asking me to move out of the way so that they can examine him and start getting some medication into him.

I'm numb. I don't know what to do and I don't like

it. I'm usually so in control of my life and I can feel myself starting to lose control. Deep breaths in and breathe out slowly, deep breath in and breathe out slowly. I have done these breathing exercises so many times in my life when I start to panic. They are usually the only way to calm myself down.

This time it doesn't seem to be working, one of the paramedics sees me struggling to breathe and takes me out of the bedroom into the living room part of our suite. "Now madame, take a seat and breathe in and then slowly let your breath out," she says repeatedly until I start to calm down. "Now you need to give me some information, who is the gentleman? When did you notice him getting ill? What happened today?" She's asking me lots of questions and I need to answer them just to concentrate on everything she is saying.

"His name is Chad and he is my husband. We live in New York and we're on holiday here. He has been sick on and off for the last few months and he told me it was a bug but that he kept getting better. He wasn't feeling well enough to come with me today; it's the first day of the holiday so he was staying back in the room to relax and be ready for a full day tomorrow. I haven't seen him since breakfast and I've just walked in about fifteen minutes ago. He won't answer me – what is happening to him?" I can feel myself getting hysterical again and I need to do my breathing exercises again.

I can see they've put Chad on the stretcher and are taking him out of the room and down towards the lift. I stand and follow with the paramedic I was talking to.

When we get downstairs to the ambulance I climb into the back with Chad, hold his hand and tell him how much I love him. He was ok this morning. Well he was better than he had been for a while. I don't really understand what is happening and I'm very confused.

"Chad I love you, I don't understand, when did you get so sick? How did I not realise? All I wanted to do was to go and see Mickey and Minnie. Why didn't you tell me you felt this bad? I feel so selfish, I should have stayed with you. I'm a lousy wife, I'm so sorry." I'm crying while I'm holding his hand. I'm looking at the paramedics hoping they can give me some answers, but they just look away, not able to tell me anything.

When we get to the hospital, I move out of the way so that they can take Chad out of the ambulance. I follow them through to the Emergency Department where they ask me lots of questions as they take him through to a room where I can't follow him. I don't understand why I can't go with him into the room, I'm his wife.

I start shouting in the corridor asking to be taken to him, but all they do is try to calm me down and then take me to a side room to wait until a doctor can come out to talk to me. It's while I'm in here that I ring my Mum, she is the only person I want to talk to right now.

"Mum, it's me," I sob down the phone. "Mum I need you!" I can't stop crying and she is trying to talk to me to find out what the problem is.

"Cassie what's the matter? What's the problem? Calm down and tell me what's going on," her voice manages to calm me down enough for me to tell her.

"Mum it's Chad. He's in hospital and I don't know what is going on. They can't tell me anything."

"Oh my god Cassie, is he ok? What happened?" She is frantic.

"He's not been feeling right for the last couple of months, but he told me it was just a bug. He was tired from the travelling and has been in bed all day today. I went to Disney World today on my own, because he wanted to rest so that he would feel better for tomorrow and we could go together." I start sobbing again. "Mum when I got back to the hotel room he was laid out on top of the sheets covered in blood and vomit, it was awful and then I couldn't wake him. I'm so scared Mum, so scared."

"Baby girl, your Dad is going to drive me to London so I can get on the first plane out to you ok. I'm going to come and look after you and Chad for a while. Go off and find out what is happening and keep in touch on my mobile. I'll ring you every step of the way and if anything happens ring me. I'll contact Chad's family. Don't you worry about that."

I can hear her moving around the room and instructing Dad to get the suitcase. I feel better for speaking to her, she has managed to calm me down and just knowing she is coming to be here with me makes me feel relaxed.

I hang up after giving her the details, I know she won't be here for another ten hours at least, those hours are crucial.

After about half an hour my phone rings and its Chad's Mum, Emma. "Cassie, what is going on? What's wrong with my Chad?" I try and tell her what I know, and then she asks where we are and tells me that she is going to go to the airport straight away and get on the first plane.

I know I have a couple of hours on my own before anyone comes to comfort me or keep me company. I sit in the side room and cry my heart out. I don't know what to expect in the next few hours and this frightens me. I have always been in control of my own destiny after the David incident and I always thought I would continue to be in control, now I can see that I wasn't in control at all. It seems I was just waiting for the next catastrophe to hit me.

I know I have to stop feeling sorry for myself when Chad is lying on a bed in another room and I don't even know how he is.

After about two hours a doctor comes to find me, "Mrs Morgan, how are you holding up?" he asks as he takes a seat next to me. "Chad is very sick, he was unresponsive when he arrived, we managed to bring him around, but he was passed out for a long time." He looks me in the eye and says to me, "as you know he has stomach cancer but it has spread to his lymph nodes. I'm afraid he doesn't have long left, his organs are starting to fail as the cancer is very aggressive. We can't give him any treatment because it has spread too far. The cancer is too large to be responsive to treatment. We need to think about palliative care and just keep him comfortable now."

I look at the doctor like he is speaking in a different language, what is he telling me? How can my husband be dying? We had dinner together last night and only last week we were dancing together.

"I don't understand doctor." I can hardly speak. "He was fine until today. Well, he had a bug for the last couple of months, but that's all it was. He told me he went to the doctor and it was a bug." I don't know why I'm shouting at the doctor it isn't his fault.

He looks at me and stands up. "I have to go and check on Chad now. You can come in in about fifteen minutes, but I want you to be prepared for what you see. He is not the same man you have known, he is very weak, he's asleep right now. We don't want you to wake him, so just sit there and be there for him." He walks to the door and turns to face me. "I'm sorry Mrs. Morgan." Then he is gone as he goes back in the room. I am all alone with nothing but my thoughts.

After waiting the fifteen minutes I stand and walk to the room where Chad is. I slowly open the door, not knowing what to expect. What I see is not the Chad that I know and love, this man looks similar but he is frail looking, grey and hooked up to so many machines. As I approach the bed I gasp. I can't believe that this person is Chad. He seems to have deteriorated so fast.

I cry so hard, I don't think I have any tears left. I don't know how long I sit here but the next thing I know Emma walks through the door and throws herself at me. "Cassie what's going on? What's wrong with Chad?

How is he?" I tell her what the doctor said to me, I'm crying while I tell her, I just can't believe it myself.

She goes to the bed and looks at him, she sobs.

"I'll go and get the nurse or doctor so that someone can tell us what is going on." I walk out of the room and all I can hear is Emma sobbing.

The nurse tells me that the doctor will be with us later this evening. I go back into the room and I take his hand, Emma has his other hand. We each take a chair and sit close to him. We both rub his hand and talk to him. "Chad I love you, you have to get better. We have so many plans, there are so many places we haven't seen yet, and we promised that we would see them together."

We sit there talking to him for a couple of hours when we notice that he is waking up. The two of us move closer to the bed and we both have so many questions, but know that we need to let Chad talk. He needs to tell us what is going on. He needs to explain what he has been dealing with on his own.

"Cassie. Mum" he croaks. "I'm so sorry, this wasn't meant to happen. Not here. Not now." He has a few stray tears running down his face, I lean over and rub them away with my thumb.

"What are you talking about? I don't understand." I'm confused and I look at Emma and can see she is as confused as I am.

"I have stomach cancer," he says not looking either of us in the eye. "I've known about this since we had the fertility test results. The doctor called me up a couple of days after he gave us the results and asked me to see him separately. There had been abnormalities in my blood results and after talking to me he sent me for more tests. I've always suffered with stomach problems, but thought nothing of it. I was told I had stomach cancer about three months later after numerous tests. I didn't tell you, baby, because I didn't know how to. I truly believed if they gave me drugs to take that I would get better. I suppose I was ignorant really and for that I am so sorry. I know you're probably going to be mad at me, both of you." He stops talking for a minute to catch his breath and he looks from me to his Mum.

Emma and I both gasp as we take in the fact that he knew for the last two years that he had stomach cancer and didn't tell us. How did we not know? How did we not realise how sick he really was?

"I'm so sorry! I thought we would have this trip and then I could tell you when we were all together at thanksgiving. Unfortunately, that didn't go as planned. I had treatment at the start and it shrank, but I knew when I got sick this time that it had spread and was bigger and more aggressive than before." He starts crying and I don't know what to do. He lied to me by not telling me; we talked about everything - why not this?

"Chad, I just want you to get better. There must be more drugs they can give you. There must be something we can try." I'm getting loud now. I can feel myself getting hysterical. I know I need to calm down, it's not fair on Chad.

"Chad, darling why didn't you say anything?"

Emma says to him. She is clearly battling with the same issues as me.

"I don't know, I just didn't want anyone to worry and then, before I knew it, it was too late. I left it too late and I really did plan to tell you all at thanksgiving," he starts crying again.

We all sit there quietly contemplating what is happening and what we are going to do about it when I hear the door open and my Mum and Dad walk in. I stand and throw myself at them sobbing hysterically. My Mum takes me out of the room so she can talk to me and Dad stays in the room to sit with Emma and Chad.

I tell Mum what has been going on and she is shocked and wants to know how I didn't realise he was so sick. "He kept telling me there was a bug going round at work and I believed him. He kept getting better, so why would I worry? We're married and he's supposed to tell me everything, so why would I worry?"

"He didn't tell me Mum and that breaks my heart." I pull myself out of her hug and look at her. "What am I going to do? I want to be there for him, the doctor can't tell me how long we've got but I need to make it count."

Mum hugs me and says, "you'll do what's right Cassie, you always do. I'm here for you and I'm not going anywhere".

We go back in the room and see Dad comforting Emma, then Mum goes up to her and leads her out of the room. "Come on" she says. "Let's go get a cup of coffee, Emma."

Dad comes over and hugs me and kisses me on my head. "We will stay as long as you need us to, baby girl. I'm going to find your Mum and Emma now and leave you and Chad alone for a while." He stands and leaves the room.

Chad is asleep, so I climb up into the bed and lay next to him, just staring at him. How did it come to this? What did I do to deserve this? Why didn't he tell me? I pick up his arm and pull it around me and snuggle in tight and that's how I fall asleep.

I wake a couple of hours later when one of the alarms starts beeping. What is going on? "Chad, Chad!"

I look around and see there is a nurse and she is asking me to leave the room. I'm like a robot and get off the bed and walk out. I turn at the door just in time to see them using the defibrillators on him. I run out of the room screaming for Mum. "Mum, where are you?" I say falling into the side room we were in earlier.

She gets up and runs to me. "Baby girl, what's going on?"

Emma starts to get up too and walks towards the door. "No Emma, stay here," I say and pull her into a hug too. "His heart stopped again, they're trying to revive him." He's got to pull through he just has to.

We sit waiting, crying and just reliving things and signs we must have missed.

The door opens and the doctor comes in. "Mrs Morgan, I'm sorry but Chad is getting worse. We won't be able to keep reviving him; it's only a matter of hours now. You should go and sit with him."

I look at Emma and we both hold hands and go in to see Chad. I hate seeing him like this, it's so awful. He shouldn't be suffering like this. I hope they have given him something to keep him comfortable.

"Hey" he croaks. "I'm sorry. I have a few things I need to tell you Cassie. I know you don't want to hear this right now, but you need to. I love you, I always have and I always will. You have to live your life; you're still young. You have to promise me that in time you will open your heart for someone, because you have too much to give not to share it with someone special."

"No Chad, we are not talking about this now. No!" I'm getting angry now. How dare he have had time to think about this, to prepare himself and not give us the time to prepare ourselves?

"Yes Cassie we are. You never open up and face things head on and that's what we need to do now. The next thing I need to tell you is that when I found out I was ill I arranged for all my finances to be put in your name and should anything happen to me then you get everything. I'm covered for life insurance." He holds his hand up to stop me from jumping in. "I know you don't want to discuss money either but we have to. The house in Newquay is in your name anyway and so is the apartment in New York. Everything I have is yours and I trust you to look after my Mum when I'm gone." He's sobbing how and I can't help but sob too.

Emma starts crying too and then Mum says to me, "Come on Cassie hold it together he hasn't got long, so relive some of the good times and let him leave with happy memories." I know Mum is right so we sit there talking about the good times, the fun times, and just our life in general.

We must have been sitting there for hours just talking and holding his hands when all of a sudden we hear the alarms ringing and the doctors and nurses run in. They want to revive him, but Emma and I know there's no point because Chad has taken his last breath with a smile on his face and happy memories to take with him.

The doctors agree and they pronounce him dead at four o'clock. I'll never forget this day for as long as I live.

We have to sign lots of paperwork and I'm kind of in a daze. I let Mum do most of the work and then we head back to the hotel to pack our bags. We have arranged for his body to be flown back to New York for an autopsy, even though it is pointless. We know what killed him!

"I Don't Wanna"

When we arrive back in New York, it's like I'm dreaming. I go to the apartment with Mum and Dad and I think that Chad has tricked me because I can still smell him in the room. I sit down and grab his hoodie that he left on the couch; I smell it and sob my heart out. I put it on and climb into bed, Mum and Dad start making some food, but all I want to do is sleep.

I'm in a daze for a few days and then we are informed his body is being released for the funeral. I immerse myself in the arrangements and ring Claudia to tell her my plans. "Claudia, I need to get my head around everything that has happened so I've decided I want to take a sabbatical for about six months. I hope that's ok."

"Cassie, of course that's fine. We just want you to come back to us and we want you to be ok. If there's anything we can do just let us know," she says.

"Thanks, Claudia. I'll let you know how I get on." We say our goodbyes and I hang up.

The funeral is the next day and I have to mentally prepare myself for all the well-wishers and commiserations. It's so hard, I just can't believe he's gone. I keep telling myself that I won't break down until after the funeral. Bonnie is arriving today, in time for the funeral tomorrow. Danni can't make it as its too far and she is pregnant, but I know she will be thinking of me.

When Dad brings Bonnie back to the apartment after collecting her from the airport, I fall into her arms and sob. She cries along with me, she knows how much I loved him and how much he meant to me. Mum has made dinner for us all, but we are all struggling to eat right now. I just want to go to bed and let tomorrow be over. When it is polite to leave the table I go up to bed and it's about an hour later that I feel Bonnie climbing into the bed beside me. "I didn't want you to sleep alone Cassie. I hope that's ok." She hugs me and then rolls over.

I sob silently knowing that I have to be strong tomorrow. I fall asleep eventually and have mad dreams about Chad, David and of course Jordan. Why do I always think back to David when I'm feeling upset? I thought I had got over that years ago. It makes me think about how, during that time, the only person who could ever calm me down was Jordan. I could do with a Jordan hug right now.

When I wake up in the morning the sun is shining. It's a beautiful day and I'm sure Chad is looking down on us smiling. We all get ready silently and the car comes to collect us and take us to the church for the funeral. The service is beautiful and I listen to all the nice things that everyone has to say about Chad. He was truly loved by a lot of people, I stand up when it's my turn to speak and everyone turns to look at me. I know they think I am going to break down, but I need to get through this and then, only when I'm on my own, can I break down.

"Thank you all for coming today. I'm sorry it is under such sad circumstances. Chad," I say looking up to the ceiling. "Chad, all of these people knew you and loved you in one way or another." I pause and look out to all the people looking at me. I smile. "Chad was a great person, a wonderful man who loved me very much. He wanted us to see as many places in the world as we could before he died, he just didn't tell me he was dying because he wanted me to enjoy every minute that we had together. He was that selfless that even when he was dying he was thinking of me. I'm going to have to live with that for the rest of my life. I hate to think of him suffering, but at least it is over now."

I pause for a minute to compose myself. "Emma, just because Chad is no longer here, it doesn't mean that we will lose touch. You are my family here and you will always be my family. I love you for bringing this wonderful man into this world, and eventually into my life. Thank you!"

I turn around and bow to the alter and make my way back to my seat. My Mum reaches out and takes one hand and Bonnie takes the other. They both smile at me. We sit in silence as the service finishes.

We walk outside into the graveyard and everyone shakes mine and Emma's hand and then we watch Chad being lowered into the cold earth. It is the hardest thing I have ever seen and this is the moment that I finally break down. "No Chad, No! Please come back to me, please!"

My Dad comes around and puts his arm around my shoulders and pulls me close to him. He then leads me away from the grave and off to the car. Once we are inside he sits next to me and says "Cassie, I'm here for you, you are very strong and you will get over this. You've done it before, you can do it again. We all love you and will help you."

I lean into him and close my eyes, just thinking about today. I can feel the doors open and Mum and Bonnie climbing inside. The car starts to move and we drive back to the apartment. We aren't having food and drinks with everyone, I just can't face it.

It has been a very emotional day and I'm glad to get home, the hardest thing was watching Chad being lowered into the cold earth. When I climb into bed with Bonnie by my side I say, "Bye Chad. I love you and I will never forget you."

When I wake up, Bonnie is still fast asleep so I creep out of the bed and down the stairs to the kitchen. I put the coffee machine on and sit and wait for the coffee to be ready. I look out the window, which has a view across the City. It really is beautiful and it makes me sad that Chad will never see this view again. We used to sit and look out of this window together and comment on all the places we had visited down below us. All of a sudden I hear someone behind me and I turn to see Dad coming towards me.

"Morning baby" he says as he leans down and kisses me on the top of my head. "How are you feeling today?"

"I'm not sure, but I woke with some determination today. Today is a looking ahead day, Dad." He looks at me slightly confused. "Today I'm going to think about the rest of my life." I can see he's clearly struggling to understand what I'm talking about. I know I'm rambling a bit, but I need to continue.

"I'm going to arrange some time away from New York. I've already asked for at least six months off work and there are a few places left on mine and Chad's list of places to visit. I'm going to visit two of those places and then I'm coming home for a while. I need to do this Dad, it will be the right time to start doing the house up. Chad gave it to me for my wedding present and I need a project to immerse myself in. I want to spend some time there, I always wanted that house and now I have I need to live there for a while." I look at him and he smiles at me.

"Cassie, that sounds like a great idea. Will you be all right on your own? Do you want Mum to go with you?" he asks, clearly worried about me.

"I won't be on my own. Chad will be with me in spirit, it'll give me time to say goodbye to him properly." I smile with tears in my eyes.

Mum and Bonnie must have appeared while I was telling Dad what I want to do.

Mum startles me when she says, "I think that's a great idea, but I do worry about you being on your own." She looks at me and smiles gently.

"I'll go with you Cassie and then we can go back home together," Bonnie says and I struggle to breathe.

"Would you do that for me Bonnie? What about Jezza?" I ask confused. I can't believe she would spend the time with me instead of Jezza.

"He won't mind, honestly, anything for you babe," she says walking over to hug me. "We live together, he's probably happy for a bit of peace for a couple of weeks," she says laughing.

We spend the rest of the day, booking flights and accommodation and by the end of the day we have a full itinerary for the next two weeks and we leave tomorrow.

I know some people will think that I am being selfish by going on holiday straight after the funeral, but that is the kind of life Chad and I had. We had been all about travelling for the last couple of years and I know that he really wanted to go to these places with me. This way his memories are the strongest, so he will be with me all the way.

"Firstly, we are heading to Las Vegas and we are staying in The Bellagio, this is one place Chad really wanted to go and I was planning on surprising him for his next birthday." I look up from the itinerary and see Bonnie smiling at me.

She claps her hands rapidly "I've never been to Vegas, oh my god, wait until I tell Jezza he is going to be so jealous."

I laugh at her knowing that Jezza really will be jealous, he's always talked about Vegas."Secondly, we are flying to Norway. We had both wanted to go and see the fjords; they are supposed to be very beautiful. We are going to drive around the fjords and visit many towns along the way."

"Our third stop will be home."

"Cassie, you are amazing letting me come with you, I know it won't be easy but I promise to give you lots of memories to remember." Bonnie comes over and hugs me tight.

Home! Well home for me until I go back to work. I want to decorate the house so that when I finally come home for good it will feel like it is mine. The apartment will stand empty, but the management of the building will check on it regularly and will arrange for it to be cleaned regularly so that it is always ready for me when I want to go back.

It has been a busy day and I'm very tired. We are all going to the airport at the same time tomorrow morning and I go upstairs to pack. It's about one o'clock before everyone else turns in. I can only assume Mum and Dad were asking Bonnie to let them know how I am! I don't blame them; they must be so worried about me. The last time something horrific happened to me, I tried to kill myself!

173

"Viva Las Vegas"

We all set off the next morning and Bonnie and I get on our flight to Las Vegas, first class of course. We are sipping our champagne when I see the article I read on my flight to Disney World. It makes me sad thinking of where I was going on that flight. I shake myself and I suddenly get a great idea. I'm going to run it past Bonnie and see what she says.

"Hey Bonnie, I have had an amazing idea, tell me what you think. When I was flying to Disney World a few weeks ago, I read this article about PEBBLES, it's a charity in London which helps victims of rape and sexual abuse to get back on their feet. They give them counseling and rehabilitation. It made me think about the incident with David. I wish I had had someone like this to go to. It is an amazing service and I want to donate a large sum of money to the charity – what do you think?" I rush through it so I can get it all out before she starts to tell me it's not a good idea.

"Cassie, I think that's a fantastic idea, but are you sure you want to relive it again? Just thinking about it might bring it all back, I know you have buried it deep inside you." I know she's worried about me, particularly at this sad time. "Let me read the article and then we can discuss it," she says taking the in-flight magazine and finding the article. As she's reading it I hear her gasp and I put it down to her remembering how it was for me after David. She reaches across and takes my hand, "Cassie, I think you are so amazing and for you to think of others at this sad time in your life makes you even more amazing. We can arrange all of the donation stuff when we get back to the UK," she says with a strange look on her face.

"Yeah I suppose, but I really wanted to do it when we get to Vegas. Then I was going to ask them if I can do some volunteer work with them when I get home, just for a few months until I go back to New York." She gasps again, what is wrong with her?

"OK, if that's what you want then we can arrange it in Las Vegas. Maybe make a donation and then when you are home, arrange to meet up with the charity organiser and see about volunteer work or something." She's smiling when she says this.

She's looking at me strangely, but I don't think much of it, she is obviously stunned by my offer of kindness. I would have done anything to have this kind of help back when everything happened with David.

I raise my glass of Champagne and propose a toast. "To best friends, endings and new beginnings." I have tears falling down my face when I say it.

Bonnie clinks her glass against mine and says, "to Chad" and we both have a little cry.

When the plane lands there's a limo waiting for us and it reminds me of my last trip with Chad. I'm determined to enjoy these couple of trips and I know I will keep thinking of Chad, but I know that he would have wanted me to do this. "Chad," I say. "I'm going to give you a running commentary of my trip and visit all the places you wanted to see. You'll be sick of hearing me." I smile when I say this.

Wow! Las Vegas is all it's cracked up to be and more; it's bright, it's noisy and it's fast paced. We stay in the Bellagio in their Bellagio Suite on the 36th Floor. It is the height of luxury and I know Chad would have been delighted to stay here. The elevator goes straight into the Suite and all you can see is the marble on the floor, it twinkles when you look at it, like there are small crushed diamonds in the sheer black floor. We both walked straight over to the window once we had closed the door to the Suite. We stood there just looking out with our hands pressed up against the window stopping us from falling and getting dizzy. We laugh at ourselves like we are kids again. I just know that this is going to be a good trip where I can gain some new memories.

We gamble, we go to shows, we have lovely dinners and we shop until we drop. One of the shows we go to see is O by Cirque de Soleil, it is a water based show and it is amazing. The synchronised swimmers are phenomenal and we are so buzzed after watching them. Each night we go to a different show in a different hotel. It has been such a great experience. On the last day in Las Vegas I remember that I wanted to donate some money to PEBBLES.

"Bonnie, we need to go to a bank so that I can send that money to the charity. We're leaving tomorrow so we will have to do it today. Will you come with me? I don't really know where to send the money or anything.

"Of course I'll come with you, I have the article with me, I'm sure it says in there where to donate."

"Great, come on we can ask at reception where the nearest bank is." We get our bags and go down to reception. They give us directions to the nearest bank, which is a block down the road.

When we get there we are shown into an office and told that the Bank Manager will be with us shortly. When he walks in he asks, "So ladies, what can I help you with today?"

We start to giggle because he called us ladies and then when we look at him he has a really straight face and that just makes us giggle a little bit more. Bonnie nudges me to speak.

"Sorry, I recently lost my husband and he left me a small fortune. I want to make a donation to a Charity back in England and wondered if you could help me organise that please."

"That is not a problem, do you have your bank details so that I can check your information?"

I hand him my bank details and wait while he taps the information into his computer. He looks at the screen and then looks at me again. "Do you have some form of ID? Just so that I can verify you are who you say you are."

"Of course I do," I say reaching into my handbag to

get my passport out.

He checks the passport against my details and then says "Mrs. Morgan, I am sorry for your loss and sorry for having to check your ID. It's just standard procedure you understand."

I nod. Bonnie hands him the article saying, "this is the charity she wants to donate to. It's in the UK, I hope that isn't a problem."

He shakes his head and takes the article. "There should be a registered charity number on here that I can use to find out where to transfer the funds. Just wait a moment while I go and check the details." He says as he rises out of his chair and leaves the room.

He is gone for a few minutes and we both look at each other and wonder where he has gone. When he comes back in he says, "sorry about that we didn't have enough information to transfer the money so we had to ring them. There was a number in the article. I have the information now so we can go ahead and transfer the money. How much are you looking to donate Mrs. Morgan?"

"I hope you didn't tell them it was me donating, I wanted to remain anonymous." I sound really stern, I hadn't told him that at the beginning, but I don't want someone contacting me to discuss my donation, I wanted to do this for this amazing charity without them knowing. When I volunteer to work with them, I don't want them treating me any differently to other volunteers.

"Of course I didn't tell them who was going to be donating, everyone is anonymous here madam."

"OK then," I say starting to relax. "I'm looking to donate £200,000." I hear Bonnie gasp.

"Cassie, that's a lot of money. Will you be able to donate that much and still be able to live comfortably?" she asks taking my hand.

"Yes of course I will. I really want to do this Bonnie."

"I know," she says.

The Manager looks startled, but then he regains his composure quickly, after all he is used to dealing with a lot of money here in Las Vegas.

It takes about fifteen minutes and I leave the bank almost a quarter of a million poorer, but a million times happier.

We go back to The Bellagio and sit on the terrace overlooking the impressive fountains as they dance in front of us. It truly is an amazing sight.

Then after what only seems like a few days, but has in fact been a week, we are on a plane bound for Schiphol in Holland where we will change flights to fly to Bergen. The connecting flight is an hour and three quarters and we sleep for most of the journey. When we arrive in Bergen, we are escorted to the Cruise Liner, which will be our home for a week. I'm very excited to be cruising down the fjords and I'm very happy that Bonnie has come with me. She has been great company, we have had fun and she knows when I need to have time to myself. She has been the perfect companion.

We get into our cabin and unpack for the week ahead. When we have done that we go to dinner and meet some of the other people on board. While we are having dinner I ask Bonnie, "how was Jezza when you called him earlier? I miss him and can't wait to get home to see him."

"Me too" she says. "I don't think he realised how much he was going to miss me, this might be the best thing that ever happened to us," she says laughing.

"I hope everything is ok with the two of you," I say to her worrying about her being away from home.

"Yeah they're fine. We just take each other for granted that's all, but that's what happens in relationships that have been going on for so long," she sighs.

"Bonnie he has loved you for a very long time. He is lucky to have you and you are lucky to have him."

"I know that" she says. "I love him a lot, don't ever think I don't. I just wish he appreciated me more."

I hug her. "I know you do. We're never satisfied are we?" I ask.

"No, never," she laughs. "Who would have thought that we would still be together after having met at school, not many of our friends can say they met their soul mates at school." She smiles and then looks at my face.

I can't help but think about Jordan and how happy I was with him. Was he the one that got away? We thought we were soul mates but we didn't last the distance. As soon as she looks at me she realises what she said.

"Cassie, I'm sorry I didn't mean anything by it. You and Jordan were different to everyone and we were all so shocked when you both made the decision to go your separate ways. I know how that affected you and I know that you are grieving for Chad right now, but you are allowed to grieve for Jordan too you know. You never did grieve after you left him, now might be a good time to do that Cassie."

She hugs me and we go to the bar after dinner and get absolutely paralytic drunk. When we wake up in the morning, we are sailing down the fjords and we have banging headaches, but it is so beautiful. We sit on deck and watch the amazing scenery pass us by.

There are shows every night and on one of those nights we get to dress up in ball gowns and have dinner with the Captain. It is a most memorable night and one that we will not forget.

The rest of the cruise is fantastic and so peaceful, I'm so happy we came along. I love the town of Stavanger with it's beautiful boats docked along the town. We stopped here on the final leg of our fjord cruise and we go up onto one of these boats and buy some fresh prawns straight out of the sea. There is a booth next to the boat and they are selling aioli, so we buy some and a plastic knife and some fresh french bread. We sit down at a picnic table and make our own very fresh prawn sandwiches with fresh aioli. It was absolutely beautiful and another memory to store away with the others that I have made on our special trip.

"Photograph"

After we leave Norway, we arrive in London Heathrow airport and my parents are there waiting for us. They have a big sign with 'Welcome home Cassie & Bonnie' on it. I have a tear in my eye and I realise how much I've missed them.

We talk nearly all the way home, which takes about six hours. We tell them about the places we visited and the things that we did. We both sleep for a while and then when we are coming into Newquay as I look out of the car window, I am reminded that this is my home, this is where I belong. Unfortunately, I am also reminded that I don't have Chad with me to enjoy this with anymore.

"I'm so glad we went on this trip Bonnie, thank you for coming with me. Now it's time for me to start making plans and thinking about my future."

"I really enjoyed spending the time with you Cassie, it's been so long since we spent so much time together. Thank you for letting me join you on your travels. I won't forget it for a long time." She smiles at me.

"Are you looking forward to seeing Jezza?" I ask.

She smiles and I can see it reaches her eyes as they twinkle. "I can't believe how much I missed him. I didn't think I would miss him as much as I did, I only hope he missed me as much too." She winks at me and I giggle.

"Bonnie, we're here now" Dad says as we pull up to her house. I get out with her to say our goodbyes. I know we will see each other maybe tomorrow or the next day, but I have got used to having her twenty-four hours a day and it will be strange.

"See you soon Cassie and thank you again."

"Love you Bonnie, thank you for giving me the strength to do these things." We hug each other as if our life depends on it.

"Cassie, Bonnie," I hear a deep voice coming up behind us. It's Jezza, he walks over and gives us both a hug, he surrounds us and squeezes us tight.

"I missed you guys," he said. "Especially you Bonnie."

I walk out of the group hug and he pulls her close to him and squeezes her tight. I hear him say, "I love you."

"Right then," Dad says, clearly embarrassed. "Let's get you home young lady." He jumps into the car and puts his seat belt on.

I laugh. "Yeah, get a room guys." Then I climb in and before I close the door I say, "love you both and see you soon."

They both turn and wave at me as I close the door and Dad drives off. He takes me back to their house because I'm going to spend a couple of nights with them before I go back to my own house. I need to make sure it is well aired and ready for me to move in for a few months while I think about any further decisions on my life.

We have dinner and then I have to go to bed because I am so tired. I walk up the stairs and I can't help but notice all the pictures going up the wall on the stairs. There are pictures of me; Mum and Dad at varying ages; there's a couple of pictures of me and Chad and I stop and touch the pictures remembering the time we had together.

I get to the top of the stairs and as I walk into my bedroom the first thing I see is a small picture of Jordan and I looking at each other and smiling. We look like we didn't know there was anyone else around. Just the two of us with no cares in the world. I feel a tear run silently down my face and I wipe it away with my thumb remembering the way Jordan used to do that for me. I pick up the photo and place it on my bedside table and get into my pajamas.

When I get into bed, I cry like I have never cried before. I feel like I am cleansing my soul. I cry for Chad and the good times we had together, and I cry for my one regret in life. Jordan! How could I have left him? He cared so much for me and I loved him with a passion that Chad could never match. So, why did I make it so easy for Jordan to walk away? Mine and Chad's relationship was good; we both cared a lot for each other and we had good sex. I loved him so much, we were very alike and we were great friends and we had a lot of fun, BUT there was something missing on my part. Whenever Jordan came near me, I knew it was him. Whenever he touched me, it felt like an electrical impulse was shooting through my body. That never happened with Chad, yes I loved him a lot but it's only when I think back now that I realise you only have that kind of reaction to your true soul mate.

It was that "thing" that makes you stop breathing when they look at you.

That flutter in your stomach when you think about them.

That, that, that AARRGGHH I can't explain it properly.

It's that thing that happens when two souls come together! I cry for the years I stayed away from Newquay, the years when I avoided some friends because I didn't want to hear about Jordan!

I cry for Chad and the years we tried so hard to have children and then being told that he couldn't have children. It turns out this was due to his fatal illness that he didn't tell me about.

I cry with anger, for Chad not telling me he was sick. Not telling me he was dying. Not giving me a chance to be there for him. I'm angry that he died like he did. I'm angry it happened so quickly. I cry until I can cry no more and eventually fall asleep and have a very restless night. The next morning when I go downstairs Dad has gone to work and Mum is in the kitchen brewing coffee. "Morning baby do you want a cup?" She says pointing at the percolator.

"Yeah I'd love one," I say kissing her on the cheek. "I'm going to walk over to my house later to see what needs to be done. I want to move in as quickly as possible. I've still got a few months off work, so I might ship a few things over."

I sit down at the table while Mum brings my cup over. I love the smell of freshly brewed coffee and I inhale the smell whilst wrapping my hands around the cup. "Do you really think that's a good idea Cassie? At least give it a couple of days before you go there. I'll come with you whenever you go, but just wait for a day or two," she sounds like she is pleading with me.

"Mum, I need to do this today. You can come with me, actually I'd really like you to come with me. I won't be staying there for a few days but there's a couple of things I'd like you to help me with, please." I really want to do this sooner rather than later.

She finally agrees to come with me and after breakfast we leave the house. We drive through the town and park up by the beach, then we walk across the bridge to my house. I stand on the bridge looking around at the beach below, it is truly beautiful. So many times I was that person down on the sand looking up at this house wishing it was mine. Now I own it – I still can't believe that it belongs to me; I've loved this house for as long as I can remember. We open the door and walk in, it's a bit dusty but the sun is shining in the patio doors and I fall in love with my hometown all over again. We spend a couple of hours cleaning away all the dust and opening the windows to let the air in. Mum helps me to go through the wardrobe and take all of Chad's clothes out and put them into a box. I'm going to give them all to charity soon and it will be much easier if they're boxed and ready.

We are in the house for about six hours when we decide we've had enough. We close all the windows and lock the house up before walking back across the bridge to the car. "Mum, do you fancy a glass of wine? I'm thirsty after all that hard work" I ask as we are driving along.

"Yeah that would be lovely, I know just the place," she says and drives us to The Pig and Whistle. It's a nice pub, a real English pub overlooking the coastline.

I love the sea; it's one of the many things I missed when I was in New York. The smell; the noises; just the whole ambience of a seaside resort. We sit on the terrace and drink a glass of wine. "So Cassie" Mum says. "How are you doing? You seem to be coping remarkably well!" She's looking right into my eyes, she knows that my eyes can't lie.

"I'm not doing too bad to be honest, but I keep getting mixed up emotions. I'm sad and heartbroken, but then I get angry at Chad for not telling me, for not letting me have a choice in all of this." I can feel the tears welling up and getting ready to spill. I take a deep breath and say "I think I'll be ok though, I think that maybe it's time for a change in my life!"

"I can understand you being upset and angry, it's

very difficult when you weren't able to make, or even help with the decisions, but you loved Chad and it will take time Cassie until you can move on." She reaches across the table and covers my hand in hers.

We sit quietly for a while and then I change the subject. "So, anything happening around here that's interesting?"

Mum looks around the pub and then looks at me, I can see something isn't right with her. If I'd thought about it I'd have noticed she was a bit jumpy. "Well, I heard that David is back in town, but I haven't bumped into him myself."

"WHAT!!" I grab my hand back and look around. I can feel my heart beating in my mouth. "When? Is he here for long? Has he been back since ... Since that day?" Now I can feel the years crashing in on top of me again. I've been able to suppress my emotions where David was concerned because I've been out of the country and the few times I've been back no one has ever mentioned him.

"Well I think he's only here for a few days, he came down to see his family. I spotted him when we were leaving to go the airport to collect you." She can't meet my eyes.

I stand up, drain my glass of wine and say, "I want to go home now please."

Mum stands. "Ok let's go. We can talk about this more at home."

"I don't want to talk about it. I'm just tired and need

to go and have a nap!" I stomp out to the car. The ride home is quiet and I find myself thinking back all those years to THAT fateful night! I don't want to remember it or my subsequent actions. It's too difficult to keep remembering.

When we get home I tell Mum I'm going to my room and when I get there, I lay on the bed and just let the memories come back. I cry for what nearly happened that night. I cry for the night I tried to kill myself and for how sad Mum and Dad were. I cry for myself and how that incident changed my life.

After crying myself to sleep, I am woken by voices downstairs and I get out of bed and make my way down. I can hear Mum and Dad arguing. "Why did you tell her David was here? Don't you think she has enough to deal with right now?" My Dad is yelling at Mum, I've never heard them argue, not even once.

"I know, it just came out. You know I'm bad at keeping secrets, I'm sorry, Brian." Mum is pleading with Dad.

I walk into the room and they both stop talking and look at me. "I'm sorry if I upset you earlier," Mum says. "I didn't think about your feelings and I'm sorry!" Mum comes over and hugs me.

"It's ok Mum, I need to move on and chalk it up as one of those things. I just hope I don't bump into him and if I do, I hope he doesn't say anything to me," I say rubbing her back. "Now, let's not talk about this tonight please," I plead.

"Well dinner is nearly ready, so why don't you open a bottle of wine Brian and you can set the table," she says ordering us both around.

Dinner was lovely, it was my favourite corn beef hash, I haven't had it in years. "I need to get that recipe off you, I love it" I say.

We then had dessert, which was banoffee pie, another favourite of mine. After dinner we cleaned up then took our wine into the lounge.

"Mum, Dad" I say, looking at the both of them. "When I was flying to Disney World with Chad I read an article in the inflight magazine about a charity for sexually abused girls and women. I was fascinated. They offer counseling and other services for people who have gone through similar experiences to what I did and others who went through more than I did. I was intrigued, I didn't say anything to Chad because I'd never told him about David, I wanted to forget that part of my life."

"You never told him? How come?" Mums asks totally dumbstruck.

"I didn't want him to feel sorry for me, I wanted him to know the new Cassie that I was then, not the victim. Does that make sense?"

"Of course it does baby, I'm just surprised that's all."

I smile at her and carry on. "When I flew to Vegas with Bonnie I read the article again. So when we were ready to leave Vegas I arranged a bank transfer to the charity. It took the bank manager a couple of phone calls to get the details, then I donated $200,000." Mum and Dad are staring at me with their mouths open.

I hold my hands up in the air to stop them talking. "I know it sounds like a lot of money, but I'm comfortably well off and I wanted to give something to these amazing people who can help others. I only wish I had that service available to me." I can see tears in both my parents eyes.

"I hope to do some volunteer work with the charity while I'm here, but I haven't approached them yet. I think they only have an office in London and I'm not sure I want to travel anywhere yet." I'm looking at my parents, waiting for them to say something.

"Wow! That is truly selfless and it's so great that we have such a giving and caring daughter," Mum says and she gets up and comes over to me. "I love you Cassie and I'm so glad you're able to do this."

Dad gets up and comes over to both of us. "I think this calls for a family hug," he says and joins in the hug.

When the hug is over we go to bed and I sleep really well.

"Collide"

I've been in Newquay for a month and I love my home. I love being close to my parents and my wonderful friends. I can't even begin thinking about going back to New York alone. I think I'd hate it.

I've been to see Bonnie and Jezza a few times at their home and they're really good company. I always feel like there is something left unsaid, like they want to tell me something. I can't put my finger on but probably think that they don't want to mention Jordan. I know he is a big part of Jezza's life and it's obviously just awkward. Tonight I am going out with Bonnie into town. It's the first time I've been out drinking since I've come home and I'm actually looking forward to it.

This afternoon I sit on my veranda overlooking the beach, watching the surfers out on the waves. I let my mind drift to years ago when Jordan taught me how to surf. I wasn't any good but I only did it because it meant he would rub against me and hold me tight. I smile at the memories and I look out at the surfers. I can see one just sitting on his board looking in my direction. I can feel my hairs standing up on my arms and I start to feel little electrical impulses all over my body!

I keep staring and I know then that the surfer is Jordan. I stand and walk to the edge of the veranda and lean against the rail, putting my hand up against my face to shield my eyes. It doesn't help me see any better, but I know he can see me and I believe he knows it's me.

How am I so sure it is him? I remember the night of the pool party when I could feel him watching me, that's how I feel now. Why does he still affect me? After all these years, why have I never forgotten him? Why have I never stopped thinking of him? I stand at the railing for about twenty minutes just watching him on his board and then I have to drag myself away. I have to get ready to go out and meet Bonnie.

I go back inside and climb the stairs thinking about what I will wear. I'm not going to make a huge effort, I'm not out to catch a man. I'm going out to catch up with my best friend.

I decide to wear a simple cut black dress, low sweetheart neckline with a nipped in waist which has a couple of diamantes on it. I wear low-heeled pumps with the dress. I apply a little make up and then just mess up my hair a bit and walk the short distance to the pub we are meeting at.

I see Bonnie as soon as I walk in the pub. She has on a short black skirt with ripped tights and her doc martins. She also has a purple top on tonight for a splash of colour. I smile at her. walk over and give her a big hug.

"I missed you this week," I say giving her a kiss on the cheek.

"Me too" she says. "I can't wait to catch up on everything. Why don't we go and sit at a table outside it's so warm." She has her hand on the base of my spine and is pushing me towards the patio area.

"Sounds good to me," I say, although I feel like I don't have a choice. We find a table and sit down. "Ah Bonnie, I miss this, just sitting and chatting and being so close." I rub her hand.

"Me too," she says "more than you know," she smiles at me. We sit and talk for two hours about what I've been up to. How the house has come along. What I've enjoyed doing and just generally gossip.

"So," Bonnie says, "I've got something to tell you."

I don't like the sound of this, I hate when people warn you before they say something bad.

"Well actually I have a few things to tell you; some good, some bad." She looks really nervous.

"I won't ask for the bad news first, because I hate when people say that. So just tell me what you have to say Bonnie." I smile at her as nothing can be as bad as she is making it out to be.

"Well .... Jezza proposed last night. It was our anniversary and I said yes!" She is beaming from ear to ear.

"Oh my god. I can't believe you didn't tell me this morning." I lean over the table and give her a big hug. "So any idea when you'll get married or even where?" I'm so excited for her.

"Well we want to have a small wedding and I don't want to get married in a church, so I'm going to go to the

Atlantic hotel to see if they do civil weddings. You can come with me if you like." She looks at me expectedly.

"Of course I'm coming with you," I smile.

"Great I knew you'd be happy for us and that you'd help me. Now, you know I said it was going to be a small wedding well there's only going to be about twenty five guests to the wedding and the dinner, then we will have a shin dig at night with loads of people." I nod for her to go on.

"Well, I want you to be my Maid of Honour." I have a lone tear running down my cheek.

"I'd be honoured to be your Maid of Honour." I start laughing at what I just said. "I'm a poet and I didn't know it."

Bonnie laughs with me and then continues. "Now, Jezza has chosen his best man and you need to know that this person has been his best friend for years. I don't know how you are going to take it but he is asking Jordan to be his best man." She looks at me sheepishly.

I don't know what to say, I can feel the air around me get thicker and I'm finding it hard to breathe. Deep in and slow out - I keep repeating to myself. "Oh OK. Wow! I knew they were friends, but didn't realise they were such good friends, you never mention him."

"I purposely don't mention him because I don't want you to get upset or angry that we still talk to him. He never did anything wrong!" She is searching my eyes to try and see how I really feel. "The wedding will be in about six months, as long as we can get the date we want. What do you say?"

"I'm so happy for you and Jezza. You should have who you want at your wedding. I'll do whatever you want Bonnie." She leans across the table and kisses me on the cheek.

"Thanks" she says. "I knew you wouldn't mind and I'm sure Jordan won't either." I don't know how I feel knowing that I'll be seeing HIM and talking to HIM and having to have the first dance with HIM. I can feel it getting warmer when I start thinking about his hands on me as we dance. I feel myself flush, I really need to pull myself together.

Bonnie gets a text message from Jezza telling her that Jordan was delighted to be best man and looks forward to seeing me again. "Wow! So what's the first thing we need to do?" I ask and Bonnie starts talking about what she wants and how she wants everything to go.

I drift off into "Jordan" land and I start to wonder what he's been up to all these years. I wonder how he really reacted to finding out I'm Maid of Honour. "I need to go to the toilet Bonnie, I'll be right back." I need to splash some water on my face because I've started getting warm.

As I'm walking around the bar I notice that it's pretty crowded and so when someone behind me starts pushing and shoving I don't take any notice. Although my senses feel like they are on high alert.

"I told you I'd come back for what's mine!" I hear

this heavy deep voice say.

"David, what the hell are you doing here? Let go of me!" Now I start to panic. Why does he make me feel so defenseless? I've dealt with more important people at work, but this guy just makes me feel sixteen all over again!

He's got his hands around my waist guiding me out towards the toilet. He keeps pushing me past the toilets and out the back door into an alleyway. "You struggling all those years ago really turned me on. I hope you don't disappoint me tonight. I've imagined this moment for years." He's got me pushed face first up against the wall.

"You don't want to do this David, I'll make sure you definitely get put away this time," I say with tears running down my face. I realise that the more I struggle the more turned on he will get.

He starts pulling my dress up slowly, revealing the tops of my stockings. "Oh my god, you've definitely improved with age!" I fight back by kicking him, but it's not easy as I'm face first against the wall. "I just want to feel your body - it's all I've been able to think about. I've pictured this so many times and I can't believe that my dream is finally going to become a reality," he's whispering in my ear.

I noticed he doesn't look polished like he did when I first met him; he looks dirty and unkempt! He smells of drink and cigarettes. What is he going to do to me? I hate to think. "So Cassie, this is how it's going to work. You are going to do what I say and come with me. I'm going to take you down this alley and then we are going back to the playground by the beach, where it all started! You are going to come quietly and then I want to hear you scream when I finally make you mine." He's rushing his words like a well-rehearsed speech. I'm worried that he's mentally ill or something; one thing I do know for sure is that he is definitely mentally unstable.

"No, I'm not coming with you. I'm going to fight you on this David and I'm going to scream." I shout at him to try to make him understand.

I didn't expect what happened next. He punched me right in the face and I banged my head off the wall. I can feel the blood running down my face. Now I don't even know if I'm going to make it through the night. I'm sure he's going to kill me before the night is over. He has to kill me so that I don't tell anyone what he does to me. The tears are flowing down my face, but I sob silently. I don't want him to know how scared I am, because that obviously turns him on.

"Now you WILL come with me and you WON'T make a noise. You don't know how pleased I was to see you in the pub tonight it was a real surprise," he says as he's kissing my cheek. I struggle and try to get away from him but he just shoves me back into the wall. Then he starts to pull me away down the alley and I start struggling. He just punches me in my side and pulls me closer. I can see some people coming down the alley.

"Don't you dare scream, Cassie. You can do that later when I'm inside you," he whispers in my ear. "Come on darling," he then says loudly so the other people can hear him. "Why did you get so drunk? I can't believe I have to practically carry you home. I love you baby".

The other couple look at us and have a little giggle. I hear the girl say "oh she's going to be in big trouble tonight!" and then they laugh.

If only they knew. I wonder whether they will remember seeing me when he's killed me and an appeal goes out. I hope so because he needs to be taken down.

His car is just outside the pub and I start to think he is going to drive to the playground. He is so drunk he can't drive; he will kill the two of us. Maybe that's a good thing! He opens the boot and picks out a blanket and some other things I can't see. He drags me to the beach and then into the playground. "Do you remember Cassie how nice it was that night? It was warm like tonight and we were young and innocent. But you hurt me when you kicked me. What was that all about? I know you liked me I could tell." He's talking and talking.

"No, David you're wrong. I didn't want you then and I don't want you now. Let me go and I promise I won't say anything to anyone. Please David." I'm pleading now because I know I'm pleading for my life. This isn't some teenager playing a game anymore, this is a man who will kill to get what he wants. ME!

"You do want me, you've always wanted me," he says as he pushes me to the ground onto the blanket he put there. "I can't believe that this is going to happen tonight. Cassie thank you for making my dreams come true." He's on top of me kissing my lips but I won't open them. He bites down on my lip drawing blood and as I open my mouth to scream he forces his tongue inside and he's pinning me down.

When he pulls his tongue out of my mouth he says, "I followed you to San Francisco you know. I heard that's where you were and it took me a few months but I found you. Do you remember the day trip to Alcatraz? I was so close to you I could have had you there, but you took the boat back before me. Disney World was nice too, although I wasn't happy about that guy being with you. I watched you that first day, but you never came back after that. It wasn't worth my while staying any longer once you had left. I've been waiting to bump into you since you came home Cassie. Thank you for making it easy for me."

He reaches into his pocket and gets out some tape, he kisses me once again and then tapes my mouth so I can't scream. I start wriggling and he goes into the other pocket and gets out some rope and a knife. I am really scared now! This is it he's going to rape me and then he's going to kill me. He grabs my two arms and pulls them above my head and wraps the rope around them and then he ties the rope around the pole for the monkey bars so that I can't move them.

He stands above me and he smiles. The bastard actually smiles at me and then he stamps down on my ribs. "That will keep you quiet," he says. The tears are streaming down my face now. There is nothing I can do. I close my eyes when I hear the sound of his zip and the sound of his trousers being pulled down.

I can feel him on top of me, pulling my dress up. Then he rips my panties off me and spreads my legs open very wide.

He says, "oh my god Cassie you look so beautiful right now. So much better than I dreamed of." The next thing I know he slams himself inside me. I start thinking of anything except where I am and what is happening to me. I think of Mum and Dad and how sad they will be when I'm no longer here. I think of Chad and how I will be joining him soon. I think of Bonnie and Jezza and them asking me to be Matron of Honour. This leads me onto Jordan. I think of all the nice things we did and the love we shared.

All the time David is slamming in and out of me, he is relentless. As I can feel him starting to cum he says, "I love you Cassie, I always have, but if I can't have you then no one else can." He grabs my head and he bangs it so hard on the ground as he cums inside me.

Everything goes black, I can't hear anything and I can feel my soul drifting above my body. This is it. This is death!

And I welcome it!!

Bonnie's POV

I'm so excited I'm going out with Cassie tonight. It's the first night she's wanted to go out. Usually she comes round to our house or we go to hers. It's hard work though because of our friendship with Jordan, even though he doesn't live here anymore he comes to visit regularly. So when Cassie is over it's hard to talk about what we've done without mentioning him. I made a decision years ago not to mention him because if I did she would get upset, even after she married Chad. Sometimes I wish I'd told her, but now I know that tonight I have to.

Jezza asked me to marry him and of course I said yes. I'm so excited and I can't wait to ask Cassie to be my maid of honour. I'm sure she will say yes. Jezza is asking Jordan to be his best man as they are best friends. I hope it's not going to be awkward, but I think they are both older now. I know Jordan found it very hard when Cassie left and then he moved to Toronto for a few years. When he moved back to England, he moved to London, where he set up his business. He comes home regularly though; he is staying with us this weekend. I know he's hoping to bump into Cassie soon.

I go to the pub and wait for Cassie. I don't have long to wait as she is on time as usual. I steer her outside because I thought I saw someone who looked a bit like David, but he was really scruffy looking so I'm not sure it is him. I don't want anything to spoil our night.

We sit talking for a couple of hours and then I know I have to ask her. "So" I say. "I've got something to tell you. Well actually I have a few things to tell you, some good, some bad." I feel really nervous.

"I won't ask for the bad first because I hate when people say that so just tell me what you have to say Bonnie."

"Well .... Jezza proposed last night it was our anniversary, and I said yes!" I know I'm beaming from ear to ear.

"Oh my god I can't believe you didn't tell me this morning," she leans over the table and gives me a big hug. "So, any idea when you'll get married or even where?" She sounds so excited for me.

"Well we want to have a small wedding and I don't want to get married In a church so I'm going to go to the Atlantic Hotel to see if they do civil weddings. You can come with me if you like." I hesitate.

"Of course I'm coming with you," she smiles.

"Great, I knew you'd be happy for us and that you'd help me. Now, you know I said it was going to be a small wedding, well there's only going to be about twenty five guests to the wedding and the dinner. Then we will have a shin dig at night with loads of people." She nods for me to go on.

"Well, I want you to be my Maid of Honour." I can see she is taken aback and I see a loan tear running down her cheek.

"I'd be honoured to be your maid of Honour." She starts laughing at what she had just said. "I'm a poet and I didn't know it," that was always her line in school. We both start laughing but I know I have to continue.

"Now, Jezza has chosen his best man and you need to know that this person has been his best friend for years and I don't know how you are going to take it. He is asking Jordan to be his best man." I can't look her in the eye.

"Oh OK, wow! I didn't realise they were such good friends, you never mention him," she said to me.

"I purposely don't mention him because I don't want you to get upset or angry that we still talk to him. He never did anything wrong! The wedding will be in about six months, as long as we can get the date we want. What do you say?"

"I'm delighted and you should have who you want at your wedding. I'll do whatever you want Bonnie." I lean across the table and kiss her on the cheek. "Thanks," she says. "I knew you wouldn't mind and I'm sure Jordan won't either."

My phone beeps with a text from Jezza.

"Jordan said he'd be delighted and he can't wait to see you."

I read it out to Cassie. She's looking a bit flushed.

She says that's she's just popping to the toilet. I reply to Jezza when she's gone.

"That went well at this end"

"Jordan says we should all have Sunday dinner at our house in a couple of weeks when Cassie has had time to get used to the idea."

"That's a great idea. Trust Jordan, he's always thinking of Cassie"

"Yea he is, well you know he never got over her."

"I know."

I look up and see that Cassie hasn't come back and I've been texting for about twenty minutes. I get up and walk to the toilet to see if she is in there, but no she's not there. I go back into the bar and ask have they seen her, no one has, but then it has been busy they say.

Now I'm starting to get worried. I do one more round of the pub and she's not there, so I ring Jezza.

"Did you miss me that much babe," he says and I can hear the sexiness oozing off him.

"Of course babe, but I've got an awful feeling that something terrible is going to happen. Cassie went to the toilet over twenty minutes ago and hasn't come back. Will you pop over to her house and see if she went home. She's not answering her phone." I'm talking really fast because I'm panicking.

"Calm down babe, it's going to be ok. Jordan and I will go and check the house. I'll ring you in five minutes. Stay there just in case she comes back." He hangs up.

I am pacing up and down and around the pub but

don't see her anywhere. Where could she be? As I look around I see a guy who looks familiar, I think we went to school with him, Paul I think his name was. I walk up to him, "Hi Paul, long time no see. Do you remember my friend Cassie? She hasn't lived in this country for years and we were out tonight but she's seems to have left me. You didn't see her did you?"

"Cassie? Oh I remember Cassie all right. That's all I ever hear, Cassie this and Cassie that, I'm sick of hearing about her to be honest. I hope that ends once he's got what he wants." He stands shaking his head at me. I drag him by the arm outside so I can hear him. He's pretty drunk, so I'm delighted when Jezza and Jordan come over to me shaking their heads.

"No one at the house Bonnie where do you think she is? Hi Paul, how are you doing?" Jezza says as he slaps him on the shoulder.

"Paul was just telling me that he's sick of hearing about Cassie and that he hopes it ends tonight when he gets what he wants. Do you want to elaborate?"

I'm almost spitting at him. He seems to think this is funny or something.

Jordan steps forward and grabs him by the shoulders. "Paul, seriously we are worried about Cassie. What are you talking about? Did you see her or not?"

Paul looks at him and nods his head. "Yeah she walked right past us and then he followed her. Before he did he said, "this ends tonight." I just thought he was going to talk to her, but now you are all scaring me."

Jezza and Jordan both shout "who" at the same time.

"David, of course. Who else is obsessed with Cassie? I'm sick of hearing how he wants to go back to that night and finish the job he set out to do. Then when he followed her he turned and said to me, "if I can't have her then no one can." He's pissed man, he's not capable of anything.

I feel like being sick and push my way past Jezza and Jordan and vomit in the bush. Crying, I say to them "we have to find her before he does anything to her. I'm going to call the police. Where do you think he is?"

Jordan says, "if he's going to go back to that night then I bet he's gone to the playground where he attacked her. Call the police and we will drive over there and meet them." He takes me into a hug. "Bonnie it'll be fine he won't hurt her, I promise." I can see he has a tear in his eye.

"Ok!" I pull out my phone, call the police and tell them what we think might be happening down at the playground.

Jezza drives us to the beach and we get out, but Jezza stops me. "No Bonnie, I don't want you anywhere near the playground, we don't know what he's doing to her down there. I don't want you to see anything. Stay here and wait for the police, but whatever happens do not come down, please babe I'm begging you." He has crushed me to his chest like he will never let go. I know at this minute that he is worried about what David is doing to her. I start sobbing, but agree to wait.

I watch the two of them run off to find Cassie.

I hear a lot of shouting and what sounds like fighting, but I wait and when I see the police I tell them what is happening. I don't go down there. I don't think I want to.

Jordan's POV

When Paul tells us about David, I don't know how to react. I can't believe this guy is back in Cassie's life. I never got over her and never will. I love her. I've always loved her and always will. I miss our friendship more than anything, but really I just miss Cassie.

I can't get in the car quick enough. I tell Bonnie that I won't let any hurt come to Cassie and I mean it.

When we get to the beach I hear Jezza telling Bonnie to stay put and wait for the police and not to come down. He's worried and to be honest I'm petrified of what we might find in the playground. Jezza and I run down towards the playground and as we turn the corner I see David. He has hold of Cassie's head and I see him slam it down hard. It's then I notice that he is balls deep inside her. I am like a raging bull. I run over and drag him off her and start punching him and punching him. I don't want to stop. I see Jezza checking Cassie.

"Jordan, you need to stop." He's trying to pull me off of David. "You're going to kill him and then who's going to make sure Cassie is ok? Come on Jordan, be there for her."

Wait! Jezza said she's still alive. I drop David and make sure Jezza stands with him so he won't be going anywhere. I run over to Cassie, my god she's in a mess; her pulse is weak, but I can hear her breathing. I find the knife on the ground and cut the tape around her beautiful hands. I rub them to get some circulation back in them.

I pull her up to me and hold her against me. There is blood everywhere. I don't know how she is alive. "Cassie, everything is going to be ok. I'm here. I'm going to take care of you. Please don't leave me, not now when I've just found you again. I should never have let you walk out of my life, but I know for sure I won't be doing it again." I kiss her face being extra gentle. I hear Jezza ringing for an ambulance and I can hear the police talking to him and arresting David. I don't want to talk to them I just need to be with Cassie.

"Come on Jordan, the ambulance is here, they need to check her and make sure she's going to be ok. They need to give her some pain relief and then they will take her to the hospital." Jezza is rubbing my back. I step back and allow the ambulance crew to do their thing. I hold her hand all the time. I just can't fully let go.

"I'm going with her in the ambulance Jezza. Will you ring her parents? Please. I just can't do it." I have tears running down my face, but I don't care, I need to be strong for my Cassie.

We get in the ambulance and go to the hospital. I think she stopped breathing on the way because they were pushing on her chest and there was a lot of shouting. The sirens were blaring and the lights were flashing. We need to get to the hospital quick.

When we get there they make me wait while they take her away to assess her. It is the longest hour of my life.

In the meantime, her Mum and Dad arrive and they are crying. They come up and pull me into a hug with them. I have kept in touch with them and always visited whenever I was down. I needed the contact to know she was all right.

We all cry and then Jezza and Bonnie join in the hug while we are waiting for the doctor to come out.

Eventually, the doctor comes out and asks us all to take a seat. Oh no, I hope she isn't dead. She can't be. "Cassie is a very lucky lady, she has broken ribs; a dislocated shoulder; a huge gash in her head which we have stitched up, but there is no other damage to the skull. We have medically induced a coma to give her body time to recover and it is only then that we will know if she has any lasting brain damage or not."

He stops talking to hand out the tissues. "We also carried out the necessary tests in situations like this and we have that information for the police. She wasn't badly injured down below, but there is a lot of bruising. I know it all sounds bad, but she's actually a very lucky girl. Now I know you're dying to see her, but I'm sorry it has to be two at a time and don't forget she is in a coma. They say that they can hear, you so keep talking to her," he smiles at us and then walks away.

"You both go in first" I say to her Mum and Dad, they both grab hold of me for a hug and then walk into her room.

"Jezza, I can't believe the bastard did this to her. She's having a hard enough time with losing her husband to then have to deal with this shite." I break down crying, I can't control it. "I thought I'd lost her, I thought I'd lost her again."

Jezza comes over and gives me a man hug. "I know Jordan I know. When she comes round, which she will, you just need to be there for her. You helped her the first time, you can do it again." I nod and hope that he is right.

Her Mum and Dad come out crying. "Bonnie, you and Jezza go in, I want to go in on my own," I say to them. I see them both go into her room and I wait. I ask her Mum and Dad, "how does she look?"

Her Mum replies to me shaking her head. "She doesn't look great to be honest Jordan. She has bandages around her head, of course, and she has bandages around her ribs and her shoulder. There are tubes everywhere and she looks fast asleep." Her Mum gasps and turns to Brian, "she didn't look like our baby girl." She starts sobbing.

It feels like Jezza and Bonnie are in there for hours. When they finally come out Jezza has Bonnie pulled into him tightly, as she is crying.

They look at me and Jezza says, "it's not good mate, just go in there and talk to her." I walk towards the door and stop just before I go in. I try to compose myself so that I can talk to her and not concentrate on her injuries. I open the door and walk in slowly. I hold my breath when I see her. She looks terrible and there are tubes and bandages everywhere. I can feel the tears running down my face, silently.

I walk towards the bed and sit down next to her. I take her hand. "Hey baby it's me, Jordan. I've really missed you. I'm sorry that I just let you go so easily. I should have fought harder. I won't let you push me away again. I'm going to take care of you and I'm going to keep you safe, if it's the last thing I do." I keep rubbing her hand while I tell her what I've been up and how I've coped without her. I tell her how I saw her on the veranda today and how my heart started beating faster and how I held my breath until she turned and walked away. She was the most beautiful sight I had ever seen.

"I told you that we were soul mates and that our souls would find each other again," I say, as I'm crying. After about an hour or so I climb up on the bed next to her and put my arm around her gently. I kiss her on the cheek and tell her I love her, I always have and then I lie down next to her and fall asleep.

"Going Crazy"

Cassie

After everything goes black I feel floaty, so many things go through my mind. I can hear the ambulance man shouting and pushing down on my chest. I can hear Mum and Dad crying and telling me they love me and that I have to hang on. They tell me that my time isn't up yet.

I hear Bonnie and Jezza talking to me about their wedding and what colour dress I am going to wear. Why did this happen to me on a night when we should have been celebrating their engagement? Life isn't fair.

It goes quiet for a while and I start drifting again. I hear Jordan next. What is he doing here? Why is he here? He's telling he loves me, he's telling me he shouldn't have let me go. I want to cry but tears won't come. I feel his arm wrapped around me but I can't move.

I drift away again and this time I can hear the doctor telling someone that they are going to leave me for another day before trying to bring me out of the coma. It's a very strange feeling - being able to hear everyone but not being able to see them or touch them.

I hear sobbing and I realise it's Mum. "Baby girl" she says. She's always called me baby girl, it's her nickname for me. "I know you can get better. If you're able to hear me, please come back to us. We all need you to come back. We all love you so much. Jordan won't go home, I've sent him for some food and then he'll be back. He loves you so much, don't let him go." She has hold of my hand and I can feel her. I just want to cry, but I just can't do it.

I drift away again, but I am woken by this horrible tugging sensation in my throat. They must be taking the tube out that has been helping me to breathe. It feels awful, so uncomfortable. When they have taken it out I can hear a lot of voices, I try to make them out, it's like a little game for me.

There's Mum. "Baby girl, come on we're all waiting for you."

There's Bonnie. "Cassie come on honey, we have to go wedding dress shopping, I can't do this on my own. I need my best friend to come with me."

There's Dad. "Baby girl. (He never calls me that.) I need to do some decorating in your house. I need you to come home and tell me what to do."

There's Jezza. "Come back Cassie, we all love you and need to see your smiling face."

There's Jordan. "Baby. My soul needs your soul. You have to come back to me."

I hear a doctor shuffling around. I feel a bit dizzy, like I'm going to be sick. My eyelids are heavy but I can move my eyes, the numbness I've been feeling is starting to go away. It's feels like a bad case of pins and needles in my fingers. I need to clench my fist to make them go away. When I do all I can feel is a warm hand in mine and I hear a gasp.

"Cassie. Oh my god, she moved her hand. Get the doctor. She moved her hand." Jordan starts to get louder, but he never lets go of my hand, he's rubbing his thumb over the top of my hand.

I slowly open my eyes and I don't think I will ever forget the first thing I see, which is five pairs of eyes staring at me. They all have big smiles on their faces and I try to focus and look at each one of them until I land on the most gorgeous pair of turquoise eyes I've ever seen. I see so much love in all of them.

"Hi guys," I say trying to smile. My voice sounds so different and it is hard to swallow.

"Baby girl, I'm so happy to see you." Mum says as she comes round to hug me. I notice it hurts when she hugs me and I wince.

"Where's the doctor?" Jordan says. "I'll go get him baby, he'll give you more pain killers." He let's go of my hand and instantly my hand feels cold. He leaves the room.

Bonnie comes over and leans down and kisses me on the cheek. "I missed you honey, we need to do some wedding shopping," she says. Then she moves closer to my ear and whispers, "Jordan brought you here and he's been here ever since. He hasn't even been home once."

She smiles at me.

The doctor comes back into the room and asks everyone to leave so he can examine me. I smile weakly and nod my head.

They all get up and leave and the doctor asks me how I'm feeling and checks all my vital signs. "I'm in a lot of pain when I move and I have a really bad headache," I tell him.

"I'll increase your pain relief and you're to take it easy. You're going to be in here for a short while. We need to make sure that you're well enough to go home. We need to talk about what happened to you and how you ended up in here. Do you remember what happened?" The doctor asks me.

I was hoping that no one would ask me that question, but in my heart of hearts, I know they all will. I also know that I need to talk about it, I'm just not ready for that right now.

"Yes, I do remember. I remember every single detail. His smell, my fear and every feeling from start to end." I feel a tear falling down my face.

The doctor comes over to the bed and says, "I know it's hard remembering all the details and it will bring it all back to you, but you will need to talk to the police. They have been coming every day to see if you're ready to talk to them."

"NO! I'm not ready to talk to them" I shout. "I don't want to talk about every detail. I'm just not ready yet."

I'm shaking and can feel my anger.

"It's ok, I've told them that you're out of your coma, but that I've sedated you, so they're coming back tomorrow," he says, understanding my fear.

"You will also need to talk to a counselor, but we can talk about that tomorrow too."

"Thank you," I say having calmed down a little bit. "Thank you."

He starts to walk towards the door. "You know you've got good family and friends, they care a lot about you. One has not left this hospital the whole time you were in a coma. Just remember to talk to them; they love you a lot. I'll be back in a while to check on you again. Let me know if you need more pain relief." With that he turns and walks out the door.

As soon as he had stepped through the door Mum and Dad come back in. "Hi" I say to them and they rush over to me.

"How are you feeling?" Mum asks. "I can't believe we nearly lost you again. You're too precious to us Cassie, we need you in our lives, you are our lives". She is crying and leans over to hug me gently.

"I love you guys so much and I'm sorry for the pain and anguish I've caused you, yet again." I'm crying too now.

"No, baby girl you've not caused us the pain and anguish, David has and we need to talk about that tomorrow when the police come. We've told them they can't interview you without us here," Dad says. He's struggling with his words.

"I know and I will talk about it tomorrow with the police, but I don't want to think about it tonight, please let's talk about something else." I plead.

"Ok" Mum says, although I can see she isn't happy; but she understands. "I'm only going to say this once so listen to me please, do not keep it all to yourself like last time. You can talk to any one of us, we are here for you, we all love you, each and every one of us." She kisses me on the forehead.

Dad does the same. "Just remember we love you. We are going to go to the cafe to get some food and a coffee, do you want anything Cassie?"

I get all panicky at the thought of being on my own and I ask "where are the others? Will someone stay with me? I don't want to be on my own." I can feel the fear rising in my body.

"Don't worry; Bonnie, Jezza and Jordan are outside they won't leave you on your own. There has been someone with you twenty-four hours a day since you came in. Just remember we ALL love you," Mum says as she goes to the door and opens it. They both walk out and my three friends walk in.

Bonnie runs up to me and gives me a gentle hug and kisses me on the forehead. I can see she is trying really hard not to cry. "Cassie you gave us such a fright, I thought .... I thought he'd killed you."

"Bonnie, stop. Leave it until she's feeling better."

Jordan says looking at me. "I'm sure she doesn't want to talk about it right now. Let's wait until she is ready to talk to us." He smiles at me and I feel myself blush. I'd forgotten how handsome he is.

"It's ok Bonnie, I will talk to you all, but I don't want to talk about it today. I have to talk to the police tomorrow, so when I have got that out of the way I will talk to you, I promise." I take her hand and rub over it gently.

"Jezza and Jordan I can't thank you enough for coming to rescue me like that. I don't know what would have happened if you hadn't arrived when you did. Thank you." I can feel tears coming to the surface.

"Jordan, I understand you've been here all the time and I want to say thank you, but you don't have to be here, I'm sure you have other things you need to be doing." I can hear the catch in my voice as I give him a chance to leave.

He walks over to me in the bed and takes my hand, I flinch a little feeling his warmth spread through me. "Cassie, I have nowhere else in the world I would rather be right now. I want to be here. I want to look after you. I need to look after you." He's looking deep into my eyes. I see a shadow pass over his eyes.

"But if you don't want me to be here then I'll just go. Tell me what you want. Do you want me to stay or to go?" He looks so sad, like someone has taken away his favourite toy. "You were my best friend and I've missed that so much. I want to be your best friend again, please let me."

Bonnie shouts at him, laughing "err that's my job mister."

He laughs back at her and says, "well I'm sure Cassie has enough room in her heart for both of us."

"What about me? Don't I exist" Jezza says and we all start laughing.

"Well, you are all my best friends, I don't deserve you all, but you're all stuck with me. Jordan I am including you as one of my best friends, because you always were. Thanks guys."

All three of them are around the bed and give me a gentle hug. I can feel Jordan's warmth through the three of them. I'm very aware of him, I would recognise his hug anywhere.

We all talk about nothing at all, avoiding the subject of David and I'm grateful for that. When Mum and Dad come back, the six of us chat about Bonnie and Jezza's wedding, it helps to take my mind off things.

Soon enough it's time for them to leave. Mum and Dad are the first to go, "we need to leave you to rest baby girl, but we will be back first thing in the morning so we can be here for your police interview. Hopefully you'll be allowed home soon." Mum says as they both kiss me goodbye.

After about ten minutes Bonnie says "yeah we need to go too. Good luck in the morning babe. I'll come and see you after work."

Her and Jezza leave the room and that leaves me

and Jordan alone together. I don't know what to say to him, because we haven't seen each other for so long. "Do you need to go too?" I ask him tentatively. "You don't have to stay if you have somewhere else you need to be". I can't quite look him in the eye, I want him to stay, but I understand he needs to go home too.

"If you want me to stay then I'm not going anywhere," he says pulling the chair closer to the bed and taking the seat. "There is nowhere else I'd rather be than here with you." He smiles as he leans towards me on the bed.

We sit quietly for a few minutes and then he says "tell me about your life in San Francisco Cassie, we have a lot to catch up on."

We spend the next hour or so talking about my life in San Francisco and New York and his life in Toronto and then London. We laugh a little and then I start to feel sleepy. "Jordan, will you stay with me until I fall asleep?" I ask. I know I don't have the right to ask him that, but he makes me feel safe.

"Of course, baby. If that's what you want." He takes my hand, lifts it to his mouth and kisses it. I watch him as he moves it to his mouth and I see the hint of a tattoo on his arm as his shirt sleeve rides up. I never thought he would be the type to get a tattoo. I remember that I don't know him anymore and that thought makes me sad. I hope he allows me a chance to get to know him again.

I lay down fully and feel myself drifting off. My eyes are really heavy and just as I feel the dark washing over me I hear him say, "I love you Cassie. You are truly my soul mate." I feel a little kiss on the corner of my lips and then I drift away.

"A Million Love Songs"

After a couple of hours I am woken up by someone screaming. It frightens me, I wonder who it is. Then I feel someone touching my hand and a weight on the bed. The screaming gets louder. "Cassie, Cassie it's ok, it's me, Jordan."

I open my eyes, the screaming has stopped and I realise that I'm crying and that it was me screaming. Jordan is looking at me with tears in his eyes as he leans over to hug me. "Can I hug you?" he says, obviously wanting to make sure I'm ok after my nightmare; but aware that I might not want anyone touching me.

"Yes please," I say with my heart beating so fast.

He leans over me and hugs me. I feel safe. It feels like I've come home. "I missed your hugs," I say to him quietly. He continues to hold me close for another five minutes.

He pulls away slightly and smiles at me. "Me too Cassie, me too. I'm going to see the nurse and ask if she can give you something to help you sleep." He stands and starts to walk to the door.

"No, Jordan. Don't go!" I can feel myself panicking. I don't want to be on my own and I don't want him to leave me just yet.

He rushes back to me and grabs my hand. "It's ok Cassie, I'm not going anywhere, I promise." He leans over and presses the call button for the nurse to come into us.

It is only now that I take in the dim lights outside my room. "Jordan what time is it?"

"It's three o'clock in the morning," he says as if it's noon.

"How come you're still here? Why haven't you gone home to your family?" I don't want him to get into any trouble at home.

"I promised you that I wouldn't leave and I never break my promises Cassie. You know that." He's looking deep in to my eyes when he says it.

The nurse comes in at that time so I didn't get to ask him whether he has someone at home waiting for him. I really want to know but at the same time I am scared to find out he has a wife and kids.

"I'm going to give you a mild sedative Cassie just to let you sleep a bit better. Tomorrow is going to be a hard day for you," the nurse says as she gives me a pill to take.

I can feel the tablet starting to take effect and I say to Jordan "I never stopped loving you, you know." Then everything goes black and sleep takes me away.

I'm woken by the bright light and the sound of a

trolley with cups clattering on it coming into my room.

"Morning sweetheart, do you want breakfast this morning?" says a very cheery voice.

I try to sit up but it's too painful. I notice Jordan isn't here and I feel sad at the thought that what I said to him might have made him run from me. I should never have said it. I didn't have the right to say it.

"Tea or coffee sweetheart?" The tea lady says, bringing me back to the present moment.

"Eerm tea please" I say smiling at her. She starts to pour my tea.

"What about your friend, what does he want?" I look at her because there is no one else here. "He's just popped out to make a phone call," she smiles at me. "He'll be back in two minutes. He normally has coffee, will I just make the usual for him?" I stare at her with my mouth open and just nod slowly. So, he did stay the night, somehow this makes me feel better and not so panicky. I smile at her.

Just then Jordan walks in the door. "Ah I see you're awake babe, thank you Betty for the coffee," he says and takes both drinks from her.

"You're welcome," she says and hands him some toast for me. "I'll see you later," she says as she takes her Trolley out the door.

"How did you sleep?" he says coming over to kiss me on my forehead. I like it when he does that, he always knows how to make me feel safe.

"Out like a light and very well thank you," I say smiling at him. I wonder if he will say anything about what I said last night.

"I know you don't want to talk about David, but you know the police are coming in today to interview you. Do you want me to stay with you or do you just want your Mum and Dad?" he asks. He has hold of my hand and is absentmindedly running his thumb across the palm of my hand, this is obviously just a natural reaction for him. I don't even think he knows he is doing it. I smile at him.

I just can't believe that he wants to stay to hear what happened. Do I really want him to know all the horrible details? Does he really want to hear them or is he being polite? I know he witnessed some of it but will he think differently of me if he hears it all?

"Cassie, I want to help you as much as I can but if you don't tell me what happened then I can't help you. I WANT to be here for you, but if you find it too uncomfortable then I'll wait outside. Your choice!" He says looking me in the eyes.

"I want you to help me." I say almost in a whisper, I don't want to seem weak, but I really need him right now. "I don't know that you'll want to know me when you hear what he did." I'm crying as I say this "I'm damaged ..."

"Stop Cassie," he says putting one finger up to my lips. "Stop. I've always wanted to know you; from the first moment I ever set eyes on you, you know that. You never have been and you never will be damaged. You are my sole responsibility right now and I want to be here for you when you talk to the police. Never think that anything would make me not want you in my life." He leans forward and very gently kisses me on the cheek.

I don't know what to say to him, because I know I am going to cry. "Yes I want you there, but I don't want you to get mad or think badly of me," I say. I know this will be one of the hardest things I will ever have to do. I don't think it will be easy for him either.

"Never babe, never," he says as the door opens and Mum and Dad walk in.

"Jordan, did you stay last night as well?" Mum asks him. "You didn't need to stay, we knew she was going to be ok."

"Jean, I wanted to stay to make sure she was ok, she had a nightmare in the night, so I was glad I stayed. I'll be staying tonight too if she doesn't go home today," he says to my Mum. Not in an arrogant way, but in a way that leaves no room for argument.

"Oh, well then I'm glad you stayed if she had a nightmare and needed you. I just didn't want to take up any more of your time. I know you need to go back to London soon. You can't be able to have this much time off," she says.

"I was taking some time off anyway. They know where I am if I'm needed, I've got some good people working for me that can take care of the place without me. I'm not going anywhere right now," he says and my

Dad walks over and shakes his hand. Jordan walks up to my Mum and kisses her on the cheek and whispers, "she needs me right now and I am not going anywhere." He said it loud enough for me to hear and turns and winks at me.

I smile, he can make me smile even on one of the darkest days of my life and I love him for that.

Jordan's POV

When Cassie told me she wants me to be there when she talks to the police, it made me very happy. Not because of what she has to do, but because of the fact that she wants me there while she does it. I know it will be one of the hardest things she will ever have to do and I will do my best to ease her pain.

Her Mum and Dad come in and I can see they are shocked to see me here. Jean says "Jordan, did you stay last night as well? You didn't need to stay, we knew she was going to be ok."

It makes me a little bit mad, because they know she is not ok and she needs all of us right now. They know how I feel about her, they know I haven't left her bedside in the whole time she has been here.

"Jean, I wanted to stay to make sure she was ok, she had a nightmare in the night, so I was glad I stayed. I'll be staying tonight too if she doesn't go home today," I say to her. I think she can tell by my voice that I'm a little annoyed.

"Oh, well then I'm glad you stayed if she had a nightmare and needed you. I just didn't want to take up any more of your time. I know you need to go back to London soon. You can't be able to have this much time off," she says.

Is she serious? Does she really think I can leave right now? How can I desert Cassie when she needs me the most? I know I have my business and my life in London; but she knows I would do anything for Cassie.

"I was taking some time off anyway. They know where I am if I'm needed, I've got some good people working for me that can take care of the place without me. I'm not going anywhere right now." Brian walks over and shakes my hand. I then walk up to Jean and kiss her on the cheek and I whisper, "she needs me right now and I am not going anywhere." I said it loud enough for Cassie to hear and when I turn to look at her I wink and catch her blushing, she smiles at me. Her smile makes me the happiest man in the world. Maybe she feels the pull we have as much as I do.

I know her world is going to come tumbling down around her when she has to relive that night, I want to be here for her when it does. I know I'm going to find it hard to hear, but I need to know everything so that I can help her.

I've never stopped loving her and I'm so happy she's back in my life. I know that I need to be a friend to her first and foremost but I'll take whatever contact she gives me so that I can be here for her.

She is my soul mate, I've always known that and my soul will wait, if it needs to.

"Scars"

Cassie

Mum, Dad and Jordan are here when the policewoman comes into the room to interview me. When she sees everyone in the room she looks at me "We won't be long," she says to Mum.

"We are not going anywhere, the three of us are staying They all tell the female officer that they are staying. She looks at me and asks "is that ok with you, Cassie? Are you sure you want them to hear what happened?"

I look at the three of them and know that to be able to help me they need to know every detail. I nod my head "Yes it's fine with me, I love these people so much and I need them to hear what happened, so that they can help me."

She smiles at me, "of course, I totally understand. They obviously love you a lot because they have been here every time we have come to talk to you."

She starts to walk towards the bed. "Do you mind if I sit next to the bed so that I can write everything down?"

"Of course, that's fine." Jordan moves from his chair so that she can sit down. He squeezes my hand before he stands up though.

I spend the next hour telling her everything that happened the first time round and then what happened a few nights ago. It is heartbreaking that this has happened to me, but I need to be strong so that eventually he can be put away for what he did to me.

When the policewoman leaves the room, Mum is crying and holding my hand. Dad is holding my other hand and Jordan is pacing the room. I can see he's angry. I know he was there at the end, but the pain and torture of what David did to me will affect him as well.

Dad is crying and holding Mum who looks like she is going to collapse. I forgot they didn't know all the details as they weren't there that night. I'm sad because they've been through so much, I've put them through so much. Jordan looks at me and I can see the anger and disgust in his eyes.

"Cassie, I'm going to get a coffee. Does anyone want one?" I know he just needs to get out of here because he found it hard to hear what I'd said to the police.

Maybe he doesn't want to know me anymore, maybe he thinks I'm damaged goods. I don't know how I'll feel about that. Now that I've got him back in my life I don't want to let him go. "Are ... Are you coming back?" I say with tears in my eyes.

He looks at me and I see the anger drain from his

face. He walks over to me, takes the hand my Dad is holding, puts it up to his mouth and kisses it. "I'm only going for coffee babe. I promise I'll be back. I just need a bit of fresh air." He kisses my hand again and then leaves.

Mum rubs my other hand. "You know it was hard for all of us this morning. I think he just needs to think for a while. He was pretty angry when the police were here. I'd say he just needs to let off some steam."

"I didn't think about that. I was just dying to get through the interview," I say crying.

"I know," says Mum. "You did a good job baby girl and I'm sure they will put David away for a long time. You were fantastic. Now the doctor wants to come in to talk about counseling, then he can discuss when you can come home. We need you to come home baby girl, as soon as possible. We miss you so much."

We all sit in silence for a while and then the doctor comes in to check my pain levels. "I've arranged for a counselor to come and see you this afternoon. We will have a chat once I've spoken to her, ok?" He says.

"Yeah I understand," I say. I really want to go home and recuperate not stay in this poxy place.

Jordan comes back after about half an hour, I'm delighted he came back, I really am. I wasn't sure he was going to, but when Mum said he was going to let off some steam I had a little grain of hope that he would. We tell him about the doctor and the counselor. "I hope you're allowed to go home, it will be easier to recuperate there," he says with a smile.

After lunch the counsellor comes in and asks Mum, Dad and Jordan to leave so she can speak to me on my own. They all come over and kiss me on the forehead and leave for a while. I see Jordan talking to the counsellor before he leaves the room, she nods at him and he hugs her. Strange!

The counsellor introduces herself as Joyce and asks me how I'm feeling. We sit and just talk for about an hour. She's not judgmental and I feel so much better. She tells me it's not my fault and I'm starting to believe her.

She says that she'd like to see me once a week to start with and see how I get on. I like her, she has really put me at ease and I feel like I can talk to her openly and honestly. I agree to see her weekly.

When Mum and Dad come back in Jordan isn't with them. "Where's Jordan?" I ask. It's strange I'm so used to seeing him in here that the room feels so empty when he isn't here.

"He's gone home to shower. I told him he was starting to smell," Mum says laughing. "He hasn't left your room since he brought you in. He needs to have some time to understand everything that's happened. He will be back in about an hour."

We talk about what Joyce had said to me and I tell them that she will visit me once a week at home where I can relax rather than going to her office. I like that idea. We wait for the doctor to come in. I am quite jittery because I really want to get home and start putting all this behind me.

Jordan comes back after an hour and the sight of him walking in my room is breathtaking. He is so handsome in his tight jeans showing off his gorgeous thighs. He has a white button down shirt on and he smells of my favourite after-shave that he always used to wear, Kouros. I can see the outline of more tattoo's under his white shirt. There are lots of them, I wonder what made him have so many. "Hey Cassie" he says walking over to me and kissing me on the forehead. "How did it go with the counsellor?"

"It was fine, Joyce really helped me. I'm going to see her once a week and she is going to come to my house because I'll feel more relaxed there than in an office." I smile.

"Ah Joyce is really good. You've landed a good counsellor there Cassie" he says with a smile.

I wonder how he knows Joyce, but I don't ask any questions.

At that moment the doctor comes back in and we all stop talking and look at him. "So Cassie, I've spoken to Joyce and she's happy for you to go home. I understand you've agreed to see her once a week for now and that's perfect. You will need to rest for a couple of weeks and then we will start some physio. If you do too much you could do more damage and then you'll need surgery. Do you understand me?" He says looking at me.

"Don't worry we'll make sure she rests." Mum, Dad and Jordan say at the same time. We all start laughing.

"I'll go and get the discharge papers and I'll give you a prescription for some pain killers and sleeping tablets to help you through the next two weeks," the doctor says to me.

"Thank you so much for all your help doctor, I appreciate it." I say smiling because I know I'm going home.

Jordan helps me out of the bed, I sign the discharge papers, pick up my prescription and pack my stuff into my bag.

Jordan holds my arm as we walk to the lift and then to Dad's car, he helps me into the front seat and then gets in the back with Mum. We stop at the chemist on the way home to get my medication.

When we get to the house, we all walk in and Jordan brings my bag in, but then he says, "I'm going to head off and leave you with your parents Cassie. You'll need your rest tonight. Don't forget to take your sleeping tablet and if it's ok I'll come back in the morning to see how you slept?" He stands, walks over to me and kisses me on the forehead.

"Do you really have to go?" I say whining like a spoilt child.

"Thanks Jordan. Don't worry she'll be fine and of course it's ok for you to come over anytime. You know that," Mum says.

I watch him walk out the door and hope that he's not walking out of my life. I feel really sad. I start to cry and Mum comes over to me, "come on Cassie, he has his own life to live. He'll be back in the morning, but you know he has to go back to London soon, don't you?" Mum says looking at me very carefully.

"I know, but I just got him back in my life and I need him to help me through this," I moan.

"I know baby, but you have us and Bonnie and Jezza too," Mum says and I can hear she is getting annoyed.

"I know Mum, I know" I say and resign myself to Jordan not being around as much as I want him to.

I get into a daily routine of doing my exercises to help my shoulders. Jordan came over the second day and helped me with them all. On the fifth day, a Friday, he tells me that he is going back to London on the Sunday evening as he has meetings on the Monday. I start crying because I know I will miss him. He has been my rock.

He comes over before he leaves. "Cassie I'll be back in a couple of days as I just have a few meetings to go to." I can see he doesn't really want to go, but it doesn't make me feel any better.

"I know you shouldn't put your life on hold for me Jordan. I know you have a life in London, you don't need to rush back for me." That was the hardest thing I've ever said and I just want to cry, but I keep strong and try to hide it from him.

"Cassie come on, I've been here every day for the last two weeks. I have some commitments that I have to keep; but I promise I'll be back as soon as I can. I don't want to leave you. I just have to," he says.

He walks over and goes to kiss me on the cheek; but I turn my head at the last minute and he ends up kissing me on the lips. When he realises what I did he doesn't pull away straight away, but I feel his kiss getting softer. When he does eventually pull away he looks me in the eyes and says, "soul mates remember!" He walks away and out the front door.

I feel really sad but I get up and walk into the kitchen. "Dinner smells nice Mum. What are we having?" I ask.

"Corned beef hash and it will be ready in five minutes. Can you lay the table for me, please?"

We sit down and eat dinner, then I tell Mum and Dad that I'm tired and want to go to bed. "Make sure you take your sleeping tablet Cassie and don't forget you've got your meeting with Joyce tomorrow. She's coming here at ten o'clock in the morning."

"Ok, I'm going to go upstairs and read for a while. I haven't read in ages." I kiss them both on the cheek and say good night. When I get undressed and get into bed I take out my book and start reading, but I just can't concentrate so I take out my mobile phone and text Jordan.

"Hey did you make it back to London ok?"

"Hey babe. Yeah I got back to my flat about an hour ago. It was cold in here and didn't feel welcoming at all. How are you?"

"I'm good. I'm in bed trying to read but I can't concentrate. I've taken my sleeping tablet, so I guess I'll

be asleep soon. I just wanted to say thank you for everything you've done and for being here for me. It has really helped me. Thanks Jordan x"

"I've told you before, I'm here for you whenever and wherever just remember that. Now you go and have a good night's sleep and make sure you ring me after Joyce has been ok. Thinking about you x"

"I will. Thanks night night x"

"Don't let the bed bugs bite xx"

I laugh as he always used to say that when we were saying goodbye. I can feel my eyes getting heavy and I drift off into sleep.

The next morning I wake up, have breakfast and then wait for Joyce to come to the house. She asks me how I'm feeling and we talk for an hour about nothing in particular, I think she is easing me into this counseling thing. She asks me to take a walk with her. I know it's just to get me out in the fresh air, but I start getting panicky. I keep looking around me to see if he is there. Every little noise makes me jump and squeal a little, so we only walk to the end of the road and back.

She's says she will see me next week and I ring Jordan to let him know how it went.

"When I come down on Friday I will take you for a short walk," he says.

"I look forward to it. See you Friday, Jordan."

"Take care, Cassie." He hangs up.

I'm a little bit sad that I have to wait five days to

see him, but I understand he has to work. My days become a routine of breakfast, read, lunch, a short walk, dinner, read and bed. Nothing exciting, but it's enough for now.

I wake up on Friday and feel a little bit excited that Jordan will be coming back today. I can't wait. After breakfast I go upstairs to get ready and put on some nice clothes instead of just my tracksuit. I want to make an effort today, he said we will go for a walk, so I want to try and look nice. My phone rings at lunchtime and I see it is him calling me. I smile and pick up the phone.

"Hey Cassie, how are you today?"

"I'm good today, I want to try and go a little bit further on my walk today. When will you be arriving? Will I wait for you or will I just go with Mum?"

"I'm really sorry babe, but I won't be able to come down until Monday. I'm sorry."

I can feel the tears coming to my eyes, but I clear my throat and say "That's ok, I know you have other things to do. I can't monopolise all your time."

"I really am sorry Cassie."

"That's ok, I'll see you on Monday some time."

I hang up the phone because I don't think I can say anything else to him.

I tell him it's ok, but it's not. I've come to rely on him and I miss him. After lunch I tell Mum and Dad that I want to go for a walk and I head out to go to my own house.

I'm tentative when I open the door, but when I walk in I immediately feel at home. I put the heat on, to take the chill off, and drag my armchair over to the patio doors and curl up with a book and my blanket. This is heaven, this is what I need.

Time must have skipped past me as my phone starts ringing at about six o'clock. "Where are you Cassie?" my Mum asks me.

"I'm at my house reading and looking out the window" I reply. "Do you want to bring dinner down here tonight? The view is beautiful this evening."

"Yeah that's a great idea, I will. See you in ten minutes," Mum says and I can hear she is worried.

When they arrive, Mum gets the food out and sets it on my dining table. I have to literally drag myself over to the table. I just feel so tired. We eat dinner in silence.

"Mum, Dad, I want to move back in here. I feel that I need to do it sooner rather than later. I want to have my own routines and start getting my life back on track. I have a few decisions I need to make and I need to really think about them. I believe that I will be able to think more if I am here in my own house," I say. I find it hard to look them in the eye. They have done so much for me and I know that they will worry about me.

"If that's what you want Cassie, but I'm not overly happy about it," Mum says standing up from the table. She starts clearing the dishes, making more noise than is necessary.

"Mum, I can't stay at your house forever. I'll never

recuperate that way. I need to be more independent or I will end up relying on you and dad all the time. I think I'm going to start by staying here tonight and see how I get on." I hate saying it to her, but it's the truth and she knows it.

"Ok, if it's what you want, but I want you to check in with me all the time. I will be checking up on you, baby girl." She kisses me on the forehead. "I can't just let you go that easily." She smiles at me and then she hugs me. We talk for a few more minutes and then her and Dad leave.

I sit there and wonder what I have done. Why did I decide to do this tonight? I know that I need to be on my own, I am always going to be on my own now that Chad is gone. I have a lot to think about and I need to be on my own to do it. I need to make the right decisions for me!

"Let Me Go"

I wake myself up screaming. It scares me stupid, my mind works overtime and believes that someone else is screaming and that's what woke me. It takes me a few minutes of heavy breathing and fast heart beats to realise that it was me who was screaming. It takes me a couple more minutes to realise that I forgot to take my sleeping tablet last night.

I can't believe the first night I am on my own I forget to take them and that the nightmares come screaming back. I lay in bed with my heart racing, I know I wasn't really ready to be on my own, and I need time to digest everything that has happened to me. The biggest decision that I need to think about is whether or not I want to go back to work in New York? I know Mum and Dad will find it even harder if I did, especially with everything that has happened, but I love my job and I'm not sure I'm ready to leave it. I need to think about what is the best thing for me to do.

I get up and make myself a cup of coffee seeing as I can't sleep anyway. I grab a blanket and go to the comfy armchair, which is next to the patio doors. I curl up with my blanket wrapped around me; my hands are wrapped around my coffee cup and I look out the window. I smile, this is my new favourite place. I can see the moon just above the horizon on the sea and everything looks so peaceful and calm out there.

For a split second I believe that I am calm, that everything is alright, that I am alright. But it is only for a second and then I wish I could forget. I hate that this has happened to me. I was a strong and independent person until David came into my life and damaged me and by doing that he destroyed my confidence. I sit there for about three hours just looking out into the dark and just thinking about everything.

Mum rings me at half eight in the morning to check on me and make sure I slept ok. I don't want to tell her that I forgot to take the sleeping tablet because she will only say that I should still be staying with them. I don't want her to think that I can't cope on my own.

"Hi Mum, yeah I slept well. I've got a lot of thinking to do, so I won't be over today. I'll make myself dinner and then I'll come over to you tomorrow for dinner if that's ok?" I say hoping she won't mind.

"Ok baby girl, I'm not happy about it, but I suppose you are old enough to look after yourself. I'll ring and check up on you later. I need to do that for my own peace of mind," she says sounding worried.

"Yes that's fine. I think Bonnie might pop in later for a cuppa, so I won't be on my own all day. I really have lots of decisions to make," I say hoping she believes me.

"Ok, then we will see you tomorrow for dinner. Ask Bonnie and Jezza if they want to come over too." I can hear in her voice she is smiling.

We say our goodbyes and I make a cup of coffee and go back to my seat by the patio doors.

So, the first thing I need to think about is work. Do I want to go back into the publishing world? It's very cut throat and I'm not sure I want that anymore. I don't feel confident enough to be in crowds at the moment. I hope that will change, but at the moment I don't feel like I can do it. It's nearly time for me to go back to New York and back to work. I haven't told Claudia about what happened, I am supposed to be taking time off so she doesn't really need to know, does she?

I think I'll have to hand in my notice. I know Claudia will be upset; I have been working with her since I first went over to San Francisco. She has been like a surrogate mother to me.

I would love to write my own book, so maybe I need to start making some notes and seeing whether I can become a writer. I have worked in the publishing side of things for all these years; I should know what makes a book and what doesn't. I smile to myself; thinking about this has just made me feel lighter already.

I am glad that I have come to a decision about work, all I have to do now is set the ball rolling. I will ring Claudia on Monday to tell her my plans; maybe I can freelance for a bit. I am sure I can work from here for a while until they find someone, I have internet access and everything. I can always start making inroads in writing my own book. I'm not sure how Mum and Dad will take it, although I think they will be pleased that I will be closer to them and not across the Atlantic.

Saturday passes by with me not talking to anyone or answering my texts. I feel detached from my life and just sit staring out the windows and sleeping. The only person I do talk to is Mum and I'm sure I'm not fooling her either.

It's very difficult to explain why I feel this way when I don't know myself. I feel like I did in the hospital, when I was floating above the bed and could see everyone. That's how I feel now. I don't feel like me. I start thinking about what happened with David and all of a sudden I have to run to the toilet to vomit. I don't think I've allowed myself to think about it properly, until now. Now I know why Mum didn't want me to be on my own.

I feel damaged beyond repair, no one is going to want to be my friend. Why would they? They'll only feel that they'll have to walk on eggshells around me. Maybe I should go back to the States and write, then at least there won't be any reminders. No one needs to know back there, I can carry on with my life as if nothing ever happened.

Although, if I'm honest with myself, can I ever really make myself think that? I don't want to look into their faces and see what they are thinking about me. How they all feel sorry for me. How they believe I need help all the time.

Why does Jordan even want to help me? I haven't

spoken to him for years and then when we finally get to meet each other again, it's when I am at my most vulnerable. Why would he want to know someone who is weak?

Do they all think it's my fault? Did I lead him on? I realise that I'm sobbing hysterically and I can't stop. I don't know how long I've been sitting here, but I must have cried myself to sleep because when I wake up I'm still in the same seat and it's getting dark. I haven't eaten anything, because I think I might vomit again. I can't bring myself to stand up and walk to the kitchen.

I remember feeling like this before I walked into the sea. All I can do is look out at the sea and remember how liberating it felt. I can feel it inviting me to come in and to say goodbye to the turmoil and weakness in my life. If I just do it, then I wouldn't feel like this anymore. My friends and family won't have to suffer anymore.

I hate myself for thinking this way but I can't help it. I need help, but I don't want to ask for help. I don't want to seem weaker than I already am. I can hear my phone buzzing and I see I have four texts from Jordan; two from my Mum and a missed call from each of them. I ignore Jordan because he is better off without me as a friend and I can feel the tears flowing down my face at that thought. It's for the best. Mum wants to know how I am, so I send her a message.

"Sorry Mum. I fell asleep. Feeling good now and have been doing lots of thinking and making decisions. Will tell you about them when I've finalised everything ;-)"

"Baby girl I was worried about you. I'm going to bed and I'll see you for dinner tomorrow around five o'clock ok"

"Thanks Mum, you don't need to worry about me, honestly I'm fine. Just taking some me time to work a few things out."

I stay sitting in the chair and keep staring out of the window, even though I can't see anything because it is so dark outside, but I can see plenty running through my mind. Why can't I forget what happened? You hear about girls who are attacked and they forget because of the trauma, why not me? Why do I have to remember everything? Arrggh, I am so angry I throw my mobile phone across the room. I don't know if it has smashed or not, I just don't care.

I sit in the chair until I fall asleep with the blanket wrapped around me. I have my recurring nightmare and I wake myself screaming. At least I manage to fall back asleep quite quickly tonight, that's much better than last night.

On Sunday morning I decide I have to move out of the chair, so I go to the bathroom and then make a cup of coffee. I go back to the chair and continue staring out the window. This is like a new job for me, I feel so much better when I stare out at the sea. It seems to calm me for some reason. I'm so glad Chad bought this house overlooking the sea.

I think about Chad then, I can't believe he's really gone. That reminds me that I will need to ring his Mum at some stage, when I am feeling a bit more sociable. I need to see how she is, she has lost her son and as much as I am hurting, she will be hurting even more. She was like a mother to me when I was in the States, she was always there for me when I needed her. I'm not ready to contact her just yet, I don't know if I can pretend everything is ok, when it really isn't. What have I ever done in my life to deserve all of this? I know I don't have the answers and I don't want to think about it anymore.

I must have fallen asleep because I wake a few hours later to the sound of my phone ringing. I ignore it because I don't have the energy to talk to anyone or to move. I haven't eaten anything since Friday and I'm too lethargic to move, the only thing I can do is think! After another couple of hours, I realise that I have to get out of the chair because I need to let Mum know that I'm not coming for dinner, so I get out of the chair and pick up my phone from the floor. I see a couple of missed calls and texts from Jordan and my Mum, I ignore Jordan's and send Mum a message.

"Hi Mum, sorry I've been busy trying to organise things, I won't be able to make dinner. I'm meeting Bonnie instead – hope that doesn't mess things up for you xx"

"Hey, that's a shame we were looking forward to seeing you, but as long as you are good that's all that matters. I will come over in the morning and bring Joyce with me for your meeting."

Oh crap. I forgot I was seeing her tomorrow. What am I going to do? Maybe I might need to lie my way out of this, I hate doing this to Mum but I can only think about myself.

"I forgot to tell you that Joyce text me on Friday night to cancel, she said she would come back to arrange another day"

"Ok I see, well I'll call round later on tomorrow for a cup of coffee and a chat ok?"

"Yeah that sounds like a good idea – love you Mum, see you then xx"

I'll have to think of another excuse tomorrow, I really don't want to see anyone right now.

I make another cup of coffee and go back to my seat, I haven't even showered or changed my clothes since Friday. I don't see the point, there's no point in doing anything right now. I just need to sit and think some more.

Sunday passes with me drifting in and out of sleep and ignoring my phone. I think at one stage I heard someone knocking on my door, but I ignored that too. I certainly don't want anyone to see me looking like this, but I don't have the energy to do anything about it. I feel like I'm drowning and I remember that feeling and it was so good. It helped me to forget what happened. I sleep some more and I wake again hearing the knock at the door, its Bonnie.

"Cassie, come on open up, I know you told your Mum you were having dinner with us today, what's happening? Please answer your phone or answer the door." I can hear she is panicking and I hate that I'm doing that to her, but I don't have the energy to go and open the door. She keeps banging and then she stops suddenly, she must have finally given up.

It's dark again now and I'm really tired, so I drift off again and once again I wake up screaming. I'm getting used to it and immediately fall back to sleep.

"She Will Be Loved"

Before I know it the sun is rising. I know I have to move and do something today. I have a headache and it's really pounding, then I realise it's the door. Why won't they leave me alone?

I can hear Mum shouting through the letterbox. "Cassie, come on I know you're in there, you need to open the door. We need to talk to you."

"I don't want to talk to anyone," I shout. "Just leave me alone today please. Just another couple of days." I'm sobbing and shouting at the same time.

"Cassie, come on please. I know you lied about Joyce, why are you lying to me? Please." She's starting to cry now too.

I can hear a scuffle and some deep voices outside talking to Mum.

Then I hear "Babe, come on let me in, if you don't want your Mum to come in then just let me in. Let me help you, please." It's Jordan.

I don't want him to see me like this, I really don't. "No Jordan, I don't want to see you or anyone today, please just leave me alone. I'm not worthy of anyone's love or help."

I don't know how I can speak, I'm sobbing so much.

I feel like I'm going to vomit, so I get up and run to the toilet. I just about make it in time, I hate feeling like this!!

I'm still sitting on the toilet floor leaning over the toilet when I hear an almighty bang. What the hell is that?

"Cassie where are you?" I hear Jordan, he sounds frantic. "Cassie?" He then spots me on the floor in the toilet. He comes in.

I hold my hand out to stop him. "Go away. I don't want you to see me like this, please go away."

He ignores me and gets down on the floor next to me. He pulls me close and holds me while I sob. "Cassie, don't you know that everyone wants to help you, you don't need to do this on your own. We all love you babe, come on, please let us help." He's kissing my head and rubbing my back. He stands and lifts me up into his arms and my head rests on his chest. He must be strong because he doesn't even break a sweat when he lifts me. He lays me on the bed after carrying me through the house and up the stairs, where he lays down with me.

He rolls onto his side and rests his head on his bent arm. "Cassie, I know you are a strong independent person and you have dealt with many issues in your life on your own. But you have got to realise that you're not on your own, you have family and friends who want to help you. Do you see that?"

I stop sobbing and say, "Jordan, I don't want to be

a burden to anyone, I didn't ask for this to happen to me. My life was just starting to get back on track. I feel like everyone always has to look after me, I don't like it."

My Mum must have been standing outside, because she comes in to sit on the bed and takes my hand. "Baby girl, you are never any trouble. Do you know how much I miss looking after you? You went off to San Francisco and didn't come back for years. I never got the opportunity to look after you. I want that opportunity. I don't want to smother you, but it's my job to look after you. That's what being a mother is all about." She leans down and hugs me.

I can start to feel my eyes closing and I fall into a deep sleep. When I wake up, the duvet is covering me. Everything is quiet and I realise I didn't wake myself up screaming and I had just naturally woken up. I get out of the bed unsteadily and walk to the stairs, I hold the banister and start to walk down. After a few steps I stop, the sight below makes me want to cry, but cry tears of happiness this time. The dining room table is set ready for dinner for six people and the smell from the kitchen is unbelievable. I haven't eaten for a few days and I didn't realise how hungry I am.

I silently walk down another couple of stairs, I don't want to be seen or heard. There is a drill in the background and from the sounds I think they must be fixing the front door where Jordan burst his way through. I hear Dad saying "No one is going to be able to get through that door with the added security you've put in there, son!" It brings tears to my eyes that firstly,

Jordan broke through the door to get to me, and secondly Dad called him Son.

I continue moving down the stairs and I hear Bonnie and Jezza in the kitchen talking to Mum. "She will be fine Jean, she has us to help her. She is the closest thing I have to a sister and I will make sure she knows it," Bonnie says, then I hear Jezza, "I've always looked out for Cassie, I love her like a sister too and have done since we were at school. I don't like bad things happening to her, she doesn't deserve any of it. We will be here for her and we will take care of her. She just needs to understand that we all love her and want to help her."

I get to the bottom of the stairs and everyone stops what they are doing and stare at me. Mum is the first one to come over to me. "Baby, did you have a good sleep? You look so much better than you did earlier. We are going to be having dinner in about half hour, the lads should be finished by then," she says looking at Dad and Jordan.

I turn to them and smile and then walk over to Mum and give her a hug. "I love you Mum don't ever forget that." Then I go over to Bonnie and Jezza, I hug them and say "you guys are the best and I'm sorry if I keep putting you through these pains. I promise I won't do it again, ok." I'm crying. "You are both family to me and I love you both."

I walk over to the front door and give Dad a hug. "Love you Dad." That's all I need to say, he gives me a kiss and then I go over to Jordan. I give him a hug and whisper in his ear, "thank you for coming to get me, I won't forget it."

He looks at me and says, "Always baby, always."

Mum says, "Right, come on help me bring the dinner out and let's sit down." We all go into the kitchen and bring a dish out to the table. We sit down and Jordan comes and sits next to me. We spend dinner talking about just general stuff until we start talking about Bonnie and Jezza's wedding. We sit at the table for three hours. Wow, where did the time go. I realise that I have been smiling for three hours and it feels so good. Is this what normal feels like? I haven't felt normal in so long. We take the dishes out to the kitchen and Mum starts loading the dishwasher. We put the kettle on to make coffee and then we all go and sit on the veranda, I bring out the blankets and we all wrap ourselves up. We just chat about anything, the weather, the beach, the town and after another hour or so Mum says they have to go home.

This is when I start to panic a bit, because I realise they are all going to leave me on my own again, but I try to hide it, I don't want them to be worried about me anymore. I go to the door to say goodbye and Mum says "Night baby girl. I'll talk to you in the morning. Jordan is going to stay with you for a few days, instead of staying with Bonnie."

I can't believe my ears. "What? No! Why?"

Jordan is stood behind me and gently touches my shoulders. "Because I want to, that's why."

I turn to look at him and then back to Mum and I see it makes her happy to know someone is going to be staying with me. I smile. "Ok Mum, I'll see you tomorrow." I give her and Dad a kiss on the cheek.

While I'm standing at the door, Bonnie and Jezza come over. "Cassie, do you think you'll be up to going to see a venue tomorrow? We can have lunch there and see what it's like, but only if you're up to it." I can feel the panic start to rise into my throat at the thought of having to go outside and try to pretend to be normal.

"Bonnie, I'd love that," I say and she kisses me on the cheek.

"See you tomorrow then," she says and flounces out the door.

"Look after her," Jezza says to Jordan.

"I'll always look after her," Jordan replies.

I watch them all walk down the path and then I slowly close the door. "Is the door fixed Jordan?" I ask.

He laughs and says, "Yeah me and your Dad bonded over that door today." He goes to put his arm around me then stops himself and puts his hand in his pocket instead. "Come on let's get this place tidied up, then we need to talk," he says. We quickly tidy everything away and go back out to the veranda and lean against the balcony looking out to the dark sky and sea.

I can feel he wants to say something, but doesn't know how to start. "Ok Cassie, I need to talk to you and I want you to listen. I'm not going to tell you what to do because I can't do that, but we need to talk about what's going on and how we can all help you."

He's very nervous, so I turn to him and I put my hand on his cheek. "Jordan, I wanted to try this on my own, but I know that I don't have to, I have people around me who love me and want to help me."

He puts his hand over mine on his face. "Yeah, we all love you Cassie and we all want to help you put this behind you so that you can start living again, you have so much to give." He takes my hand and kisses my palm. He doesn't let go of my hand and he pulls me into the house then he locks the door.

"Take a seat," he says pointing at the couch. So I sit down. "The first thing is that I will be staying here for a while until I know you are going to be ok."

I go to interrupt him and he puts his finger to my lips. "No, I'm not finished yet." I smile a little and he continues. "Now I want you to take your sleeping tablets for the next couple of nights because you need to rest so that you can start to recuperate."

I know he's right, so I don't say anything. "Tomorrow after breakfast we will talk some more about counselling and then you can start getting your life together. Ok?" I can see he's nervous, because he doesn't really have the right to tell me what to do. But actually, maybe as a friend he does!

I stand up and hold out my hand for him to take, he takes it. I link my arm in his arm and say, "Ok you're right, but I'm tired and I want to go to bed."

He smiles and then he moves away from me. "You need to take your tablet first." He goes into the kitchen and gets me a glass of water to take my tablet with. "Come on then, let's get you to bed."

I follow him up the stairs and into my bedroom, he puts the glass on the bedside table and starts to walk out the room. "I'll leave you to get ready for bed, I'll be back in a minute," he says and then he's gone out of the room. I stand there for a couple of minutes not knowing what to think. Then it hits me that he will see me in my pj's so I rush in the bathroom and do my teeth and then I jump into my pj's and rush to get under the covers, I don't want him to see me with my shorts on.

He comes strolling back in a few minutes later with a pair of shorts and an old t-shirt on. "I see you're tucked up safely in bed, do you mind if I sit on the bed and just talk for a while?" he says making his way over to the bed.

"No I don't mind Jordan, it's fine." I say, but I can't stop looking at him. He looks like he did when we were going out together and I gasp as the memories start coming back. I can feel tears in my eyes for what I gave up. Then I remember that I should never regret any decisions I have made in my life. They were made for the right reason at that time.

He sits down on the bed next to me. "Did you take your tablet?" I nod at him. "Good, you'll start to drift away soon. I'm looking forward to Jezza's wedding, you know he's my best friend right? He's kept me updated as to where you were and what you were doing in life. I

261

don't know what I would have done if I didn't know how you were." He brushes one of his fingers across my cheek.

"I'm so happy for him that he finally asked Bonnie to marry him, it took them so long. It won't take me that long, when you really love someone - you just know."

He looks at me and I snuggle down into my pillow, "yeah I know what you mean," I say smiling at him. I can feel my eyes getting heavy. "Jordan, I'm getting sleepy. Thank you for, well just for being you. I'm very lucky to have you back in my life," he looks at me and then smiles at me.

"No, I'm the lucky one babe," my eyelids close and I drift off with happy thoughts in my head for a change.

I don't have any nightmares and I don't dream of David, instead I dream of Jordan and the fun we used to have at Pebbles Café with Mr. Stanley. When I wake up I feel really warm and I can't move. I start to feel panicky. I open my eyes and I see an arm wrapped around me, I slowly turn around and I am looking straight into Jordan's face. He must have fallen asleep on my bed last night. Instead of feeling panicky and scared I feel safe, and I snuggle back into his arms.

A few minutes later I hear, "I know you're awake Cassie. Sorry for staying in here last night, but I wanted to be close if you needed me. If I was next door then I might not have heard you." He's pulling me back closer to him.

"It's fine. It's the first time I've felt safe since … well you know," I say.

He rolls onto his back taking his arm with him. I feel cold and it feels like he is withdrawing from me, it gives me a sense of loss. "Come on, we need to get up, we've got a lot to do today," he says and jumps out of the bed.

I roll onto my back and say, "just another minute please". He reaches down and pulls the duvet off me and runs out the door.

"No way. No time for being lazy today."

"Oh you're so going to get it Jordan when I catch you." I say jumping out of the bed and running after him. He's down the stairs before I can catch up with him and he is on the other side of the dining table. I go one way, he goes the other, then he starts to slow down, I think he wants to be caught.

I run up to him and jump on his back and put my arms around his chest. It hurts when I jump and I didn't really think about it before I did it, then the pain hits me. "You're not that fast Jordan." He's laughing and he sets me down again. He turns to look at me and I swear we have a moment. A moment where everything goes silent and you can hear our hearts beating.

"You can go and put the coffee on, seeing as I caught you," I say to break the heat between us. It doesn't make me uncomfortable, but I don't know his circumstances, we haven't talked about his family or personal life…

We have coffee and Jordan makes me eat a good breakfast, then we go into the lounge and sit on the couch. I sit at one end and Jordan sits at the other end, but he sits facing me with one leg bent up on the couch and his arm along the back of the couch. He is rubbing the couch with his hand, its strangely erotic. I can see his sleeve of tattoos and I trace them with my finger. I look up at him and he is watching me with a smirk on his face.

"Tell me about your tattoo's, I never thought you would be the type to have so many. When did you have your first one?" I keep my finger on his arm, outlining each and every one of them.

He smiles, I don't know if that's because he's ticklish or because he is thinking about his first tattoo.

"I had my first one the day after I left the last message on your answer phone in San Francisco. Do you want to see it?" I nod, not taking my eyes off him.

I watch him as he slowly lifts his t-shirt to reveal a lot of tattoos, I gasp at all the colours and the amount of them. He looks me in the eye before pointing at a very small one just under his heart. It says '*Our souls will meet again,*" and there, where there should be an exclamation mark is an infinity symbol vertically with '*Cassie*' at the top of the left circle and '*Jordan*' at the bottom of the right circle. I take my finger and trace the outline of the symbol, it's beautiful. He starts moving as it is obviously tickling him.

He reaches out, takes my hand and holds it flat over the tattoo. "I needed to keep a piece of you close to my heart. I always said that our souls would meet again, Cassie."

"It's beautiful. I bet it has been hard to explain to all the women in your life." I laugh. Secretly I don't want to know, but I am curious.

He smiles, "yes it was awkward at at times. Some of the women were jealous of 'Cassie' because I wouldn't brand my body with their names. It wasn't a stupid thing to do because I always knew we would meet again. We were destined to be in each other's lives."

I can feel his heart start to quicken under my touch, he is staring at me with those beautiful turquoise eyes. My heart is racing too. I need to pull myself together, but I can't look away.

He lets go of my hand and I continue to look at his tattoos and he tells me about some of them, what they mean and when he had them done.

We both go quiet for a while and then he says, "So, we need to talk about counseling."

I hold my finger up to him "No, I want to talk first please. I need to tell you something and see what you think."

I turn around to face him on the couch. "OK, I know this might sound silly to you, but when I was on a plane to Disneyworld before Chad died, you know who he was don't you?" He nods at me, looking quite sad.

"Well, I was reading the inflight magazine and there was an article about a charity called PEBBLES. It caught my attention because that's the name of our favourite café, I read it and it was really interesting. It's for people who had been abused or sexually abused. They, not only have counsellors to help victims, but have other services to help girls, boys, women and men who have been in these type of situations."

Jordan is just looking at me listening, not even attempting to interrupt. I had better finish what I am going to say. "When I read the article it brought back memories of David and what he did to me when I was at school. After what I did, if it wasn't for my friends and being able to talk openly about it, I don't know what I would have done. Well maybe we do."

I can't look him in the eye, but I know he is staring at me. "I found it a really interesting article and I suppose because of its name, it made it more poignant. I had said to myself that I was going to contact them and see if there was anything I could do for them to help spread awareness for them. I didn't do anything about it at the time because of everything that happened on that trip. However, when Bonnie and I were on our way to Vegas, I saw the same article and it really spoke to me. It was like the articles were put there for me to do something about them."

He still hasn't tried to speak, so I carry on. "So, when I was in Vegas, I sent an anonymous donation of £200,000 to the charity to help with their services." Jordan is sitting with his mouth open.

"Cassie, wow, I can't believe it."

"I haven't finished yet Jordan. I gave my notice on my job in America the other day. I'm moving back home and I've decided to write my own book. I have been dabbling in writing for years now and think I want to give it a go. I don't want it to be a regret that I didn't try it. I am financially stable so I can do this. However, when you mentioned counselling yesterday I got to thinking about how I'd like to have counselling through the charity PEBBLES. Then eventually, I want to volunteer with them to help others who have to cope with what I've been through. Hopefully it will make their life easier. What do you think?"

I look at him and he is just staring at me. He leans towards me and kisses me on the lips. "Sorry if that freaks you out, but you are the most selfless person I have ever met. The fact that you gave to this charity, you want to offer your services, to listen to other people's stories and help them is amazing." He leans back, I'm still thinking about his lips on mine, wow, that was amazing.

"OK, it's my time to talk now," he says with a smile on his face. "First of all you are an amazing woman, to give that amount of money to a charity is phenomenal and to do it anonymously too shows how selfless you are. A lot of people want recognition for any charity work they do. You, however, want to do it as a benefit to other victims."

He takes a breath. "I need to tell you a bit about what I have been doing since you left. As you know, I went to Toronto and my contract was extended and I stayed there for a few years. When it was time to come home, I decided I didn't want to come back to Newquay because you wouldn't be here." I blush when he says that.

"I never got over you Cassie, I went to London and stayed with friends for a while, then I was left some money by an uncle I forgot I even had. I bought a place in London and decided that I wanted to do something worthwhile with my money, but I wanted to do something that would help others who have been abused or sexually abused. I wanted to help these victims because I couldn't help you anymore; you weren't here for me to help. You weren't mine anymore."

I sit there looking at him, is he telling me what I think he is telling me? "I set up PEBBLES so that I could help others who had suffered like you had. We offer counselling services; we offer relocation, if necessary; we help them to integrate into groups; help them with jobs; build their confidence and make them feel more at home in their environments. I have helped a lot of boys, girls, men and women and every time I do, I think about you."

He moves closer to me on the couch, I can feel my heart beat rising again. "I received your donation and didn't know it was from you, Bonnie told me about it when she came home. She knows all about my charity, she helps out sometimes too. In fact her and Jezza help out a lot. I'm just glad I can help others, you were my inspiration for that Cassie, you!"

"Wow Jordan!" I stand up and pace the room not knowing what to say.

He stands up and walks towards me. "Cassie, I never forgot you; I know our relationship is different now from the way it was back then, but I hope I can be in your life as your best friend and I'd love for you to volunteer with us. Joyce is actually one of our local counsellors who helps out, she is very good. I know she will be able to help you too."

"Jordan, I never forgot you either. I'm so touched that you would do all of that because of what happened to me all those years ago. It means so much to me. Do my Mum and Dad know?" I ask.

"Yes they do, they help out too when we have activities or events," he looks sheepish.

I walk over to him and take both his hands in mine, "Jordan you are an amazing man and I would be delighted to call you my best friend." Then I hug him. He wraps his arms around me and pulls me in tightly to him. I feel a little sad that he just wants to be my friend, but then I have been through a lot. I don't know how I would feel if he has a girlfriend.

"Jordan, can I ask you something?"

He's still hugging me and rubbing his hands up and down my back. "MMM mmm," he says.

"Are you sure you can spare the time to be here with me? Don't you have to work or … don't you … don't you have a family you have to go home to?" I falter when I ask the last question.

I brace myself for his reply. "I've taken time off work, there are other people who can help in my absence. They know how to get hold of me if they need to. As for family; I have all the family I need right here, Cassie. You ARE my family. You will always be my family and I will do whatever it takes to make you enjoy life again." He kisses the top of my head.

I step back a little and then my phone rings, breaking the moment we were having. I see it is Mum calling. "I'd better get that before she starts panicking," I smile to let him know that I'm sad I have to move out of his arms.

"Hi Mum, yes I'm good. We've had breakfast and were just talking about counselling. I can't believe you didn't tell me about the charity and it being something that Jordan set up."

"Are you mad with me?"

"No I'm not mad. How can I be when you all give so much to help him with it."

"Would you and Jordan like to come over later, so we talk about this now that you know about the Charity?"

"Yes, we can come over to yours, but I'm going to lunch with Bonnie. We will come round in a few hours." I put the phone down and then turn around to look at Jordan. "She wants us to go over later, is that ok with you? I'm not putting you out am I? Did you have something else planned?" I ask.

"No, I had nothing planned, although I would like

you to talk to Joyce. She can come over here or you can go and meet her, whichever suits you the best. I know you probably think you don't need to, but its best to talk it through with a third party." He smiles at me, I know he thinks I won't do this, but I will do it for him and for me.

"Its fine, she can come here if she wants. You can stay too if you want, I don't have any secrets from you Jordan." I smile sheepishly at him.

"I'd like that, but I don't want you to feel uncomfortable Cassie, I have spoken to Joyce myself about the way the whole situation affected me." I didn't think about how it affected anyone else, I wonder how it did affect him. "She does know how I feel, but if you want me to stay then I will." He comes over and says "now go and get dressed, I can only look at you in those little shorts for a short period of time." He grins and wiggles his eyebrows up and down. I laugh and run up the stairs to get dressed, feeling happier than I have in years.

I stop to think about that while I get dressed, I wasn't this happy when I was with Chad, was I? I was always trying to be someone else because I didn't want my memories to come back and I didn't want to cloud anyone else's life with my issues. I had never told Chad about David and I don't think I ever would have. That Cassie was not the woman that Chad knew. Our relationship was always comfortable, but it was always at his pace and I was willing to just be carried along with whatever he wanted and not really thinking about anything. It was easier that way! I did love Chad though, he helped me to become the woman I am today. He made me push past my insecurities and made me do things that were out of my comfort zone. It made him happy when I managed to do them, it made me happy too. I finish getting dressed and go back downstairs where Jordan is dressed and waiting for me.

"I've spoken to Joyce and she is on her way over. You can change your mind and I can go if you want to talk to her on your own."

He looks nervous, I just look at him and say, "Jordan I wouldn't ask anyone to stay and listen to all this if they don't want to. But I don't want just anyone; I want you to stay, but only if you're comfortable."

"Of course I'll stay Cassie, I want to be with you and I want to help you, but more than that I want to be here FOR you." He comes over and hugs me. "Come on let's make coffee and sit outside until Joyce comes over." He releases me and walks into the kitchen to put the coffee percolator on.

He makes the coffee and then comes and joins me on the veranda. He gives me my cup and then sits down just staring out at the sea. I wonder what he is thinking about, I don't get chance to find out as the front door bell rings and he gets up to answer the door.

"Hi Joyce, sorry about yesterday. It was a bad day, but I'm ready now" I say glancing over to Jordan. He has made her a cuppa and brought it outside to her.

"It's fine Cassie, I understand. I'm sure you know

by now that I work for PEBBLES and I know your history. I also know that you're in very capable hands with Jordan here," Joyce says and I can feel myself blushing. I can't help but look over at him and smile when he lifts his head to look at me.

"I know he is staying with you to help you get through this quicker, but if you need to talk to me without Jordan here, then just call me ok?"

I nod my head and say, "Yes Joyce I understand, although I have no secrets from Jordan." I look at him and smile.

We spend the next hour just talking about David and what happened the first time, years ago. How he had obsessed on me and the fact that I hadn't done anything to encourage him. He must have been slightly imbalanced, even back then. It seems he had been thinking about me and he'd even been to San Francisco looking for me after I had left for New York. Thank god he didn't find me. He'd made it his life's work to find me.

We were only just touching on what happened the other week when it was time to go to Bonnie's. I say goodbye to Joyce and I while Jordan is showing her out, I sit staring at the sea it's such a tranquil place up here looking down at the sea just washing in and out over the sand.

He comes back outside to me quietly and comes up behind my chair. "Are you ok Cassie? You did really well, do you know how proud of you I am?" he leans down and kisses the top of my head.

273

I tilt my head up to look at him and say, "thanks Jordan that means so much to me." I can't help looking at his lips, he sees me looking and leans down and kisses my forehead.

"Come on, it's time to go to Bonnie's and see this venue," he grabs my hand and starts to drag me to the front door.

"Wait up, I don't have as long legs as you," I say laughing.

He slows down and we leave the house, making sure it's locked up before we get into Jordan's car. He drives to Bonnie's house and we go in. She is so excited. "Cassie, wait until you see this place it's amazing," her enthusiasm is catching and I can't wait to see it. "Jezza and Jordan are coming too hope you don't mind," she says.

"Not at all, the more than merrier," I say smiling at Jordan.

Jezza drives us to the Atlantic Hotel. We explain that we would like to see the room for weddings and ask if they can show us around. Bonnie is right, it's an amazing hotel, I can just see her in her wedding dress walking down the aisle to Jezza stood at the altar waiting for her. I'll be in front of her walking down towards Jordan. Wow, where did that come from? I can't let my thoughts drift there, we are friends and that's it. We stop for lunch in the restaurant and we get to try some of the wedding food, it is such a great afternoon, we laugh and have fun and it makes me feel extremely grateful for my friends.

Bonnie and Jezza go to talk to the wedding coordinator about dates and wedding things. Jordan and I walk outside and sit down, looking at the sea, which looks like it surrounds the hotel. It really is an amazing place. We sit quietly and don't say a word, then I have to break the silence.

"Jordan, I really appreciate everything you're doing for me, I really do. You'll never know how much this means to me." I can't look at him because I have tears in my eyes, I realise that I love him so much it hurts. I don't want him to do this because he feels sorry for me, I hope he's doing it because he loves me too.

He comes and kneels in front of me and takes my hands. "Cassie, I'm doing this because I want to. I want to help you. I want to be there for you. I need to know that you are ok."

He's still kneeling in front of me when I hear, "Jordan are you proposing or something down there on one knee." Its Jezza and he's laughing.

"No I'm not" Jordan says. "It will be far more romantic than that when I propose," he says looking in my eyes.

"Have you both sorted everything out? Do they have the date you want?" I say, we both look expectantly at Bonnie, she starts smiling and nodding her head. I jump up out of my chair and run over to her and grab her in the biggest hug ever. "I'm so happy for you. Right Bonnie, we need to write a list of things to do. When are you coming over? How about tomorrow for dinner? Then we can start planning." I know I'm gushing, but

I'm so excited.

We get into Jezza's car and start to head home. "Yeah we can come over for dinner tomorrow, can't we Jezza?" Bonnie says. "Will you be there Jordan? You and Jezza can help plan too," she ask hesitantly.

"Of course he'll be there," I say, I don't even think to ask if he is going to be anywhere else. I start laughing at the thought of the two lads organising a wedding.

"What are you laughing at Cassie," Jordan says looking at me.

"I'm laughing at the thought of you and Jezza organising the wedding. Bonnie maybe you should let them do it – you know like in that TV programme 'Don't tell the bride.' I smile at him to show I'm only joking. He smiles back.

"No freaking way, they would turn it into one of those weddings at their favourite football pitch the way these two like football. Can you imagine Cassie? That would be terrible." She laughs though at the thought of it.

After Jezza drops us back to at Bonnie's and then we get into Jordan's car and head over to Mum and Dad's, we collect Jordan's car and head to Mum and Dad's. I'm smiling when we pull up and I get out of the car and run up to the front door. "Come on Jordan keep up," I laugh.

Mum comes out of the kitchen and catches me as I run up to her and hug her. "Wow, where did that come from?" she says hugging me back.

"Oh Mum I had a great day, the hotel was amazing and we just had so much fun!" I can see Mum has a tear in her eye.

"I'm delighted Cassie, you deserve to have some fun. Now come through to the lounge and tell us all about it."

We sit in the lounge for a few hours just talking about lots of different things. I tell them about the hotel for Bonnie's wedding and about my meeting with Joyce. Then I talk to them about my idea of counselling others when I feel better myself. They think it's a good idea but don't want me to jump in without feeling one hundred percent better. I tell them that Jordan won't let me anyway, he wants to make sure I'm not having nightmares and have talked about everything with Joyce before he lets me do any counseling.

It's soon time to go and when we get up to leave Mum says, "Jordan, can I have a word with you in the kitchen please?" I look over to Jordan who just shrugs and follows her into the kitchen. I can't hear what they are talking about and I'm really curious, but Dad stops me from following.

"Cassie, they need to talk about a few things. Your mum is worried about you and she knows that you will listen to what Jordan says, so just let her look after you the way she knows best." I nod in agreement.

About fifteen minutes later Jordan comes out and says "Come on Cassie let's go, it's time to get you into bed, it's been a busy day, you must be so wrecked". At the front door Mum and Dad both hug me and then they hug Jordan too and say thanks to him. We arrange to go over for lunch the next day.

On the journey home I say to Jordan; "I'm going to be the size of a house with all this food I'm eating."

"You're beautiful and you will always be beautiful." I blush.

Once home I go upstairs to get ready for bed. Jordan gets a glass of water so I can take my tablet and he leaves it on the bedside table. He's laying on my bed when I come out of the bathroom, I'm a bit surprised to see him there - but not in a bad way. "I just wanted to make sure you fall asleep ok and then I'll go into the spare room," he says looking sad.

"No, you can stay here with me Jordan. I know you want to protect me and I know you'll behave," I say, secretly hoping he won't.

"Yes Cassie, I will behave and I will protect you" he says. Once I'm in bed he leans over and kisses my forehead. "Sleep tight babe, I'm here if you need me."

I feel my eyes closing and I start falling asleep when I think I hear him say, "I'll protect you until my last breath Cassie. I love you. You're my soul mate and my soul isn't letting yours go this time." I swear I feel him very gently kiss me on the lips. I snuggle in and feel his arms go around me and pull me in tight.

We continue our routine for about a month; we see

Joyce every day and I'm starting to feel much better. Jordan and I talk about everything that happened when we were apart and I feel that he knows everything about me.

We are now only two months off Bonnie's wedding and I can't wait until the big day. Her dress is beautiful and so is mine. We had so much fun when we went to choose the dresses, she tried on so many different styles and we kept laughing. She is and always has been a tom boy and I know she was worried about wearing a dress, but after trying on about ten dresses, she walked out in this most beautiful dress. It is quite plain, but they finished it off with a sparkly sequined and beaded belt around her waist. When she walked out I cried. I couldn't speak to her – I just cried and when I looked at her she was crying too, her mum was crying and the three of us looked a right mess.

When I wake up I decide that I need to speak to Joyce on my own. I'm not sure how Jordan will take it, he's been here for me every day, but there's something I can only talk to a woman about.

When Jordan comes downstairs I am sitting in the lounge looking out the window, daydreaming. He goes to make coffee and as I watch him with the coffee machine I ask him "Jordan can I ask you something? I don't want you to be upset or anything."

He laughs, "You know you can always talk to me."

"I don't want you to take this the wrong way, but I need to talk to Joyce on my own today. I know I said that I don't have any secrets from you and I don't, but there are just a few things I need to ask which I would be embarrassed to talk about in front of you." I hope he's not going to be mad.

"Cassie, I knew there would be a day when you wouldn't want me there and I understand totally. I'll go and make a few calls when she comes over, no big deal." He smiles at me and I know everything is ok

When Joyce knocks at the door, Jordan let her in then he calls out "See you girls in a while," and heads out the door. Joyce looks at me and asks, "What's going on Cassie, did you two fall out or something?"

"No," I say laughing. "I wanted to talk to you on your own about something." We take the coffees, which I've made, and go and sit by the patio doors, it's not as warm out today.

"Joyce, I'm slightly embarrassed, but I wanted to talk to you about Jordan." I look at her sheepishly.

She smiles at me and says, "I knew this time would come Cassie – let's talk."

I'm really embarrassed but I know I just need to say it. "Joyce, I love Jordan with such a passion that I have never known, so much more than when we were at school. He means so much to me and I want to know whether to take it to the next level or not. I'm afraid to lay it out there for him, I know you can't talk to me about whether he likes me that way or not, but I want to talk through the whole intimacy and sex thing." Now I'm blushing really bad and Joyce starts laughing and clapping her hands.

"I'm so excited and pleased that we are at this point in our talks Cassie. This is a real milestone in your recovery. She hugs me and then we both sit back down.

"I'm worried about making a move with Jordan just in case it might not be what he wants. I don't want that to come between us. He might not like me like that and I might have just taken his kindness the wrong way. Most importantly, what if I make those types of advances and then freeze when it comes to being intimate. No one has touched me since David and I don't want anything intimate to trigger those memories. I don't want to have David at the front of my mind, he needs to be kept at the back out the way, otherwise I'll be back to square one." I'm crying while I'm talking because it means so much to me.

"Cassie, the fact that you want to talk about it, means that you are ready to start exploring your sexuality again. That's great progress, as to whether you should do that with Jordan or not; only you know that. My view is that he wouldn't spend all this time making sure you are improving if he didn't care so much about you. I know that if you wanted to move forward sexually, then you couldn't choose a better person than Jordan."

We talk about it for another hour before Joyce has to leave. Jordan still hasn't returned and I realise that this is the first time I have been on my own in the house for weeks. It feels strange without Jordan here, I go upstairs and lay on the bed. Talking to Joyce has worn me out.

I think about Jordan and I can feel myself getting turned on, I don't know where he is or when he'll be back, so I take this opportunity to fantasize about him. I imagine him coming up to the bed and leaning over me and kissing me with all the passion that he has.

I run my hands over my breasts imagining they are his hands, I can hear myself panting. I slowly move my hands down towards my waistband and slip my fingers under my pants. I'm embarrassed I'm doing this, I've never felt the need to do this. I am sexually frustrated and I don't want to start something with Jordan that I can't finish. My fingers move down between my legs and I run them up and down my lips, slowly pushing them inside. It feels amazing. It doesn't feel weird. It feels good. I thought it might hurt after what David did to me, but it has been a few months and everything has healed.

I hear myself moan as I plunge two fingers in and arch my back, then I pull my fingers out and lick them, they taste amazing. Then I rub them over my clit and I am finding it hard to hold onto the orgasm as it rushes through my body. I cry out "Jordan" when I cum. I relax back onto the bed but my breathing is really heavy. I can hear noises in the house and I start to get scared.

"Cassie where are you? Cassie?" Oh my god, Jordan is in the house. I hope he didn't hear me. I'm so embarrassed. I get up quickly.

"Jordan, I'm here I'm just getting into the shower, I'll be down in a few minutes." I strip my clothes off and jump into the shower. I let the hot steamy water fall over me while I think about what I just did and what this might mean. I want Jordan and I hope he wants me too. When I've finished I dress quickly and go downstairs.

"How did it go with Joyce today? Are you ok?" Jordan looks worried, I suppose he has been with me for every meeting and he doesn't know what I wanted to talk about.

"I'm fine Jordan, everything went well. You can stay tomorrow for the meeting; honest everything's all fine. I walk up to him and hug him so tightly. He smells so nice.

We hang around for the rest of the day and then when we go to bed I say to him, "Jordan I don't want to take my sleeping tablet tonight, I think it's time for me to see how I cope without them."

He looks at me and smiles. "I think that's a great idea Cassie, come on then let's be rebels."

I get into bed and we lay facing each other. "I hope I sleep well tonight." I smile when I say it as I remember my earlier release.

"I'm sure you will Cassie, now don't forget I'm here if you need me. Whenever you need me." I lean over and kiss him on the lips.

"I know you are Jordan." I roll over and lay facing the ceiling. He does the same. I don't fall asleep as quickly as usual, but I roll onto my side and move back to snuggle into Jordan, it feels so natural and he puts his arm around me to move me in closer to him.

I want to say something, to try and move this along, but I don't know what to say. I don't want to ruin what we have, but if I'm getting frustrated then surely he is too. I slowly start to drift off and Jordan must think I'm asleep because I feel him rub my cheek.

I hear him say "Cassie, that was the most erotic thing I saw today. When you called my name when you came, it was so amazing. I love you so much I don't want to lose you, but today you made me realise that you love me too. You've made me a very happy man. I love you." He kisses the side of my head and I fall asleep smiling.

"You Raise Me Up"

I slept very well that night and every night thereafter. I don't need to take my sleeping tablets because Jordan is here to protect me.

I don't let on that I heard what he said to me that night, I was embarrassed because he had seen me masturbating and calling out his name. Our relationship only got closer, but neither of us wanted to be the first one to take the next step.

A month before Bonnie's wedding, Jordan is going out for Jezza's stag night. I know he's looking forward to it and has arranged for Bonnie to stay with me for the night so that I won't be alone. The guys are staying at Jezza's, so we don't have to wait for them to come home.

On the day they are going out, Jordan and I go for a walk on the beach, he holds my hand to help me up and down the steps and then he just doesn't let go. It feels so natural that I don't pull away.

We stop at Pebbles Café, like we always used to. We love that café, it's so quaint, but it's in need of a lick of paint. Mr. Stanley says he doesn't get much trade anymore and he's thinking of selling, but there's not much interest. It's a shame because it's a bit of a landmark with the locals.

We have lunch and talk about Jezza's stag do. Jordan is looking forward to going out with Jezza and some of the other lads from school. They're only going into town, they're not the type of guys to go abroad for the weekend or anything, they can party hard wherever they are.

When we get back to the house, Jordan goes upstairs to get ready to go out. When he comes back downstairs I have to take a deep breath, he looks amazing. He smells wonderful and all I want to do is to kiss him, to make sure he remembers me when he goes out looking like that. I feel territorial, I'm not sure I've ever felt like that before.

I go over to him and hug him, I just can't help myself. "Have fun tonight Jordan, you deserve it. You've been looking after me for long enough."

He hugs me back tightly. "I will. Will you be ok tonight? I know you have Bonnie, but I'll still worry about you. I can't help it, I've always worried about you."

"I'll be fine Jordan, honestly. Just go and have fun! I'll look after you tomorrow when you have a hangover," I laugh.

He laughs too, "Deal."

I hear the doorbell ring, so I pull back from my hug, it's Bonnie and Jezza, they're both laughing. "Now Jezza if you're sick tonight, I'm not cleaning it up tomorrow," Bonnie says in between laughs.

"That's ok Bonnie, Jordan will do it," Jezza says

slapping Jordan on the shoulder. Jordan just shakes his head.

"Right guys, time for you to go and enjoy yourselves," Bonnie says pushing them towards the door.

When we get to the door, Jezza takes Bonnie in his arms for a hug and kisses her deeply and then he turns to go out the door. Jordan stops and comes back to me and takes me into a hug too. He then whispers in my ear, "If you need me, you know I'll come running Cassie." Then he pulls away slightly and kisses me quickly on the lips. I stare at him, I don't know what to say, so I don't say anything at all.

We wave goodbye to them and then close the door after watching them walk down the road. We are having a girlie night with a takeaway and a bottle or two of wine. Now that I am not on my sleeping tablets I can have a few drinks, so I am looking forward to them tonight. We open a bottle of wine and go and put a dvd on, it's a girlie chick flick and we soon finish the bottle. The take away comes and we drink more wine, it is so nice to just have fun and relax. We talk about the wedding, Bonnie is getting very excited, I am too!

She asks about Jordan, but I don't have anything to tell really, yes we are close, yes we spend every day together and we talk about everything. But there is nothing else to say really, we haven't moved our relationship forward, of course we start giggling and speculating about how good Jordan is in bed. The more we drink, the naughtier we get.

We both laugh, my stomach starts to hurt because I've laughed so much. When we go to bed, I wobble a bit going up the stairs but I just keep giggling. We get undressed and then we both get into my bed laughing. "Cassie, it's been years since we've done this, I've missed it and I've missed you."

"Me too Bonnie, I don't think I've laughed so much in years either." We both lay on the bed looking at the ceiling and I can feel my eyes getting heavy. "I wonder what the guys are up to?" I ask.

"Lots of fun, I hope," she says sleepily.

"Yeah me too, I can't wait for your hen night tomorrow night," I say as I feel myself drifting off.

I'm dreaming that David is in the house, climbing the stairs towards my room. I can hear his footsteps coming closer to me. Boom boom. My heart is racing in time with his footsteps. Boom boom. He comes in the room and walks towards my bed. Boom boom. I start screaming for him to get out of the house, to leave me alone. All of a sudden I feel him touch me on the arm.

"Cassie, Cassie wake up," he says.

"No! Go away. Leave me alone." I'm still screaming.

"Cassie, Cassie come on wake up you're scaring me." I can feel my body being shaken from side to side. I wake up and realise that it's Bonnie shaking me and she looks scared.

"Cassie it's me Bonnie, wake up you're scaring me"

Bonnie is shaking me and crying. When I eventually wake up, I just sit there staring at her. She leans towards me and takes me into a big hug. "Cassie it's going to be ok. I'm here, I'm going to look after you," she's crying.

"B B Bonnie?" I say in between sobs. "It was a dream? David isn't really here?"

"No Cassie he's not here, it was just a dream," she says. I can feel myself relaxing now that I know it's a dream.

She hugs me for about half an hour and then I say, "I'm ok now Bonnie, I'm sorry if I scared you, that hasn't happened for a long time. I don't know why tonight is different".

We both lie down and stare at the ceiling. "It must have been the drink, I haven't had so much to drink for a long time." I can feel my heart beating really fast. Why did I have this dream?

"Maybe Cassie, maybe it's because Jordan isn't here looking after you. Maybe you need him more than you think." She has a big smile on her face.

"I did think of that Bonnie. I love him you know. I never stopped loving him. I let him go because we were young and needed to concentrate on our careers, but he's always been in my mind. He's always in my heart. He never strayed far from my thoughts, I just didn't allow myself to think about him too much, it wasn't fair to Chad." I feel exhausted now.

"Cassie, I know why you did that all those years ago and maybe it was the right thing at the time. He's back in your life again; don't waste that opportunity. If you want to have a relationship with Jordan then you need to make the move. He needs to know one hundred percent what you want. He won't risk your friendship if he's not certain that you want him as much as he wants you. After everything you've been through recently he won't make the first move, you need to do that."

"I know Bonnie. I just don't want to lose his friendship. I know how he feels about me, but it's hard to take that first step." I sigh.

"I know Cassie, it'll happen. Now let's go back to sleep, it's the middle of the night." I agree and we fall silent. My mind is very active so it takes me a while to sleep. When I do I dream of Jordan …

"Truth Is"

When we get up in the morning the first thing we do is make coffee and sit in the lounge looking out at the sea. "Are you sure you're ok Cassie? I was worried about you last night."

"I'm fine, honest Bonnie it was just a nightmare," I say trying not to think of it. Every time I do I feel my heart start to race, not because of David but because of telling Jordan that I had a nightmare.

"Ok, if you're sure. We need to go into town today to get some stuff for my hen party tonight," she says excitedly.

"Of course we do. We can have some lunch too. Maybe the guys will be up and ready to meet us?" I hope they can, I've missed Jordan and can't wait to see him.

We get dressed and go into town to buy outfits for tonight. About twelve o'clock we both get texts from the guys asking where we are. They have gone to my house and were worried when we weren't there.

"Are you ok Cassie? I'm worried about you. Where are you?"

"I'm fine Jordan. We're shopping in town. We're going to stop for lunch about one o'clock. Do you want to meet us?"

"Yes of course we will, just tell us where to meet you. I missed you last night."

"I missed you too. It was strange not waking up to your smiley face. See you soon xx"

Bonnie tells Jezza where to meet us so we can wander around a little longer.

As soon as I walk in to The Crib Bar, I know Jordan is here. I can feel his presence. I turn around and see him walking towards me, slowly. It's like he's taking me in. In that moment I don't see anyone else or hear anything else other than my name on his lips. I start walking towards him in what feels like slow motion then I run the last couple of steps and throw myself at him.

"Oh my god Jordan, I really missed you last night. I can't believe how empty the house felt without you there."

He's hugging me so tight. "I was worried about you and then when you weren't there this morning my heart started to beat really fast and I didn't know what to do. I'm so glad you're ok." He kisses me on the top of my head. He slowly lets me slide down his body to the floor. I didn't even realise he had lifted me off the floor when he hugged me. I look up to him and smile, then I take his hand and we go and find Bonnie and Jezza.

They don't take any notice of us holding hands, they're so wrapped up in each other.

We order lunch and Bonnie and I have a glass of wine just to get us in the mood for the hen party tonight. The guys tell us about their night out. It sounds like they had loads of fun.

After lunch we all go home, Bonnie to hers and we go to mine. When we get to the house Jordan asks how I slept last night. I panic a little because I thought I was moving on and didn't want to start going backwards. I tell him about my nightmare and he pulls me into him.

"Thanks for telling me Cassie, I already knew though because Bonnie was worried and thought I'd be able to help. I was worried you were going to keep it to yourself and not tell me." He's rubbing my back and it feels so nice.

I look up to him and say, "I told you Jordan, I have no secrets from you. Remember in school we learnt the phrase 'WYSIWYG' - 'what you see is what you get,' well that's me!" I'm giggling remembering my school days.

"Well I like what I see," he says and I can feel his heart speed up a little. I panic a bit but then he steps backwards and takes me out on the veranda. "So what are you doing tonight?"

I tell him all about our plans for the night, poor Bonnie doesn't know what's going to hit her. "Are you staying with Bonnie or are you coming home?" he asks me and I get butterflies in my stomach. He called this home.

"Will you be here? If you are, then I'll come home but I don't want to stay by myself," I say, looking up at him.

"Of course I'll be here. I'll look after you and make

sure you sleep." He smiles that gorgeous smile.

"Thanks Jordan, I don't know what I've done all this time without you, you make me feel safe and complete." I stand up because this conversation is getting too personal. "I'm going to go and have a bath and get ready for tonight, I'll see you in a while," I say as I walk out of the lounge to go up the stairs.

"Ok I'll cook some food. Do you want to eat before you go out? You know soakage!" He laughs, he knows I can't drink much.

"Cheeky, yeah I'd love some food. Maybe I'll have a bath, put my make up on, do my hair and then we can eat. I can get dressed after dinner." I blush as I realised I just said I'd have dinner with him in practically no clothes.

"Can't wait," he says smiling again.

I go up the stairs and start running the bath, when it's boiling hot with the bubbles nearly overflowing, I get in and slowly sink into the hot water. I lay in the bath thinking about my life; about Jordan, about Chad and David. I know I've come to a point in my life where my life can change for the better and I know what I have to do to achieve that. I wash my hair then I let the water drain out slowly and it feels like all the negative things in my life are being pulled away from my body and are draining out through the plug hole.

When I get out of the bath I do my make-up and style my hair. Then I put my dressing gown on and go downstairs for dinner. The smell is delicious. "What are we having Jordan, its smells amazing," I ask walking up behind him.

"I made corn beef hash, I hope it's still one of your favourites," he says. He turns around to talk to me and stops and stares at me. "Wow Cassie, you look beautiful."

I laugh. "I don't even have my clothes on." I blush realising what I said.

He looks me up and down and stops when he gets to my eyes. "Just perfect." He turns back to the stove and then says, "sit down dinner is ready."

Dinner is as good as it smells, delicious. After dinner I go and get dressed and then, when I'm coming down the stairs, Jordan is waiting for me at the bottom, just like he was all those years ago. Memories come flooding back to me and it makes me a little sad, I know what I have to do and I hope it doesn't ruin our friendship. That would be just so devastating.

"You look just like an angel Cassie, take care tonight."

I go over to him, I reach up and kiss him very gently on the lips, then I say, "thank you for being here for me." He kisses me back very gently, but doesn't increase the pace, he is following my lead. I pull back.

He seems startled. "I'm going to take you into town and wait until the others get there. I don't want you to wait on your own. Is that ok?" He asks.

He really is too good to be true. "Come on I can't be

late, I'm the chief bridesmaid you know. I didn't want to wait on my own, so thank you." He drives me into town and waits until Bonnie gets there.

He whispers in my ear, "take care, if you need me I'll be straight here, don't forget that." He kisses me on the cheek.

He says to Bonnie, "have fun, don't do anything really bad I don't want to have to bail you both out. Look after Cassie for me, please," he says looking at her.

We have a great night. We stay in The Cribber for a few hours because it's buy one get one free on the cocktails and we had to try a few of them to see which ones we liked. We go to the nightclub after that and dance, dance, drink and then dance some more. Bonnie has a 'bride to be sash' and I have a 'chief bridesmaid' one so we get bought a lot of drinks. It is lots of fun.

When we are ready to leave the club, Bonnie rings Jezza to pick us up. When we get back to my house, Jezza walks me to the door and Jordan opens it and looks at me and then at Jezza. "Don't look at me like that. I've got one of my own in the car," he says walking back to the car laughing.

Jordan helps me into the house, he has his hands on my waist supporting me. I can feel the heat coming off his hands. "Come on, let's get you to bed Cassie," he's steering me towards the stairs. When we get to the bottom of the stairs he stops, looks at me then looks up at the stairs, then he bends down and picks me up wedding style and carries me up the stairs.

I squeal a little bit and then I start cuddling into his neck. "I could get used to this," I say and I cover his neck with little kisses.

He walks into the bedroom and lets my legs down, but I still cling hold of his neck. "Cassie, what are you doing? You're drunk, don't do something you'll regret tomorrow babe."

"Don't you want me to kiss you?" I can feel myself pouting, is he turning me down?

"Of course I do, but I'd rather you were sober and knew what you wanted," he says.

"Jordan, I know what I want." I walk backwards and suddenly I hit the bed and fall backwards onto it. I start laughing again. Jordan stands over me shaking his head, but he's smiling.

"Come on let's get you changed for bed." I just nod. He slowly takes my clothes off and folds them up in the corner, he seems to be taking his time coming back with my pyjamas. He brings them over, helps me into them and then I crawl across the bed and get under the covers. I watch him as he takes his clothes off and gets ready to climb in beside me. When he gets in I move so that I'm closer to him and I put my arms and legs over him.

I snuggle into his neck, then I raise myself up slightly and lean down and kiss him ever so gently on the lips and say, "I love you Jordan. Thank you for saving me." I wait for about one second and then I put my lips back on his and kiss him urgently. Thankfully he kisses me back. I push my tongue into his mouth and then take his lip into my mouth and suck it, he groans. Then he pulls away.

"Cassie, Cassie, you've had a lot to drink. I really want to keep kissing you, but I don't want you to wake up tomorrow and regret it. I want you to want to kiss me, if that makes sense. I'd feel like a shit if I carry on kissing you and taking advantage of you when you are so obviously drunk," he says.

I'm so embarrassed. I jump out of the bed, run into the bathroom and start crying. He doesn't want me. I've probably ruined everything now. Why did I have to drink so much?

I hear a gentle knock on the door. "Cassie, come on what are you crying for? Open the door, please, let me talk to you."

"No, I don't want to talk Jordan. I'm sorry. I just couldn't help myself. I've wanted to kiss you for so long and I just, I just had to taste you. I'm sorry Jordan." I move away from the door and open it. "I'm sorry, will you forgive me?"

I don't get a chance to apologise again before he moves into the bathroom and lifts me up so that I'm sitting on the counter and he opens my legs and steps in between them. He looks angry. "Don't you ever be sorry for anything you do Cassie. You do things because you want to. No regrets, remember. I just want to make sure you know what you are doing and that it's really something that you want. I want nothing more in this world than to taste you, to love you, but only if it's what you really want." He has his head leaning against my forehead and he is looking right into my eyes.

This is it, this is my chance and I intend to take it. "Jordan, I know I'm drunk and I know I'll have a hangover in the morning, I know it's not the right way to tell you this but "I love you and I don't just want to be your friend anymore. I want more and I hope you do too because I can't lose you from my life again." I have a few tears running down my face because I'm not sure how this is going to go. Will he agree with me? Or have I just lost my best friend in the world ever.

He wipes my tears with his thumb and then it feels like a lifetime before he says, "Cassie, I've never stopped loving you. No one can hold a candle to you. They never have done. Not since the first day I saw you through the window at school. I wanted to possess you that day and every other day since then. I want you more than I need to breathe, we are soul mates and we need to be together. Now I'm going to kiss you and prove to you how much I love you. Is that ok?"

I nod at him and he slowly moves his lips down to mine and then he does what he says and he devours me. It's the only way to describe the kiss. It's like all the years that we were apart come together in this moment.

I put my arms around his neck and kiss him with all the emotion I can muster. It is amazing, all the good memories I have of him come flooding back to me. I never forgot them, but they float in my mind like I'm watching a beautifully coloured movie. I don't understand, but it's beautiful. I must be drunk because this is all a bit weird. I pull back slightly because it is so intense and I want to look at him. I want to see if he feels it too.

He looks at me and smiles his beautiful smile. "I think it's time for you to go to bed. We can continue this ..." he indicates between me and him, "conversation in the morning or after your hangover has gone," he laughs.

He takes my hands and put them both behind his neck, I wrap my legs around his waist and he carries me over to the bed. As I climb under the duvet, he climbs in the other side, then he pulls me over so that I am against his body. He rolls me on my side and pulls me closer to him and then he wraps his arm around me. "This is the best night ever. I hope you remember this in the morning Cassie. I love you." He kisses me on the back of my head and then I drift off to sleep.

"I Believe In You"

When I wake up, I can feel something heavy on my leg, what is it? I look down and see Jordan's leg over mine, his arm over my body and I can feel his face in my neck. It's wonderful to wake up with Jordan lying all over me. I have a dry mouth and can see a glass of water on my bedside table along with two painkillers; he must have brought them up for me last night before I went to bed.

I think back over the night, I giggle because we had so much fun, drinking, dancing and more drinking. Some memories were definitely made last night; I wonder how Bonnie's head is this morning.

I'm smiling and then I remember what happened when I got home. Oh my god, I'm so embarrassed. Did I really throw myself at him? I turn my head so that my face is in the pillow and I groan. I hope things aren't awkward today. I'd hate that.

"Morning Cassie, what are you groaning about? Does your head hurt?" Jordan says laughing at me.

"Yes it does, I had far too much to drink last night." I can't roll over to look at him because I'm afraid. Afraid he might not want me in the cold light of day.

"There's two headache tablets by your glass of water, I got them for you last night just in case you had a

301

headache this morning, I thought you might." He's still chuckling.

I slowly sit up and reach for the tablets and the water and swallow them down. I look over to Jordan who is now laid on his back with his hands behind his head and he's smiling at me. I really don't know what to say. I lay back down and lay on my back too, I groan because it was such an effort to move.

"Is it bad? You were pretty drunk last night," he says.

"Yes the room is spinning a little bit," I say laughing.

"Do you remember everything? Or do you have blank bits?" he asks with a little trepidation in his voice.

"I think I remember everything, you know there's always something you forget until someone reminds you." I smile at him. "I remember what happened when I got home though," I say blushing.

"Do you? And have you changed your mind?" He's rolled onto his side now and he is only a couple of inches away from my face.

I look at him and see his love for me in his eyes. It's like I've allowed myself to see what everyone else could already see. "No, never" I smile at him.

He smiles his beautiful smile, leans closer to me and kisses me on the lips very gently, I close my eyes, but he doesn't take the kiss any further. When I open them he is smiling and I can see laughter in his eyes.

"I'm going downstairs to start making some breakfast for you. Stay in bed and sleep until your headache is better, then we can talk." He starts to roll over to get out of the bed when I reach out and grab his arm.

"Please Jordan just a small kiss, it'll make my head better." I give him a sweet smile, he starts laughing, then he leans in and kisses me from his heart. Wow!

He pulls back still smiling, "now sleep and get rid of that headache, we need to talk when you come downstairs." He turns and walks out the room, closing the door behind him.

What? He's such a tease. I lay in bed with my head pumping, with a big smile on my face and then I think about what he wants to talk about. Is he going to say it was a mistake? Does he really want to make a go of it? I'm fretting and I need to stop. I feel like I'm a teenager again. I laugh, then I close my eyes to try and make the headache go away.

I must have fallen asleep because when I wake up suddenly I give a little shriek because Jordan is sitting next to me on the bed. "Wakey wakey," he says. "You've slept nearly the whole day away, don't mind breakfast it's tea-time," he smiles.

"What? Why didn't you wake me up?" I ask sitting up quickly, I'm delighted to realise that my head doesn't hurt anymore. "You should have woke me up Jordan, have you been downstairs waiting for me all day?"

"I've been downstairs, but I've not been waiting for you. I did pop out for half an hour to buy some things for dinner tonight. I'm cooking you dinner tonight, a nice dinner. Let's call it a date!" he smiles at me.

"A date" I start laughing, "why?"

"Well, we've progressed past the first date and then all the other stages in a relationship and moved directly onto living together," he grins at me. "So I just thought it would be nice to have a date. What do you think? Are you game?" he's looking at me, searching my face for a clue.

"Ok, yeah, sounds good. I like the sound of that," I giggle. "I might go have a bath and relax before getting dressed ready for our date." I play along with his idea. The more I think about it, the more I like it.

"That's fine, but we aren't staying in all evening. We're going out for a drink." I groan, I'm not sure I can drink anymore. "Only one or two, before coming home to have dinner, then we can talk," he says, smiling at me. He comes over to me and kisses me gently on my lips, I'm enjoying this. I could do this all day. "Now you go and relax, then you can get ready while I go into the other bathroom to get ready," he stands up and walks to the door. "No checking my bum out either you" he laughs as he walks out of the room.

I lay on the bed laughing, it feels good to laugh so much. Once I am up I go to the wardrobe to see what I can find to wear. I need something dressy if we are going out, but then I don't want to appear overdressed when we get home. I find a lovely woollen black dress that is figure hugging, but I'll wear my boots with it to dress it down a bit. I pick my accessories to make it look more colourful, then I go to the bathroom and run a bath which I can sink into and relax.

I lay there thinking about how my life has changed in the last twenty four hours. I'm so glad I made the move last night with Jordan, it was risky, but I feel so happy that I know it was the right thing to do.

"The One I Love"

When I get out of the bath, I get dressed, do my make-up and finally my hair. When I'm happy with the way I look, I go downstairs to find Jordan. He's not waiting at the bottom of the stairs, so I go looking for him. Once again there is a beautiful smell coming from the kitchen, I look in and he's not there either. I look in the dining room and see the table has been set with a fresh red rose in a vase in the middle of the table. He's not in there either.

I go into the lounge and then I see him out on the veranda and just the sight of him makes me catch my breath. Can guys look beautiful? Because that is exactly what he looks like. He has lit lots of tea lights and they are all across the railings and on the table and on the decking floor.

It's amazing! He turns when he hears the doors open and smiles at me. "Hi Cassie, you look beautiful again." He comes towards me and takes my hand, "the view here is so amazing, I love looking out of your veranda, it's just so peaceful."

"Do you remember the dreams we had of living here one day? We used to lay on the beach just looking up here and imagining that it would be like to actually live her. Now you know, you've achieved that dream."

He leans up against the railings and breathes deeply. "Jordan, you've made it look so gorgeous out here," I say looking around.

He pulls me close to him and he wipes a stray hair off my face "no Cassie you have, you make any place beautiful when you walk into a room." He kisses me gently. "You are gorgeous and light up everywhere you go." I don't know what to say so I just stay quiet and stand there looking up into his face. He moves slowly around the veranda while gently blowing out the tea lights and I watch the smoke spiraling up into the air. I love the smell of the smoke from a quenched candle, I don't know what it is about it but it's very calming.

He laughs and then says, "Come on let's go out for our date. Are you excited?"

"I'm a bit nervous really Jordan, what if I don't like your company." I look at him all serious and then I can't keep a serious face any longer and burst out laughing. He joins me, links my arm with his, pulls me out through the house and out the front door.

We walk down to the town holding hands, it feels strange and yet it feels normal at the same time.

We go into the Cribbers Pub on the seafront and have a couple of drinks. We've talked a lot over the last couple of months, but as we sit here and chat it's like meeting for the first time. We discuss previous relationships, friends and how we've been over the last few years.

As we are walking back to the house for dinner, we

walk past Pebbles and Mr. Stanley is locking up. He really is getting old, Jordan goes to help him pull the shutters down and then we walk a while with him.

"How are the plans to sell going?" Jordan asks him.

"I haven't had an offer yet and it's on the market at a low price. I don't understand it, everyone likes a seaside café don't they?" He sounds so sad, it's like his life's work is being pulled away from him at a time when he should be enjoying his life.

"I can't believe that. We love this place don't we Jordan?" I say because it holds so many memories for us.

"I know you do, I remember when you both started coming in together. Everyone could see how much you loved each other. I was as shocked as everyone else when you left Cassie."

"I know, I was shocked myself, but I didn't want to ever think 'what if?' I didn't want Jordan to think that either if he didn't go to Toronto. We had to do it - no regrets." I say the last bit looking up to Jordan. He smiles and leans down and kisses me on the head.

"Ah, I see you lovebirds have finally realised what everyone else saw in you both." He says smiling at both of us and nodding down to our joined hands.

"Yes we have." Jordan says, wrapping his arm around my shoulders and pulling me close. "It's taken a while, but I always knew we would be together again."

"You will both have to come in next week for a hot

chocolate, just like the old days. If I don't get a buyer soon, then I will just have to close down. It will be sad, but I really can't stay open any longer."

I hug him because it is so sad, he hugs me back very tightly. "Thank you for all the times you let us just sit there nursing one drink for hours."

He laughs. "All the kids did it. I just enjoyed the company. This is my car, I'm going home now. I can't keep going like I used to." He says laughing.

"See you soon, we will come down for a hot chocolate. I promise." He smiles and climbs into his car. We watch him drive off.

"It's a shame isn't it." I say snuggling into Jordan's side.

"It is, unfortunately. It will be sad to see it close down. We have a lot of memories there."

When we get home all thoughts of Mr. Stanley have gone from my mind as the smell of food is so delicious. "I hope the dinner tastes as good as it smells." I go up behind him and put my arms around his waist to hug him tightly. "Do you know how long I've wanted to do this when you been beavering away in here? A really long time."

"Mmmm that feels so good Cassie." Jordan turns to face me and takes me in a big hug. I look up to him just in time for him to look down and kiss me. I can feel his hunger for me in his kiss and I reciprocate, I can't explain how I feel, I just need to be closer to him. He pulls away and clears his throat. "We need to eat or the dinner will go to waste," he starts busying himself with putting the dinner out on the table. I wonder why he stopped kissing me. It felt nice.

I sit at the table and he opens a bottle of wine and serves up the dinner. The food is amazing and we talk about what foods we like and dislike.

After dinner we grab blankets and go out onto the veranda. I have a patio heater outside, so Jordan turns it on and we sit underneath it with our drinks.

He takes a deep breath and then he starts to talk. "Cassie we need to have this conversation before we take our relationship any further. You understand that don't you?"

I nod my head because I'm afraid to speak. I think I might cry.

"I truly believe that you are my soul mate, you are the reason I breathe every day. I need to know that you believe that too. This it for me, I won't let you go again. I will fight all the way for you. You are my future, without you my life won't be complete!" What he says is so beautiful. I have tears running down my face.

"Jordan, I feel the same, I never felt contentment like I do right now. I think you're right, my soul was searching for yours so that it could become whole. You have proved to me over the last couple of months that you want my mind, friendship and soul more than you want my body, for that I am grateful. This is it for me, I want you now and for the rest of my life."

He takes my hands and moves me so that I'm sitting

on his lap; he puts one arm around me and takes my hand with the other. "Thank you Cassie, you've made me so happy I can't even begin to explain. I know we can overcome any issues we might have, together! I love you and I want to tell the world that you're mine." He leans forward and kisses me and we start making out.

I stop to take a breath and rest my forehead on his. "I love you Jordan, so much it hurts. I can't imagine being apart from you again."

We sit and talk for a while, none of us touching on the subject of sex; Jordan because he doesn't want to push me and I don't mention it because I'm scared. We will overcome this together, I just know we will.

We lock up and go upstairs. He holds my hand as he walks in front of me. When we get into the bedroom, I start to feel shy, why does this feel different to any other night? It shouldn't do, we know each other so well, but it all feels so exciting.

I walk to the chest of drawers and get my pj's out, then I stand in the middle of the room and slowly take my clothes off, all the time I'm looking into Jordan's eyes. His eyes don't leave mine, although I can tell he's dying to look at my body, but I know he's seen it so many times already. He takes his clothes off and puts on his shorts, but I notice he doesn't put a t shirt on. I put my PJ's on and move towards the bed, he does the same.

I climb under the covers, so does he. It feels a bit awkward, maybe I should say something. "Will you hold me tonight? Close to you? I want to feel you on my skin."

He opens his arms for me to climb inside, which I do. We are both facing each other, his leg is over mine and he's pulling me in closer with his foot. I put one leg in between his. Jordan tilts my head up towards him, "I want to get closer to you, but I can't. There's no gap between us, but it's still not enough. I feel like I've got you back after all these years and I just need to consume you," he says,.

We both laugh because we can't get any closer. We kiss and cuddle for what seems like hours. When I run my hands up and down his body, he doesn't touch me back. I know he's worried about my reaction, but I need him to touch me. "Jordan please touch me. I need you to touch me, I need you to see that I can do this. Remember no regrets. What HE did brought you back into my life, always think about the positives. Please touch me," I say as I move my hand up his thigh towards his groin.

All of a sudden his hand flies out and grabs my hand very gently. "No Cassie don't. I've waited so long for you to touch me like that again I know I'll explode." So I take my hand back and rest it on his back. "Roll over Cassie. Roll onto your back, please," he says and I do what he asks.

He leans up on one arm and then takes the other one and cups my face to his so that he can kiss me. He breaks the kiss and I watch him as he slowly moves down my body placing small kisses everywhere in his path. Down my neck, along my collar bone, then he moves so he's over me and he starts kissing very gently down to my breasts, all the time he's watching me for a sign to say stop! I don't, he keeps going.

He very lightly kisses my nipple; it's so soft I nearly didn't feel it and then he does the same to the other one. He looks into my eyes and he waits for my permission, permission to take it in his mouth. I nod and he very slowly, painfully slowly, opens his mouth and takes my nipple into it. It's so hot in his mouth, it feels so good. I moan, he leans over and takes the other one and does the same. He kisses down my body, until he reaches my shorts. He's still looking at me and I want him to take them off and ravage me, but I know I might not be ready for that although my body seems to be.

He sees the hesitation in my eyes for a split second and then he starts to crawl up my body kissing me as he comes closer to my lips. When he gets to my lips he kisses me and I know how much he loves me because his lips tell me.

He lays back down beside me and he pulls me into his body. "You're so beautiful, I am so lucky."

"Yes you are," I say and giggle.

We both start laughing and I can feel my eyes getting heavy. "Thanks for a lovely date Jordan, I really enjoyed it."

"It was the best ever" he says, kissing me on the back of my neck.

"I Just Wanna Make Love To You"

After we have had breakfast Joyce comes for my daily session. We make her coffee and then we all take a seat in the lounge, these meetings are casual at this stage.

"So Cassie, how was the weekend? Did you have a relaxing one?" she asks.

"The weekend was amazing, Jordan had the stag night and I had the hen night. We had lots of fun and then yesterday Jordan and I went on a date." I can't help saying it I want her to know.

She looks surprised, but I think that's because she wasn't expecting me to say it out of the blue like that. She stands up, comes over and hugs me. "I'm delighted for both of you," she says. "You both deserve to be happy." She goes back to her seat and sits down.

"So, what are we going to talk about today? Cassie is there anything worrying you about your relationship with Jordan? How do you think you will cope with being intimate?" Trust Joyce to come out and just say exactly what I was thinking.

"Well," I'm actually embarrassed. "I'm not sure how I'm going to cope sexually to be honest Joyce." I can't even look at Jordan, and I know I'm blushing. "I

314

want to have sex, but I'm worried that when it actually comes to it, I won't be able to." I look at the floor, I can feel the tears starting to come to my eyes. What if I can never have sex? Jordan will leave me then, won't he?

"This isn't unusual Cassie, a lot of people who have been through what you have find it hard to have sexual relations with anyone. Others find someone who understands what they have been through and help them move on. Most importantly they help them to love themselves and love their own body. This is really important because, unless you can love your own body, you won't allow someone else to. Does that make sense?" She's looking from me to Jordan.

"I understand what you are saying Joyce." Jordan says as he reaches over and takes my hand. "Cassie, I'll help you to love yourself and your own body. I'm not going to push you into anything that you don't want to do. I understand what you've been through; I've been here with you when you have been in your darkest moments. I know you can move forward and I want to help you to do that. I hope you let me do that."

"I know you will Jordan." I then ask Joyce, "Are there any sexual psychologists who work with the charity, you know who can help victims with rebuilding their sex lives?" I know it's a strange question, but I can feel an excitement that I haven't felt for a while. I've had lots of thoughts over the last couple of months and I've been thinking about what I want to do with the rest of my life. I think I've just put the last piece of the jigsaw into the puzzle. I smile a really big smile and then I look at the two people who are staring at me wondering what is going through my head.

"There are a lot of phychiatrists working in PEBBLES, I know that Brenda is a sexual psychologist, why?"

I smile at her. "Joyce, you have been wonderful to me during the last couple of months and I appreciate every conversation we have had. You are an amazing person and you have helped me overcome the worst and hardest thing in my life. Without you I would be a walking disaster, but I'm not, I feel like I can overcome anything." She smiles at me and then I turn to Jordan.

"Jordan, you have always been the best thing that has ever happened to me and I love you for what you've done for me." I look at the two of them and they are staring at me with no understanding, I don't even think I understand what is going through my head right now.

"What are you thinking about Cassie?" Jordan looks at me like he can see the cogs turning.

"I'm just thinking about what happens next. I've let David control my life for too long. I need to think about the rest of my life. I need to move on, put what happened behind me. I want to help people like me and I think I know how." I'm so excited it's all slotting into place, I can't believe I didn't think about this before.

"Do you both fancy a walk. I want to show you something," I ask and hope they take me up on it.

"I'm intrigued by the look on your face, so that's a yes from me," Joyce says.

I look to Jordan, he looks confused. "Please Jordan, I need you to come too. This involves you in a big way." I move towards him and take his two hands in mine.

He looks down to me. "I was worried there for a moment you wanted your future without me."

I go up on my tiptoes and kiss him forcefully on the lips. "Jordan, I have no future without you. You are my everything."

He smiles his beautiful smile then says, "Come on then, let's go for a walk and see what plans you have for us all."

We put our coats on, leave the house and walk down towards the seafront. Jordan and I are holding hands while Joyce, on my other side, has our arms linked. I've got to know Joyce very well over the last few months and I like her a lot. She is very good at her job and she has helped me tremendously. She's funny and can get you to talk about things without you even realising you're talking about them.

When we get to the beach I steer them towards Pebbles café. "Let's go in here and have a drink." I can feel them both looking at me with lots of questions in their eyes.

"Just go with flow guys," I say laughing. Jordan opens the door for us and Joyce goes in first, I go next and Jordan puts his hand on my lower back to guide me through. I love it when he does that, it feels territorial.

"Morning Mr. Stanley, how are you today?" I ask. He looks tired today; I can see it in his eyes.

"I'm ok, a bit tired and getting worn down with the idea that I might have to close up. What would you like to drink?."

"I'm going to have one of your special hot chocolates please!" Jordan and Joyce place their orders, when they have finished I ask Mr. Stanley "Is there any chance we can have a look at the other rooms that you have here first, please? I'm interested in helping you sell this place. I would hate it to be closed down, it holds a lot of good memories for me." I smile at him and he returns my smile. I think that's the first genuine smile I've seen on his face for a very long time.

"Of course you can, let me put up a closed sign on the door for a few minutes. Now, I've not used all of these rooms so some are empty, but come on follow me." We all stand up, Joyce and Jordan look at each other before following me out the back of Pebbles..

We go through the door which leads to the toilets, I always knew there were other doors out here, but I never really thought about them. Through one of them we come to a few more rooms leading off a corridor. He uses one of them as a stock room and another as a small office. Then there are two other rooms, which are empty, and it's such a shame because they are huge rooms. My mind just keeps rolling my ideas around in my head and I can feel I'm getting even more excited now that I have seen them. I know I am smiling widely.

After he has shown us out the back, we walk back into the cafe and Mr. Stanley flicks the sign back to 'Open'. He busies himself with making our drinks and it's only after he has brought the drinks over to us that Jordan turns to me and asks "Ok Cassie I'm very curious. Will you just tell us what you have going on in your mind?" I think he might have guessed because he has a smile on his face.

"OK guys, bear with me. Let me just speak and try and get this out right, it's a bit jumbled in my mind, but I know what I want to say." They both nod and take a sip of their drinks.

"So, I've been wallowing in my own self-pity for too long and I need to move on and do something constructive. Now, I've quite a bit of money coming to me from America and I've been thinking about what I can do with it. As you know I donated £200,000 to your charity a few months ago," I say.

"Oh my god, that was from you," Joyce says. I forgot she didn't know.

"Yes, I'll explain how that happened another time, but I want to work for you and become a counsellor. I have personal experience and can use that to relate to other peoples cases."

"That would be amazing" Joyce says. Jordan just nods his head and smiles, he's heard me say this much before.

"Anyway, I love Newquay and, if I'm honest, I don't want to move away from here again. I missed this place when I was away and nowhere else ever came close." I'm looking at Jordan because I know he can't live here indefinitely because of his charity in London. I hope it doesn't mean our time will have to come to an end.

"How would you feel about opening an office here in Newquay? I know that, with it being a tourist town, there's a lot of people coming and going and I'm sure there's a lot of things going on that aren't nice. I'm sure we could help a lot of people, not just from Newquay, but around and about." I look from Jordan to Joyce and back again.

"That would be a great idea Cassie, it would be great to help the local community," Joyce says. I notice Jordan isn't saying anything; I need him to want to do this as much as I do.

"Jordan? What do you think?" I look at him and reach over and take his hand.

"I think you are amazing Cassie, that's what I think. In the middle of your crisis you think of other people and how you can help them. I think it would be great to open an office here, but it would have to be in the perfect location though," he says. I don't say anything for a minute and then I see the light come on behind his eyes, he's caught up with my line of thinking. "Ah I see," he says.

"Yes, what about if I buy Pebbles? I've loved this place for years and it holds all my memories of us, Jordan. We could still run the cafe, I'd hate for that to go. Then we can turn the rooms out the back into counselling rooms and offices, maybe even a community centre type place for people to come and get help about sexual diseases and everything else that goes hand in hand with a tourist town like this." I'm getting really excited as I say it all out loud. Everything starts clicking into place.

"Jordan you are an amazing cook, you can come up with some ideas for the cafe, we could even make it a bistro at night or something to make this fabulous landmark a bigger part of the community. What do you think?" I hold my breath while I wait for them to reply.

"I think it's a fabulous idea Cassie, I can't believe you've only thought of it today, it seems like something you've been planning for a while," Joyce says.

"No, I was just thinking while we were talking this morning, it hit me and then the idea just ran away with itself, it was like a runaway train building up momentum in my head." I'm still waiting for Jordan to speak, he's being very quiet. Maybe I should have spoken to him on our own before I mentioned it in front of Joyce.

"Jordan, I know I'm kind of jumping the gun here, but I'm excited and just wanted to see what you think. Don't be angry with me for not waiting and talking to you about it first, please."

"I'm not angry with you Cassie, I just think that what you're suggesting is unbelievable and I can see how excited you are. My mind is thinking of what we could do to this place and how we could get this to work. I love it as much as I love you." He leans across the table and kisses me passionately. I hear someone clearing their throat, it's Joyce.

"Ok lovebirds, calm down," she laughs. "I love it

Cassie, but are you sure about this cafe, it's very tired looking and looks like it should be knocked down."

"No way!" Jordan and I shout at the same time.

She laughs, "Ok, ok just asking."

"Sorry Joyce, this places means a lot to Jordan and I, we could never knock it down. I'm going to ask for another drink and then see if Mr. Stanley will join us," I say standing up.

"Hi Mr. Stanley, can we have another round of these gorgeous drinks please. We'd love to talk to you about something really important, so why don't you make one for yourself, then come sit down and talk to us," I say smiling at him. He smiles back and goes off to make the drinks.

We chat through some more ideas until Mr. Stanley comes and sits down with our drinks.

"So, what do you want to discuss with me Cassie?" He smiles.

"I love this place, it holds a lot of memories and I don't want to see it knocked down. We were thinking that we could buy it off you and keep it as a cafe and then maybe a bistro at night. The real reason we want to buy it though is because we want to turn the back rooms into a community centre type place for sexually abused victims. We want to offer counselling them and help them get back into society without being scared of their own shadow. Maybe they can work here, I don't know, we have to work on the ins and outs."

I look at him and he's quiet for a while, then I notice some tears in his eyes. He leans over and takes my hand. "Cassie, it is amazing that you would take this cafe and keep it as a cafe/bistro, but the fact that you want to turn it into a place where people can get together and be helped through such awful times of their lives, means so much to me. I know what happened to you all those years ago and what you have recently been through, I think it takes a very brave person to be able to see beyond the hurt and come out the other side such a giving person."

He takes a few deep breaths and then I see the tears welling up in his eyes. "My daughter left Newquay and went to London when she was a teenager, we were annoyed because she didn't keep in touch. Then one day we got a phone call from a police officer to tell us she was in hospital. My wife Belinda and I drove straight to London. When we got there we couldn't believe our daughter had been raped. She was in a terrible way; her attacker had raped her then left her for dead. She took a long time to recover physically, but she never recovered emotionally. There was no one to help her, she wouldn't let us help and to be honest we didn't know how. She was institutionalised for many years in Truro, Belinda went every weekend to see her. One day about ten years later we got a call to say she had died, she had hidden some of her tablets and then took them all at once, she committed suicide."

He stops to rubs his eyes then he continues "She never got over her experience Cassie, you have great support, but then you are a fighter, you always have been. Belinda never got over Sarah's death and she died six months after Sarah. I've thrown myself into this place ever since, but I can't keep going. I'm not getting any younger. I can't think of a more appropriate use for this place." He takes my hand and kisses it.

I really don't know what to say; he has totally blown me away with his story. I have never heard anyone mention it, I must ask Mum and see if she knows about Belinda and Sarah, it is so tragic. When I look over at Jordan and Joyce, I don't think they have heard it before either.

"Mr. Stanley, thank you for sharing your life story with us. I never knew any of this and you're so brave to tell us now. I feel like you've been a part of my life with Pebbles for as long as I can remember, as I said before, I have many good memories here and I hope to have many more. I'd love to buy Pebbles, but I'd love you to stay a part of it." I can feel my own tears welling up.

Jordan gets up from the table and walks over to Mr. Stanley. "We want to do a deal for Pebbles, but then we want to offer you a job." Jordan obviously knew where I was heading with the conversation, I look at him with such admiration in my eyes. "Will you come for dinner tomorrow night at Cassie's? I'd love to cook for you and make some plans," he says shaking Mr. Stanley's hand.

Mr. Stanley smiles up at him "I'd love to. You've done amazing things with your charity. I've followed you for years. I wish there had been somewhere that would have been able to help my Sarah, but if you can use Pebbles to help others, then it would be the best sale ever." He shakes Jordan's hand and pulls him in for a hug.

We all start talking at once, Joyce has been quiet for a while. "Joyce are you ok?" I ask.

"I'm overwhelmed by your generosity, Cassie. You are so selfless and what you want to give to others is just unbelievable," she says.

"Joyce, you have been the one who has selflessly helped me, you have given up your time every day to come and help me. I know you were retired before that, but if you're interested I'd love you to be an integral part of this project. I really value your opinion on things. I will never be able to thank you enough for what you have done for me, nothing I could do would ever come close to expressing my thanks to you. Please help us." I know I'm pleading, but I need her to make this work.

She looks at me with tears in her eyes. "Cassie I've loved helping you because you are an amazing person. I would be delighted to help you with this project," she starts sobbing.

"Joyce what's the matter?" I ask her taking her hand.

"I don't have any children of my own, but you have included me in your plans and made me feel like I'm part of your family. That is just so amazing."

"As far as I'm concerned you are family. I will never forget what you've done for me," I say with tears in my eyes too.

"Ok, this is all getting too emotional. We need to go and make some plans," Jordan says.

"Yeah you're right Jordan," I say trying to pull myself together. "Mr. Stanley, we have to go now, but will you come to our house tomorrow say about seven o'clock?" I ask.

He smiles at me and says, "Cassie I'd be delighted too". We all stand up and shake hands, but Mr. Stanley takes me into a hug. "See you tomorrow at seven o'clock."

We say goodbye and when we walk out Jordan takes my hand and Joyce links my arm exactly as we were on the way down, except now we are all deep in thought.

When we get back home we thrash out a few ideas, then Joyce says she has to go. After we've said goodbye, we go and sit on the veranda, it's my most favourite place. "Cassie we need to talk about this. It's amazing that you want to do this, but there is so much work involved, are you sure you want to do this? Are you ready to commit to this? I've done this before and it's hard work, it's emotional work, but it is very rewarding. Are you sure you won't miss your life in New York?" He looks sad.

"Jordan, I have only ever been as certain as I am right now about one other thing in my life and that is how much I love you. I had a great life in New York, I would never say any different, but my life never felt complete like it does now." I kiss him passionately. "You are my future, you are my forever and I want to give back a part of what you have given me."

He pulls me onto his lap and wraps his arms around me. "I love you Cassie, more than I can explain, I always have done but are you really sure about this?"

"I'm so excited about this Jordan. I know that this is what I'm meant to do. What happened to me was the most horrific thing. Before you came along I thought he was going to kill me. I can share with others what happened to me, I can relate to them and what they've been through. I wouldn't be anything without you though, or Joyce for that matter. I want to save someone like you two saved me." I kiss him.

He leans into me and rests his head on mine. "I love you so much Cassie."

He then scoops me up into his arms and stands up. I throw my arms around his neck and snuggle in tight. He laughs at me, and then carries me to the stairs, takes a breath and then carries me up them. When he gets to the top he walks into our bedroom and he gently puts me down on the bed.

He stands over me, looking at me, not saying a word. He slowly removes my clothes, all the time he is watching me intently. He takes his clothes off and I get to see him naked for the first time in years. He is magnificent, gorgeous and I hold my breath because I can't believe he is mine. His tattoos are gorgeous and I can't wait to learn about each and every one of them.

He crawls up the bed until he is leaning over me, he leans down and kisses me like his life depends on it.

Neither of us speak as he starts moving over my body, kissing every spare inch. He kisses me between my legs and I move my hips up closer to his mouth. After he has kissed me down my legs to my ankles he works his way back up. Then when he reaches my face he kisses me again. While he is kissing me he slips a finger inside me, I moan into his mouth. He slides it out and then inserts two. I groan really loud, he slides them out and then inserts three. It's a tight fit but I take his fingers, I'm waiting for something else. He slowly withdraws his fingers and continues kissing me. I moan because I miss his fingers. He moves above me, pulls my legs open wider and slowly inches himself inside me.

I groan with pleasure at every inch he gives me. We still haven't said anything as we continue kissing. He slowly enters me until he is buried deep inside, only then does he starts to pull out slowly. I've had enough, I don't want him to pull out so I reach out, grab his arse and push him back in. He groans in my mouth and tries to pull out, I let him for maybe an inch then I dig my nails in and push him in fully.

He realises I don't want him to pull out, "Babe I need to move, I have years of love to give you." He starts to pull out again. I let him this time because I know it'll be worth my while. He starts pumping in and out and it feels wonderful. I curl my legs up so my ankles are pushing into his arse.

I can't hold on, I've wanted this for years, even when I was with other guys I always thought about Jordan. I start moaning because it feels so good; it feels so natural.

"I'm sorry Cassie, I can't hold on I need to cum. It feels so good," he has tears in his eyes. He starts to pump faster and I keep pulling him back in. I need every inch of him; I've missed him so much. We fit so well together; we are so good together. I let go of his arse, I need him to finish, to show me how much he loves me.

"Jordan, give me every inch of you, give it to me hard and deep. I need you," I whisper as I lift my hips to meet him.

That is his undoing, he starts pumping in and out like a mad man. I come undone and scream out his name, when I do he stills and I can feel him throbbing inside me. He falls on top of me, sweating, breathing heavy. We are both breathing heavy, then he leans up and looks at me, "Welcome home baby" and kisses me hard.

He pulls out of me after a while and rolls over into his back. "I missed you so much when you were away Cassie, I thought you were going to come back when I did. When I heard you got married I went out and got drunk every night for a month. I thought that was it for us, but I couldn't move on, no one ever came close for me. I kept my tabs on you, I couldn't let you go completely. I can't believe you are here with me, staying with me. I love you so much Cassie, it hurts when you're not with me."

"Jordan it was the hardest thing I ever had to do - leaving you. I always believed we would go home and be together after a few months. Then those months became years and I thought I'd lost you forever. I see now that I never lost you, I just needed to find you again." I roll over to face him and snuggle into him and I can feel myself falling asleep.

When we wake up it's early evening. I'm a little embarrassed that we made love during the day, but the feeling I felt when Jordan gave himself to me makes me smile.

"What are you smiling at?" Jordan says to me. "Come over here and kiss me instead," he says pulling me in tight to his body.

"I've never made love during the day before, it's so naughty." I laugh because I feel like a teenager.

"We can do that as often as you want Cassie, I really enjoyed it. Nothing has ever felt like that, it was like our two souls were entangling."

"Come on lover boy, we need to get up and make some plans. Shall I ask Bonnie and Jezza to come over tonight? We can tell them our plans." I ask.

"Yeah that's a great idea, they might have some ideas too," Jordan says as he gets out of the bed. I forgot he was naked and I gasp as I see him in all his glory. He truly is gorgeous inside and out. His tattoos are really beautiful, they were a shock at first but they really suit him, they have a story attached to them. It was his way of trying to erase me from his mind. While he is getting ready I get out of bed too, I get dressed and go downstairs to ring Bonnie.

We have just opened a bottle of wine when Bonnie

and Jezza arrive. "What's this about? It's only Monday night," Bonnie says looking between the two of us.

We both smile and then Jordan tells them our plans. They are both very excited for us and there is a lot of hugging and shaking hands. "We wanted to see what you think before we go and tell Cassie's parents tomorrow. Mr. Stanley is coming over for dinner tomorrow night so we can try and make some plans. We want to move on this quickly and start straight away."

We talk about what we have planned and what we want to do with the cafe and then how the charity will be run as a community centre in the back rooms. "So Cassie, are you going to change the name of the cafe to something more suitable for its purpose?" Bonnie asks.

"No!" Jordan and I say at the same time, then we start laughing.

"No, I love Pebbles and want to keep the name, everyone around town knows it as Pebbles. It can be like stepping stones to success for victims. Anyway the charity is called PEBBLES, so we don't need to change the name" I say, there is no way I'm changing the name.

When we finish talking about Pebbles, we move onto the subject of the wedding. I snuggle back into the couch and Jordan is sat beside me. Instinctively I cuddle into the crook of his arm and he starts playing with my hair.

Bonnie looks at Jezza, then at us. "Ermm guys is there something you want to tell us," she asks with a huge grin on her face. I look puzzled, "you know between you two," she says looking from me to Jordan and back.

Jordan starts laughing and he pulls me in closer. "Oh you mean us? We are a team, business partners and friends," he stops and takes a breath, I can see Bonnie just waiting for more. "We are a couple, we have found each other and this time neither of us intends to leave the other one behind." He leans in and tips my face up to meet his and then he devours me.

I hear Bonnie saying "Yay!" and clapping her hands. When he's finished kissing me, I slowly turn my face round to see Bonnie about to jump on me. "I'm so happy for you both," she says as she hugs me so tight I find it hard to breathe.

I start laughing. "About time," says Jezza. We all laugh and I'm so glad they are happy for us.

They leave soon after and as we close the front door, Jordan pushes me against it and he takes my head in between his hands. "You're amazing Cassie, I've been waiting to do this all night," he says as he takes my lips and claims them as his. I can feel him against me and I didn't think I could want him again so quickly, but I do, I want to show him how much I love him.

"Take me to bed Jordan" I say breathlessly.

He smiles, lifts me up and throws me over his shoulder. "Do you know how many years I've waited to hear you say that Cassie? Too many." He walks up the stairs and then puts me down gently on the bed.

"Jordan, tonight I want to explore you, I want to

make love to you, will you allow me to do that?" I ask as he starts taking my clothes off.

"Baby, if that's what you want then I'm not going to stop you, believe you me I want that so much," he growls.

I spend the next hour exploring his body; every scar, every mark, every tattoo and every inch of his body. When I take him inside me I know he can't hold on for long, I don't want him to. I move slowly but deeply and then I reach a peak and start falling apart around him. He starts to swell, then he explodes inside me. It is the best feeling in the world.

We cuddle all night, never moving apart, always touching and it feels amazing. I feel like I've finally come home. This is where I'm meant to be.

"You Raise Me Up"

After breakfast I ring Mum to ask if we can go over. She says it's fine, so we go to their house around lunchtime. When she sees us walking up the drive holding hands she smiles and says "about time kids." She kisses us both on the cheek and we walk into the house. She has lunch ready for us when we get there.

We sit down to lunch and she says "Is this what you wanted to talk about?"

"No," I laugh and then I proceed to tell them about Pebbles and our plans. They are both delighted with what we plan to do , they join in with the discussions and help to iron out a few wrinkles in the plans. They want to help out as much as they can as well.

They've agreed to come to dinner tonight with Joyce and Mr. Stanley so that we can all discuss Pebbles and see what arrangements we can come up with.

When we leave Mum and Dad's, Jordan drops me home while he goes to get the food for tonight.

I stand on the balcony looking at the beach and the sea below, it's very calming. I think about how my life has changed over the last six months and I smile thinking about Jordan, my soul mate.

"What are you thinking about Cassie?" Jordan

comes up behind me and wraps his arms around me. He kisses my neck; it feels so good.

"I was just thinking about you and how good it feels to have you back in my life." I put my hands over his.

"Ditto babe, ditto" We stand like that for a while then I start to shiver. "Come on let's get you inside," he says turning me around and hugging me, then he takes my hand and leads me into the house.

When we get inside he takes me to the kitchen and he asks "Will you watch me cook for a while, we can discuss what we want from tonight," he leans over and kisses me. I sit up on a bar stool and talk while watching him cook.

Mum and Dad arrive first and I offer them a glass of wine, then Mr. Stanley comes and lastly Joyce. We show them into the dining room, where the table is set and we all start talking at once.

"We wanted to bring you all here because of our plans to buy Pebbles". I smile at Mr. Stanley. "We still want to keep the cafe, but we thought we might be able to bring more business at night by having a bistro. This would mean we would need a drinks license, but I don't think that would be a problem. I would like to redecorate but want to keep the counter and everything where it is. What do you all think?"

Everyone starts talking. "Mum you go first." I say smiling.

"I think it's a great idea, but are you sure you can

take this project on?" she asks.

"Yes I do, I need something to sink my teeth into and challenge me so my mind doesn't go back to the dark places. Which leads me onto the next part of the venture. Jordan will you tell everyone what we have talked about," he nods and smiles at me.

"We want to open a south west office for PEBBLES, we don't have one this side of Bristol and we think that we can open one at the back of Pebbles. There are plenty of rooms out the back and Cassie had mentioned a kind of community centre type environment. We will have counsellors, experts on sexual diseases and any other services which we feel would be of benefit. I'm moving back here, well I kind of already have. I'm not going anywhere that takes me away from Cassie now," he smiles at me and takes my hand.

"I don't want to close the charity in London, so one of my managers is going to run that office. We also thought that if we had anyone who needed lots of therapy then we could have them working in the cafe to help increase their confidence and we will be there to help them through any issues they might have," he takes a sip of his drink.

Mr. Stanley talks first. "I think it's a great idea and cannot think of anything better to use the facility for. I was worried about selling it because I thought someone would knock it down or completely change it and that was upsetting me. Although it's none of my business after I sell it, but knowing what you want to do makes me so happy. I'd be happy to sell it to you."

We negotiate a fee and tell him that we will get a lawyer onto it first thing in the morning.

Joyce says, "I'd love to help out with this. I've missed working and helping others and have really enjoyed our discussions Cassie. I don't think I ready to stop working yet," she laughs.

"Don't worry Joyce we want you involved, we need you. Mr. Stanley If you want a job at the cafe then there's a job for you, we don't want you to leave, but we understand if you want to give it up now you've sold," I say.

"I'd love a job there, I want to see what happens to my Pebbles" he smiles.

"Great, it looks like everything is falling into place. We will see our lawyer and get the sale moving, then we can start getting the rest of the work that is involved in opening a new office for a charity," Jordan says.

"Let's have a toast," we all raise our glasses. "To Pebbles and to Cassie for bringing us all together."

We talk about our plans for the rest of the evening and then Joyce says she has to go. Mr. Stanley offers to walk her home and they leave together.

When they've gone, Mum turns to me and Jordan and says, "I can't believe the change in you Cassie, you are totally different to a month ago. I'm delighted that you have this project to help you. Jordan, I can never thank you enough for your influence in the changes in

Cassie," she hugs him tight. I can see a tear in her eye.

"Come on let's go home," Dad says and they say their goodbyes and leave.

We tidy up, talking about our plans and then we go to bed. Jordan makes love to me for hours and we fall asleep fully satisfied and happy.

Everything starts to move really fast after the meeting with Mum, Dad and Mr. Stanley. We went to the lawyers to negotiate on the sale the next day.

I have to go to New York to finalise some details on the properties over there and Jordan is coming with me, we are going to stay for few days and I can show him around.

I meet up with Chad's Mum, Sarah while I am there, she is very welcoming and I have missed her. We talk about Chad and how much we miss him, while we are talking I tell her all about David and what happened years ago. She is shocked and upset that I hadn't told her before now. I told her that Chad didn't even know – it was a part of me that I wanted to keep hidden. I told her how he had raped me in Newquay after I went home and everything I have done to overcome it all.

She held me and we cried and I promised to keep in touch with her. I introduced her to Jordan, later that evening, and she really liked him. I'm glad because it means I can keep her in my life.

Jordan and I have sunk into a routine which feels so natural and I can't believe there was a time when he wasn't in my life.

Bonnies wedding day creeps up on us so quickly. I stay at her house the night before the wedding and Jezza stayed in our house with Jordan. It is horrible being away from him. I realise that I have big security issues still, he keeps me calm and grounded without me even realising it. I don't want to rely on him being there, I know I need to do things on my own, it's just I love him so much and need him in my life.

On the morning of her wedding day, we have champagne for breakfast and someone arrives to do our hair and makeup. Bonnie is so excited, no nerves whatsoever. "Are you nervous Bonnie? Being stood in front of all those people?" I ask her.

"No way, I love Jezza. Everyone who is coming today knows that, this is the most natural thing in the world," she smiles and she looks so happy.

I hug her before she puts her dress on. "Bonnie I love you, you're like a sister to me and I'm so glad you're still in my life, you've helped me so much over the last year and I love you for it. Now get that dress on or you'll be late!" I laugh.

"I love you too Cassie, now help me into this dress or I'm going to be late," she laughs back at me.

When we are both dressed I can feel tears in my eyes, she looks so beautiful. Her Dad is waiting for her at the bottom of the stairs and he smiles when she comes down. "Bonnie you look so beautiful, I hope Jezza knows how lucky he is. Actually I'm going to make sure I tell him later," he says laughing.

We get in the wedding cars and drive to the hotel. We are chaperoned to the room where the wedding ceremony is going to be held. As we stand outside the door to the room the wedding march starts to play, I walk down the aisle first and all I can do is look at Jordan and smile, he looks fabulous, I love him so much. It feels like I'm walking down the aisle to him, I can feel the tears welling up, I need to control my shit because this is a happy occasion.

The ceremony goes well, it's a beautiful service and the Atlantic Hotel is the perfect wedding. It's as beautiful as we all imagined it would be. A perfect day!

I sit next to Jordan on the top table and we have a great day, I can't believe Bonnie's now a married woman. I never thought she would get married! We dance, laugh and drink and have a wonderful day, the kind of day memories are made of. We go to our room when everyone starts leaving and I throw myself on the bed, I'm wrecked. Jordan laughs at me and then says, "Come on beautiful, let's take this dress of, I've been waiting all day to do this." He starts pulling me up from the bed so that he can take my dress off. I can hardly stand up I'm so tired.

When he's taken my dress off he gently lays me back down. "You looked so beautiful today Cassie, it made me think about how beautiful you would look in a wedding dress, walking towards me, joining me. I love you so much sometimes I feel like I can't breathe without you near me." He leans down and kisses me. "I know you're tired babe and you need to go to sleep, but don't think for one minute I'm going to let you out of this room tomorrow morning without me showing you how much I love you." He's taken his clothes off while he's been talking to me, he climbs into bed naked next to me and pulls me into his body. This is my own personal piece of heaven.

When I wake the next morning, the sun is shining through the window, I slowly turn around and see Jordan watching me. I smile and ask him "Have you been watching me sleep?"

"Yes I have, you look so peaceful when you sleep and you keep smiling, it's great to see," he says with a naughty little grin. "But I want to see your naughty face, I want to see your face when you cum and call out my name." He rolls me onto my back and straddles me; he takes my hands and raise them above my head. "Don't move Cassie, I'm going to show you how much I love you." He bends down and kisses me on the lips, he pushes his tongue into my mouth and I hear myself moan.

He sits back and looks at me. "Do you know how beautiful you are Cassie? I could sit and look at you all day."

"Well please don't, because I feel horny and only you know how to heal me," I say looking him in the eyes.

He then bends down and shows me how much he

341

loves me in every which way is possible, I cry out his name when I fall off the edge of my orgasm. He cries out my name at the same time and then he falls on top of me and whispers in my ear; "I love you Cassie, you have made me whole again."

We fall back asleep until the phone rings and it's Bonnie, who is down in reception. "Erm who's wedding is this? We are all waiting for you two down in reception," she starts laughing. "See you in ten minutes," and then she hangs up.

"Jordan, we fell asleep and everyone is waiting downstairs for us so that we can go to lunch. I can't believe we did that." I'm laughing and getting out of bed at the same time, "Come on Jordan get up."

"I was having such a good time Cassie, do I have to get up?" he says laughing.

I go over to the bed and take the covers off him, "Yes you do." I run off to the bathroom to get washed up and dressed. I hear him groan in the bed.

When Jordan is up and dressed, we go down to reception where we receive a standing ovation. "All right guys just because I love my lady and you're all jealous," Jordan says laughing.

We all have lunch in the hotel and then Bonnie and Jordan leave to go on their honeymoon, they're going to Egypt, I'm sure they'll have a great time.

After lunch we go back to my house and continue sorting all the necessary things for Pebbles. We have decided that we need to go to London for a few days tomorrow so that I can see how the charity works. I'm quite excited, I haven't been to London for a few years and I love it, although I couldn't live there.

When we get to the head office of PEBBLES Jordan introduces me as his partner and explains to everyone that we are opening a South West branch. Everyone is excited for us and there are lots of meetings with the counsellors and job placement people. I learn a lot in the couple of days we are there, and when we go to dinner on the third night, I nearly fall asleep in my dinner. We've been staying in Jordan's apartment, which is lovely but very impersonal. He brings me back to his apartment after dinner and we sit on the couch with a bottle of wine. "It feels strange being back here after being in your house Cassie. This is just somewhere to sleep, your house feels like my home, it feels like where I belong." He pulls me into him on the couch, he knows I'm getting sleepy.

"It is where you belong Jordan, and it's not my house it's our home." I look up to him and kiss him, "You belong wherever I am".

We go to bed and he holds me close to him all night, yes it is where we both belong.

As soon as we get back to Newquay everything starts happening at the same time, we have pushed for a quick sale and we get the keys in a week's time. We have already advertised for counsellors and other key personnel to help get it all up and running. We've already organised a fundraiser in the Atlantic Hotel, a dinner dance with a local band. We've had a lot of support both locally and in the whole of the South West.

I can't wait to get the keys so that we can move in and start working with Jordan on this project. We work very well together and it doesn't bother us that we will be working together and living together, it just feels like the most natural thing to do.

Before we get the keys, Mr. Stanley lets us in to start measuring up and start clearing up, he is going to be working with us and we know he won't screw us over. Everything is going perfectly and we collect the keys on the Friday. We are so excited that we go straight down to Pebbles and walk in, lock the door and just stand there. We can't really believe that we've done this, that we've bought our most favourite place in the world.

"Jordan, I can't believe we own this, it's just amazing," I say leaning up to kiss him on lips.

He pulls me into his body and says, "It's amazing what you want to do to help others Cassie. I love you so much, but every day you surprise me with how giving you are."

There's a knock at the door and Mum, Dad, Mr. Stanley and Joyce are waiting outside, we open the door and they all walk in smiling. We shake hands with them all and Mum reaches into her bag and brings out a bottle of champagne and some glasses. We open the champagne and sit in one of the cubicles, then we raise our glasses in a toast. "To Pebbles and to all who come here looking for food, drink, help or guidance."

"To Pebbles," they say in unison. Jordan lifts his glass and says, "To Cassie, without whom this would not have happened and wouldn't have been worthwhile doing."

"To Cassie," they all say. We take a sip and then Jordan goes out the back for a few minutes. When he comes back he seems nervous, I wonder what he was doing out there.

"I know we will be having an official opening and fundraiser next week and I was going to wait till next week to do this, but Cassie I can't wait any longer I need to know what you think and how you feel." I look at him confused, he knows how I feel about everything because I tell him how I feel all the time. I found during my counselling that it was better to talk about my feelings than bottling them up or waiting to be asked how I feel.

All of a sudden it's like everything happens in slow motion, one minute Jordan is stood at the end of the table, the next minute he is on the floor on one knee. "Cassie, I've always loved you from the first moment I saw you at school. The years when we were apart were the hardest and I was never fully happy with anything in my life, no one ever made me happy like you did. When I heard you were moving back home, I was happy and wanted to have you in my life as a friend, but then fate threw us back together and I know those circumstances weren't good, but it meant I had you with me. I always told you that our souls would find each other and they did."

He looks at me while he takes a deep breath. "Cassie will you marry me? I want to be with you forever, I didn't realise how much I need you to make my life complete, but I am nothing without you." He stops talking and looks at me, waiting for me to answer him.

I can't talk. I can't speak. I stare at him, everyone is waiting for my reaction. "Cassie?" Mum says. "Don't leave him kneeling there put him out of his misery."

I can feel myself start to cry, big snotty tears are falling down my face. "Oh my god Cassie, I'm sorry I thought you wanted this. I thought this was meant to be, don't cry babe, please," Jordan says getting up and taking me onto his lap and cradling me.

"Jordan," I say in between sobs. "I love you so much and I know we complete each other, what you said was so beautiful. I don't deserve to have you in my life. I don't deserve to be happy, but I want to be happy. I want you in my life and I want to marry you. I've always wanted to marry you," I'm really crying now.

"Did you just say yes?" He asks.

"Yes, yes, yes I did," I say smiling and looking up to him, he reaches down and kisses me. He then takes my hand and puts a ring on my finger. It's beautiful. It is a white gold band with an infinity symbol made out of diamonds. It is delicate and beautiful.

Mum, Dad, Mr. Stanley and Joyce start clapping and talking all at once. "Good job I brought another bottle of champers isn't it," Mum says. We all laugh.

About an hour later, I'm sitting in the booth and watching everyone around me. Mr. Stanley who has just sold his dream to us, I am so touched by him right now that I can't think straight. He looks so happy and I know that some of that is because he will still work here after today.

Mum and Dad look so happy and I know they are happy for me, after everything I have put them through over the years I just want them to be happy, I just want to have some of the love that they still have after all this time. Joyce sits with us, she has become a part of the family, she has been instrumental in my recovery and I couldn't do this without her.

Then there's Jordan! I sit and watch him for a while, he is hands down the most attractive man I have ever met. He is beautiful on the inside as much as he is beautiful on the outside. He has helped me through the most difficult time in my life and he still wants me. He wants to marry me and to stay with me forever. I just can't get over that! I sit smiling at him and after a few minutes he must feel me smiling at him because he looks up at me and smiles back.

"You ok Cassie?" he says taking my hand and twirling my new ring around on my finger. "Are you happy?" I nod because I can't speak right now. He smiles at me and keeps my hand in his and continues to talk to my Dad about the plans for Pebbles. Mum and Dad are going to help in the redecoration and the general running of the charity.

When it is time for everyone to leave I watch them

go. We tidy up for a while and then lock up as we walk out the door. I stand and wait while Jordan locks the door and I can't believe that we own Pebbles, the place where are dreams were made and where we became one.

We walk back to our house and when we get to the front door, Jordan unlocks it and then turns to me and gently lifts me up so that my legs are draping over his arm and he carries me into the house and down into the lounge. He had kicked the door closed on the way in, he lowers me gently to the couch and then he kneels on the floor, he is between my legs and he is leaning his elbows on them looking at me.

"Cassie, you did mean that you wanted to marry me, didn't you?" I can see the worry on his face, Did he not believe me?

"Jordan, of course I meant it. Why do you think that I didn't? I always want to be with you, it's all I thought about at Bonnie's wedding. I was walking down the aisle and could see you at the end and all I wanted was for it to be me and you that were getting married. This is what I've wanted since the day I met you Jordan. Of course I want to marry you!" I grab his face and pull it into mine and I kiss him to show him I need him to breathe.

I pull away, "Jordan you saved me when I needed saving the most, only you could do that. I needed you to do that," I have tears falling down my face.

"I'm so glad you mean it Cassie, I need you so much. I'm unhappy when you are not near me, it feels like I'm not whole. You make me whole, you complete me."

The next morning, we have so much to organise at Pebbles as we are having our first official fundraising next weekend. I'm so excited about the opening and I can't believe I am getting married to the man of my dreams. I can't wait!

I ring Bonnie as soon as I get out of bed, she is delighted for us and as they are coming home from their honeymoon today she offers to come down to Pebbles later on when they get home. She is so excited when I tell her about Jordan's proposal that I have to hold the phone away from my ear because she is squealing so much.

Jordan holds my hand as we walk to Pebbles; we are meeting the contractors for the refurbishment. It is very exciting to think that we can change everything to the way we want it. Putting the key in the door feels so amazing, and we both smile at each other.

The meeting goes really well and we are all engrossed in the plans and details when Bonnie and Jezza are walking through the door at six o'clock in the evening. We've been here all day, but we have made tremendous progress. Bonnie runs in and takes me into a bear hug. "Oh my god I can't believe it, I'm delighted for both of you, you were meant to be together." She kisses me on the cheek, releases me and then goes over to Jordan to hug him. Jezza is shaking his hand then he comes over and hugs me. I see they brought a bottle of champagne too; this is becoming a habit!

We show them what we have achieved so far and they think we've done really well. They offer to help us in the evenings this week so we might be able to open on Monday. We need all the help we can get!

"Thank God I Found You"

This week has been so busy, it's Friday already but we are almost finished and ready to open. The chairs and booths are being delivered later on today, I can't wait. The rooms out the back are organised too, there is an office with three desks, two smaller interview rooms and then one communal room.

We have advertised about the work the charity does and we have already had a couple of people coming in asking what we can do to help them. We've already spoken to a couple of them even though we were all sat on boxes and surrounded by dust and noise, but we helped them as best we can!

Joyce and Mr. Stanley are helping us out as much as they are able, they are making quite a team and they seem to get on really well.

On Saturday morning we have a lie in because we have worked so hard but also because last night Jordan made love to me for hours. I think we are still trying to make up for all the years that we lost out on.

When we eventually get up, we stroll down to Pebbles and find a few people outside. "Hi, is everyone OK?" Jordan asks them, they are teenagers like we were when we started coming here.

"Hi, we heard you were reopening and we normally come down here after football on Saturdays and just wanted to see whether you were open or not," one of the lads says.

"Well we're not due to open until Monday, but if you want to come in you can, we won't turn you away." Jordan smiles at them and looks to me for confirmation.

"Of course you can come in boys." We open the door and let them in. They stay for a couple of hours as we go about our business of making sure everything is ready for the event tonight and ready for opening for business on Monday morning! The boys come and go, there is a good turnover of them and they are all very pleasant and helpful. Some of them have helped us move some furniture and boxes around. We made them drinks and let them just hang out. I see a couple of girls and one of them is sat with a boy the same age as her, I look at her and smile, they remind me of Jordan and I.

All of a sudden I feel two arms reach around my waist and I know it's Jordan. "I know what you're thinking Cassie, I see it too. Do you remember sitting here for hours, talking, laughing and falling in love?" He twirls me around and kisses me, much to the pleasure of the group of boys who start jeering and then I hear "Put her down mister!" and "Oh you're too old for that." This makes us laugh and then he puts me down.

"Guys, we've got a few more things to do today so if you want to stay you can, just shout if you need anything." I say and go to continue finishing all the preparations. At about four o'clock we start to close up, turning everything off and tidying up. The boys and their friends have all gone with promises of coming back next week. This is what I love about Pebbles, it's a great meeting place.

We lock up and go home to get ready for the charity fundraiser tonight. We have sold over one hundred tickets at twenty-five pound each. After the dinner dance we have a local band playing and then we will finish the night with a DJ. There will be an auction of some local artists work, which we will also be featuring in the cafe and selling if anyone wants to buy them. We have had some good prizes donated to the auction from local businesses and other businesses in the South West too. It's going to be a great auction.

The dress I picked is one of my favourites because it shows off my figure and my long blonde curls. It is bright red, has only one shoulder which has diamante's on it and comes down at an angle to my waistline. It is ruched with one big diamond in the middle. I have my hair curled and pulled to one side, it is swept to the front and is held together with a big red rose.

Jordan has his tuxedo on and he looks good enough to eat. I can't believe this man wants to be in my life forever, I am so lucky.

We go off to the fundraiser, which is extremely successful. We meet lots of people from around the town and from far and wide. A lot of these people know my story and have come up to personally thank me for doing this and bringing this charity to Newquay. With it being a tourist resort there are lots of things that go on that shouldn't and because the turnover of tourists is high, people don't always tell anyone about the things that happen to them.

Dinner is fantastic. For starters there is a choice of prawn cocktail or melon followed by a choice of chicken or salmon. The dessert is a trilogy of desserts, which is absolutely scrumptious. Everyone is laughing and making new friends.

After the dinner, Jordan stands on the stage and taps the microphone to get everyone to stop talking. "I know everyone is having a good time, but I just need to say a few words before we start the auction and the rest of the evening's entertainment." The talking dies down and Jordan looks at me, smiles, then he clears his throat.

"First of all I want to say a big thank you to everyone who has come along tonight; to everyone who has donated to this evening's auction and a huge thank you to everyone who has supported my charity. A huge thank you to everyone who is involved in PEBBLES; from those who help us every day, to those who help in any small way they can. Without all of you, we wouldn't be able to do this to help others. I wanted to tell you a little bit about me and how PEBBLES got started." He looks at me with questions in his eyes. He has already asked my permission because he wouldn't talk about it without having my say so. I nod and smile at him.

"I think you all know me around here and most of you will remember that Cassie and I started dating when we were at school. I remember the first time I really saw her, she was sitting in an Economics class looking out the window when I happened to walk past. She ended up looking directly at me and I could have stood there all day, captivated by her beauty and the passion in her eyes." I blush and look down at the table.

"We eventually broke eye contact and I found myself looking for her all over the school. I was really lucky one day when I was playing football and I saw her sitting on the grass watching us. We kept staring at each other and I hoped that she could feel the amazing bond that I believed we had. I heard she was going to a party so I managed to wangle an invite – thanks Jezza – and I went along to the party with the intention of trying to steal her heart. She looked like an angel, but everyone was telling me to stay away from her, explaining they all looked out for her and protected her. I had to convince them, especially Jezza, that I really was worthy of her and how much I wanted to make her mine. We got on really well that night and we started to see each other all the time."

He takes a breath and looks at me. I nod. "Eventually, I was told the story of how she was attacked by someone at a beach party but luckily he was interrupted. She never told anyone and a few months later she tried to take her life. It makes me so mad that he nearly took her from me before I even met her."

He wipes away a tear from his eye, as do I. "Eventually we had to separate because we wanted to concentrate on our careers. However, we thought it was only going to be for a few months but we both had our contracts extended. I always thought we would go out into the world together but it didn't happen. We were soul mates and I told Cassie that our souls would find each other again because we were meant to be together."

"When I moved back to England I didn't want to live in Newquay because it would remind me too much of Cassie and I was finding it hard enough to live without her, let alone seeing her in OUR places and seeing her family all the time. So I moved to London, but Cassie had inspired me with her strength and determination that I knew that I wanted to help other people who had been through similar situations. I always believed that had Cassie felt she could have talked to someone, she wouldn't have tried to take her own life. I set up PEBBLES so that I could help those who didn't know how to help themselves. I guess you all know why I called the charity PEBBLES, but just in case you didn't – it's the place where Cassie and I used to go to be together. We made lots of plans in there and we always felt comfortable there. When I was thinking of a name for the charity I toyed with a few ideas but 'PEBBLES – the stepping stones to healing' seem perfect to me for many reasons. When Cassie suggested opening the charity in our favourite café, it just seemed like the perfect place."

Again he takes a breath and looks around at his audience. "PEBBLES has been a phenomenal success and because of this success we were featured in an inflight magazine, they were doing an article on our charity to raise awareness, particularly in resort locations. It was on a flight that Cassie saw this article and actually during her time of grief and loss, she donated a large sum of money, anonymously, to my charity. When I found this out it made my heart swell, but it also cause it to break a little because by doing that it meant that she still thought about those bad times, she was still haunted by what happened to her. It also made me realise that my Cassie was still in there, and I thought there was hope for me yet."

"Now unfortunately fate had to intervene for us to get together again and unfortunately, it was a very sad occasion as Cassie had lost her husband. When she came home to grieve, the guy who had hurt her years before brutally attacked her and raped her before Jezza and I could stop him. He didn't stop there though, he tried to kill her by smashing her head on the ground continuously. Thankfully, we got there and pulled him off her and I will never forget how I felt when we did. I wanted to kill him, I wanted him to suffer like she did. I knew that if I did then I wouldn't be there for Cassie and that is something I wanted more than anything. It was a slow road to recovery, but then Cassie found a purpose in life." He looks to me to make sure I am Ok. I smile and nod my head and he continues.

"It was her idea to set up a branch of PEBBLES here in Newquay and already before our doors have opened we have had some customers. Cassie wants to help the victims by getting them to talk about themselves and we intend to rehabilitate some of the victims by letting them work in Pebbles, to help them with their confidence, which has been lost due to their situations."

He holds his hand out for me to join him on stage. When I step up next to him every person in the room stands up and starts clapping their hands. There are many people with tears in their eyes and they are all looking at me.

I wave for them all to be quiet and sit down, when they do I say "thank you to everyone who has helped us with this venture, thank you to my friends and family for putting up with me during my darkest days. Thank you Jordan for thinking of me even when I wasn't here with you. You were right, our souls did find each other again and I am so grateful that they did." I stand up on my tiptoes and kiss him in front of everyone, he grabs hold of my waist and pulls me tight.

When we break away and everyone has gone silent Jordan continues, "We are getting married and I am so happy to be able to say that I will be spending the rest of my life with the one person who is my soul mate."

Everyone starts wolf whistling and clapping, so Jordan calms them down and then he says "right let's get this auction started and then let's have some fun."

When we leave the stage he pulls me into a quiet room and holds me close, we stand there swaying to an imaginary beat. We don't say anything to each other, because we don't need to.

I look up at him and say, "I know I have always lived by the rule 'no regrets' but Jordan you were always my one regret. We wasted so many years apart and that saddens me." I look at the floor because I can feel the tears coming to my eyes.

He puts his finger under my chin and makes me look up at him. "Cassie, no regrets remember. We are the people we are today because of that time we spent apart. We never really let each other go, our hearts were always searching for each other and we were never far from each other's minds. I'm just so sorry that it took two huge heartbreaks for you, for us to come together again. I promise you that I will never let you go again and I will always spend my time making sure you are happy. I love you Cassie and I can't wait to show you how happy you make me."

"I love you too Jordan. Now come on, let's go and have some fun!"

We kiss really deeply and then he takes my hand and pulls me out of the room, ready to face the life that we are embracing together.

The End

Or is it?

Three Years Later

"With Arms Wide Open"

"Come on Cassie, don't be a lazy bones! We have a big day ahead of us today," Jordan says in my ear. I moan and turn around slowly to face him. He is lying on top of the covers and he is fully dressed. How does he have so much energy at this time of the day?

"Go away. Leave me alone. I'm tired." He swats me on the bum and laughs. "Ok I'm getting up."

I climb out of the bed and he jumps off the bed and comes around the bed to hug me. "I love you Cassie, now get dressed, we have lots to do."

After I have showered and got dressed I go downstairs. Jordan is standing at the patio door looking out at the sea. It is such a wonderful sight; I could stand here and watch him all day. I creep the last few steps so that he can't hear me and I wrap my arms around his waist to hug him tight, well as tight as I can do with my big belly, which is full with a baby Jordan.

"Hey baby, are you excited?" he says turning around in my arms and hugging me back. He rests his chin on my head and I can breathe him in, he smells divine and I don't want to leave his arms.

"I'm very nervous, I hope everything goes well."

"Of course it will, it is going to be a great day. Come on we'd better get Lilly and go down to Pebbles." He walks out of the room and goes to the playpen in the corner. He reaches in and lifts Lilly out and into his arms. Lilly is eighteen months old and she loves her daddy, she puts her arms around his neck and rubs noses with him. Then she giggles and my heart swells with even more love for this man that changed my life.

He puts her down on the floor, puts her coat on and takes her hand. She walks with him to the front door then turns around and says "ma ma ome on" and waves at me to join them. I smile at her and take her other hand and follow them through the door and across the bridge to the street.

Walking down to Pebbles Lilly gets tired, so Jordan picks her up in one swift movement and puts her on his shoulders, she loves sitting there because she is high up and she can rub his hair.

My life has changed so much in the last few years. After the charity night when we officially opened the doors for Pebbles we became known as the 'stepping stone to a better life following abuse'. We get lots of people coming through our doors unfortunately, but we treat each one of them individually, depending on their circumstances. Some of them work for us for a while so that they can rebuild their confidence in a controlled environment, before they continue with their lives. Mr. Stanley is still there helping us out; he is very good at training them all in how to work in a café. Joyce still helps with the counseling and Mr. Stanley and her are an item. They are so cute together and we have them over to dinner regularly as they are such wonderful people.

The first year was tough because I had David's trial to go to and whenever I thought I was getting over it, the police or lawyers would ring to ask me more questions. Eventually, David got his comeuppance. He was sentenced to rape and attempted murder. He tried to plead insanity, but when he was analysed they said that he was faking it. He was sentenced for nine years and I hope that when he is in prison he takes the time to realise what he did and what he took from me. I try not to think about him, but sometimes when I am working and a young teenager comes in with a similar story then it comes back to me in a flash. I have learned techniques to bring myself back from the edge and they work very well for me.

We walk into Pebbles and everyone is there; mum and dad; Jezza and Bonnie with their son, Hadley; Tony and Danni; Joyce and Mr. Stanley and even Chad's Mum, Sarah is here. She has been over to visit us quite a lot in the last couple of years and she loves Lilly and can't wait for Baby Jordan to come along. It might seem weird to some people that she is so happy for us, but she really is a lovely person and treats me like a daughter, so it is only natural that she is here today. There are lots of the people who we have helped here today as well and I smile at each one of them. They all have their own stories to tell and we have helped them to become the people that they are today, I am very proud of that fact. I get really embarrassed because today is such a big day and I don't want it to be a flop.

Jordan and I were married two years ago today. I was pregnant with Lilly, but that isn't why we got married. We got married because it was what we were always destined to do. We were meant to be together and we both knew it. When we first opened Pebbles, we worked really hard with the café and the charity and after about six months I got sick and didn't really think about being pregnant. I was worried that I was getting cancer like Chad and didn't really say anything to anyone. Jordan noticed, of course, that there was something wrong and eventually he managed to convince me to go to the doctor. He came with me and held my hand and when the doctor told us that we were having a baby, Jordan starting crying. He had wanted this for so long and never thought he would be a father. He had never wanted a long relationship during the time we were apart and he had told me he definitely didn't want children with anyone other than me.

We had organized the wedding, so we went ahead with it as planned, it was my dream wedding. We got married on the beach beneath our house. It was beautiful, simple and the most romantic wedding I have ever been to. I was just so happy to become Jordan's wife. I remember the moment he removed my necklace that he had given me when I first went to San Francisco, the one I have been wearing every day since he gave it to me. He replaced it with a necklace almost identical to that one, but this was made out of white gold and diamonds. "I promised you that one day I would give you one made out of real diamonds and today I can fulfill that promise Cassie." He kissed me on the neck. It is so beautiful. I smiled at him, god I love him so much.

We have opened small satellite offices of PEBBLES in some of the other holiday resorts in the South West and Jordan travels around them to make sure that they continue to run with the same philosophy that we have for Pebbles. Each of these offices is run behind a café so that we can offer the rehabilitation and confidence building sessions as we do here. I stopped travelling once I had Lilly. We are so excited to be having a baby boy and I know it is only a matter of time before we meet him.

Today isn't about Pebbles; it isn't about the charity; it isn't about Lilly or our new baby – today is about me, Cassie. When I walk into Pebbles a lady approaches me. "Hi Cassie, it is such a pleasure to meet you. We have heard a lot about you and your charity. Congratulations on releasing your latest book. Can you tell us about it?" She is from the local newspaper and she is here to interview me, as today is my release day.

I had released a couple of books as an indie author and then a publishing company, penguin books, snapped me up. After many meetings with them they convinced me to write my story; write about my life and what happened to me and what I have done to turn my life around. Apparently, everyone thinks that I did something good in my life, but it was Jordan who founded the charity not me. I still can't see what everyone else thinks I did.

"I know that I write romance stories with a bit of a dark twist in them, but this book is more like an autobiography of my life. It is my story about my personal heartaches and pain that I suffered; it is about how I got through those dark days and found something so wonderful." I smile at Jordan and take his hand. "If one person reads my book and finds some comfort in my story then that would make me a very happy person."

Everyone claps their hands and I blush. Jordan hands around glasses of champagne to everyone. We are there for most of the day, eating, drinking, talking and having fun until someone says that I have made the number one spot on amazon for kindle books. Everyone starts to clap and hug me and then Jordan raises his glass and says "To Cassie's Story". Everyone holds their glasses in the air and repeats "Cassie's Story!"

The End

Playlist

If I could turn back time - Cher

If I could - Regina Belle

Another day in paradise – Phil Collins

Girls just wanna have fun - Cyndi Lauper

With every beat of my heart – Taylor Dayne

Here and now – Luther Vandross

I'll be your everything – Tommy Page

Why? - Annie Lennox

All I wanna do is make love to you - Heart

How am I supposed to live without you – Michael Bolton

If wishes came true – Sweet Sensation

Release me- Wilson Phillips

White wedding – Billy Idol

It's a nice day for a white wedding- Billy Idol

My heart will go on – Celine Dion

I don't wanna – Jagged Edge

Viva las vegas – Elvis Presley

Photograph – Nickelback

Collide – Howie Day

Going crazy – Natalie

MY ONE REGRET

A million love songs – Take That

Scars – Boy Epic

Let me go - Gary Barlow

She will be loved – Maroon 5

You raise me up - Westlife

Truth is – Fantasia Barrino

I believe in you – Amanda Marshall

The one I love - David Gray

I just wanna make love to you – The Rolling Stones

You raise me up – Westlife

Thank god I found you - Mariah Carey

With arms wide open – Creed

Acknowledgements

There are too many people to thank, so I just want to say a thank you to everyone who is a part of my life. You rock!

Sneak Peek into the Future

Some on the projects which I am working on to look out for in 2015!

Swan – Autumn 2015

It's ironic that her name is Lily Swan because she's always felt like the Ugly Duckling. The one that nobody wants …

Would you change yourself for a man?

Would you consider surgery to get the man you want?

She did …

Little did she know, it was the best decision she ever made …..

Sunshine in Amsterdam – Late 2015/Early 2016

Can true love be found in the most erotic city in the World? This is a story of six wonderful women who travel around the Cities of Europe having fun and living life to the fullest. Join the Sunshine Tour to find out!

Other Works In Progress

There are other works in progress which I will tell you about as they become closer to release!

About the Author

I know that most of you know about me so these are my other books that I have written:

Til Death Us Do Part Series

For Better or For Worse – Book 1 in Trilogy – No Longer Available
In Sickness and In Health – Book 2 in Trilogy – No Longer Available
To Love and To Cherish – Book 3 in Trilogy – No Longer Available
To Have and To Hold – Book 4 Standalone
For Richer or For Poorer – Book 5 Standalone

Sunshine Tours
Sunshine in Madrid

Christmas Novella

A Taste of Christmas Dublin Style

Anthologies

Love Reborn

When Destiny Calls

Keep your eyes on my facebook page:

www.facebook.com/authorkrissy.vas

Keep your eyes on my blog page:

Authorkrissyv.wordpress.com

MY ONE REGRET

45065277R00210

Made in the USA
Charleston, SC
13 August 2015